MW01103349

Dirty Magick: Los Angeles

edited by Charlie Brown

Story by: [signature]

luckymojopress.com

Contents

This is a work of fiction. Names, characters, events and incidents either are the product of the author's imagination or are used fictitiously. Any resemblance to actual persons, living or dead, events, or locales is entirely coincidental.

copyright © 2013 ADS Films, LLC

ISBN 978-0-9911960-0-5

All rights reserved. No part of this book may be used or reproduced in any manner without written permission of the publisher, except brief quotations in reviews or critical articles.

Cover art by Trent Oubre (http://trentoubre.com/)

ACKNOWLEDGEMENTS

First and foremost, to Marguerite Darlington, for inspiring this collection and making critical connections.

To the hosts of The Dead Robots' Society podcast, Paul Elard Cooley, Justin Macumber and Terry Mixon for helping to promote this work to would-be authors. Your generosity is appreciated by me and anyone who has listened over the years.

To Richard Rayner, Judith Freeman, Brighde Mullins and the rest of the professors at the Masters of Professional Writing program at the University of Southern California for helping me grow as both a writer and editor. Fight on.

Finally, to ConJour, may it rest in peace, and Balticon for connecting me to great authors and friends who gave this anthology variety and intrigue.

Introduction: Los Angeles, *Noir*, and the Magick In The Shadows

by Charlie Brown

The sun must have been imposing to these Germans who found themselves in Los Angeles around the time of World War II. They were used to chilly air, gray skies and cobblestone streets, all with the patina of ancient civilization where America cannot compete.

These men (Robert Siodmak, Fritz Lang, and Billy Wilder) imported their personal film style of Expressionism, which could be seen so clearly in the influential short film "The Cabinet of Dr. Caligari," a style that already put emphasis on light, dark and the difference between them (*chiaroscuro* to the Italians). But in their new city, they found shadows so sharp, they could shave their faces clean.

They had come to find work in Hollywood, as well as seeking refuge from the Nazis, but Los Angeles already had the formula for the stories they wanted to tell. Wasn't there Raymond Chandler and his hard boiled detective Philip Marlowe raving against the Santa Ana winds while punching and shooting his way through the criminal underworld? And didn't James M. Cain exploit the dry desert towns of a half-formed metropolis for his series of *femme fatales*?

These writers of the 1930s supplied the grit and grist for the filmmakers of the '40s and '50s, all taking advantage of the bleached surroundings.

Of course, three would intersect in the film adaptation of "Double Indemnity." Cain's novel became the film directed by Wilder co-written with Chandler. And, even though none of these men actually liked each other (Chandler called Cain "the offal of literature" and had to write a manifesto to get Wilder to work in a way Chandler found comfortable), it produced the first work of art that could be termed *film noir*.

By the 1960s, when the French cinematic critics actually coined the term, the B-level hard boiled movie had become cliché, not organic to the modern time, but lapsed into nostalgia. But by the end of the decade, as the hard boiled faded to black, the weird and wild began to seep out of the sewers and take their time to shine.

Filmmaker Kenneth Anger, a pioneering underground gay filmmaker who plumbed the depths of the gossip columns for his book "Hollywood Babylon," first started exploring the ritualistic world of magick with his film "The Inauguration of the Pleasure Dome," a 1954 short playing out a ceremony from the Thelema religion (founded by British occultist Aleister Crowley).

Anger photographed all of the decadence that middle America thought existed in Hollywood. By the time hippies and their drugs took over the scene on the Sunset Strip, Anger would find himself friends with Mick Jagger, Marianne Faithful, Jimmy Page and Anton LaVey.

He began work on "Lucifer Rising," which would symbolize the coming of the Aeon of Horus (derived from Crowley's "The Book of the Law"). The footage would later become "The Invocation of My Demon Brother," which starred hairdresser and would-be rock'n'roller Bobby Beausoleil who would later fall under the spell of that other Los Angeles-based dark magician Charles Manson.

Anger would also be interviewed by Richard Rayner, spurring his "Westside Witches" series, and the story contained herein "Cougar Witch Plot."

Thus Los Angeles, formerly the fedora-wearing purview of Marlowe, became the playground for freaks, hippies and the New Age.

So where do these two worlds come together? That is not just the question posed by this anthology. Have there been ideas such as those found in these pages that could show the connection of Southern California's two most famous styles?

The answer is "Cast A Deadly Spell" and its sequel "Witch Hunt," two television movies written in the early 1990s by Joseph Dougherty, who was a writer for "thirtysomething" and is now a writer and producer on "Pretty Little Liars" and "Ravenswood."

The former film, the better of the two, stars Fred Ward as H. Philip Lovecraft, hard boiled private eye (ironic in two ways: the real Lovecraft's abysmal health would prevent him from pursuing such a career while the Philip name directly recalls Marlowe) who is hired by rich Amos Hackshaw (David Warner) to find the Necronomicon. The twist is that everyone in '40s L.A. uses magick, except Lovecraft who refuses for "personal reasons."

With its Chandlerian plot fused to the atmosphere of Cthulhu worshippers, "Spell" is a small but delightful film and the main inspiration for putting together stories that find the intersection of crime, magick and Los Angeles. In November 2013, it is unavailable on DVD but can be found in its entirety on YouTube.

The Los Angeles of the following fourteen writers is a tough place, a shady place, but it's also funny and wry, eager to control the magick all around its citizens, but also unafraid to use the power to solve a conflict. Like the gun, magick can be used for good or ill, but down these mean streets, it will always be dirty.

THE FORBIDDEN POSE: A MATT BOLSTER YOGA MYSTERY

BY NEAL POLLACK

One recent morning at around 10:30, Matt Bolster lay on his back in his Venice Beach apartment, moaning in discomfort. The sliding door to his balcony was open. Two blocks away, he could see a sliver of beach, and a sliver of bums walking on that beach. The clouds appeared to be dissipating early, auguring another relaxing day in Yoga Land. But Bolster couldn't feel the vibe.

Bolster had an injury. It felt like a hamstring. Not the tender belly — those strains can easily be rehabbed in less than a month. Do a program of squats and chair poses and commit to some compression shorts that'll make your balls sweat and you'll be fine. But this injury, Bolster guessed, involved the attachment, that thin fibrous area connecting the hams to the pelvic bone. Those could nag you for months, maybe forever.

He'd been doing an easy, restorative practice, frustratingly enough. As he'd ducked back into child's pose, the tendon tweaked. Just like that. Bolster refused to believe. He pushed it further. It got hot, mocking him. No yoga for you, old man. Bolster was fucked.

In the big range of medical problems, this was nothing. But to Bolster, it mattered. He worked as a yoga teacher, and it was hard to teach yoga when you felt a hot shard of pain around the rim of your left ass cheek every time you bent forward. Of course, it shouldn't have mattered. Yoga is an internal practice, a deeply intricate system of human psychology that teaches you to discard the heavy burdens of your daily life in favor of a broader, more infinite perspective. But Bolster's students didn't want to hear that. They wanted to raise up into half-moon without stumbling. Suddenly, Bolster didn't have much to offer them. He felt depressed. The words of that song that no one younger than him remembered came to mind:

I haven't got time for the pain...

He did, however, have time to get stoned.

Bolster had recently invested in a G-Pen. Some people preferred vaporizing resin or liquid, but Bolster was old school. He liked the leaf. He vaped now because he needed his lungs intact to practice *pranayama*. Still, there was nothing like the pure taste of *sativa* flower to get him through the afternoon. It beat *ujayi* breathing every time.

He sat on his couch, inhaling. Suddenly, the day's injury bothered him less. Sure, the back end of the left side of his pelvis burned a little, but that was impermanent, like everything else in the universe. The Bolster Express would ride again.

His cell rang. The display showed that it was Bolster's former partner from LAPD Homicide, Detective Esmail Martinez. Bolster answered, thinking Martinez was calling to invite him to Friday night poker. He wasn't.

"Bolster," said Martinez.

"Of course I'll play," Bolster said. "but you're gonna have to spot me the buy-in."

"I'm in Silver Lake," Martinez said. "Better get over here."

It took Bolster about 45 minutes to drive east. He peeled off at Vermont, before the 10 merged with the 110, and worked his way to hipster town, listening to NPR all the way. It was his only real choice, given that he drove a 1998 Nissan Sentra that still had a cassette player in the dash. It was either FM radio or his high-school mixtapes, and he didn't want to dredge those up again. The morning NPR music was, as advertised, eclectic and predictably terrible, all whiny Decemberists-type crap and twee little tunes with bells. Bolster kept the volume low.

Soon enough, he pulled up in front of the address Martinez had texted him, part of that east side netherworld between Sunset and the 101 that was sort of gentrified but also sort of smeared in pitbull shit. The successful sitcom writers didn't live in the flats; this wasn't a part of town to make your Jewish mother proud.

Bolster parked four cars away from a wrought-iron-gate duplex, painted grayish blue, decorated by worthless shrubs and a ratty patch equal parts grass and shredded malt-liquor bottles. It smelled hot, rank, and unloved. There were a couple of cop cars in front, double-parked, with their sirens whipping around. Bolster recognized Martinez's tricked-out Dodge Charger. Martinez fancied himself Vin Diesel from *Fast Five,* though he couldn't drive worth a damn.

There was some police tape across the entrance to the bungalow — or what had once been a bungalow and was now a sleazy stucco duplex rental — from the sidewalk, but it hardly seemed necessary. Half the people around here didn't go anywhere near cops, and the other half were in a hurry to get down the hill, order a coffee, flip open their laptops and work on their zombie apocalypse screenplay. They hadn't even posted a guard. Bolster ducked under the tape, and walked up.

Wind chimes flanked the doorway. They tinkled pleasantly in the light breeze as Bolster crossed the threshold. Martinez was in the living room, which smelled like sweat and Nag Champa, trying to make sense of a series of yoga-instructional DVDs. He looked up and saw Bolster.

"*Rock Your Yoga: Bliss Edition*?" he said. "I don't understand this shit."

"Probably not important," Bolster said.

"It just makes no sense."

"Is this a yard sale?" Bolster asked. "Did you ask me to come down here to help you make a selection?"

"Fuck off, Bolster," said Martinez. "Look in the bedroom."

Bolster walked down a narrow hallway over wood floors that had never been finished. Hell, they'd barely even been started. People lived like animals in this town, and for what? For the rent on this shithole, you could get a 2,000-square-foot three-bedroom with a yard in the suburbs of Iowa City, probably with a view of water. But then you wouldn't have ready access to all the drugs and the assholes who were selling them. Also, the yoga wouldn't be as plentiful, or the coffee as good.

Bolster looked into the bedroom. Yoga hadn't done its occupant any favors. From what he could tell, she was a woman in her late 20s. Given the lack of video-game equipment in the living room, she was probably single, and, given the fact that she was wearing a special-edition Hello Kitty Lululemon yoga top, probably straight. Or at least she had been. She was dead, the strangest-looking corpse Bolster had ever seen in a career full of strange corpses.

The girl had short hair, close-cropped, serious-appearing, and light-gray eyes that looked totally content and serene, even in death. Her left leg had been tucked behind her head, so the crook of her knee hooked around her neck, and her foot brushed her right shoulder. Her left arm threaded that gap and balanced on the floor, fingers spread equidistant, creating a perfect platform of balance. The right leg, held straight out with foot flexed, also hovered above the floor. You had to practice for a decade before you could even *think* about doing this post. That was about of the length of Bolster's service on the mat, and he wasn't even close.

Bolster looked closer at the posed corpse. Her right arm was crooked at the elbow, hand sitting straight up. The thumb folded over the index finger, the other three fingers standing upright.

Bolster hadn't seen this *mudra* ever practiced, and hadn't even heard of it outside of an obscure collection he'd stumbled upon once in an East Asian studies library in Santa Barbara. On its own, or in meditation, it was harmless, even calming. But in conjunction with the wrong position, it could be deadly. Bolster knew what this was, but he never thought it was actually possible.

Martinez entered the room.

"Weird, huh?" he said. "A neighbor just found her like this after her door had been open for a while. No one keeps their doors open around here."

"How long has it been?" Bolster said.

"We don't know for sure," Martinez said. "Eight hours minimum. Maybe longer. Her heart stopped. But she doesn't smell, doesn't seem to be decomposing at all. She's just frozen in place, like time just stopped for her."

"This isn't good," Bolster said.

"No shit, Buddha."

"I mean, she couldn't have figured this out on her own. Someone had to teach her."

"Teach her what?" Martinez asked.

"The Forbidden Pose," Bolster said.

The dead woman's name was Renée LaRue. From what Bolster could tell, she was an ordinary yoga student, if an extremely committed one. He'd flipped through her books. A flier for the Ashtanga shala on Sunset slipped out. Bolster knew that spot. It was a serious joint.

After securing a promise from Martinez that he'd get paid,

Bolster headed over, only a five-minute drive. The sign said it was closed until 4 PM, when there'd be an afternoon led primary series. It was a little after 1:30. Bolster knew how to kill a couple of hours on the east side.

He drove Whitey up to Highland Park. This joint on York had some great goat *carnitas*. Bolster had two, with chips and salsa, and a great big lemon-lime *agua fresca* which he ate at a table with a laminate cover over colorful Mexican *loteria* cards. Of course, the only Mexicans in the place worked there, but Bolster didn't care. It tasted damn good. Jonathan Gold never did him wrong.

After, he went two doors down to the House Of Greenery. He'd had his prescription since the day they'd become available in 2005, and was on the list of at least one medical-marijuana shop in every neighborhood. You never knew when you'd need a resupply. He liked this place. It was an old Craftsman, sitting in back of the sidewalk behind wrought-iron gates and a dusty lot. At the front door, a fat black guy sat on a stool, reading a decade-old issue of *X Factor*. Bolster showed his ID, and he got buzzed in.

As soon as he entered the door, someone sounded a gong, and shouted, "CUSTOMER!" A half dozen employees came scurrying, all part of the show. Bolster knew that he was just another consumer at the ass-end of a multi-billion-dollar industry, one step away from just buying a can of Budweiser. But he didn't care. He liked the weed, and he had a web coupon. An eighth of Lemon Lift was only setting him back 45 bucks.

He got into his car, stuffed a nug into his G-Pen, absorbed some sweet THC, and thought about the situation. When you practiced yoga, you sought *samadhi,* or complete absorption into the true nature of reality. And what could be more real than death? Yoga had killed Renée LaRue. Bolster was pretty sure of it.

The ancient texts talked of a pose that was so difficult to master that accomplishing it brought final release. A Forbidden Pose. For centuries, it was lost, as the art of yoga *asana*, or postures, fell into disrepair, replaced, for a time, by the philosophical traditions of Yogananda and Krishnamurti, and then, in the '60s, by *mantra* and meditation. But a quiet physical revolution had been brewing in Indian places, famous now, but then obscure to Western knowledge, like Mysore and Pune. Gradually, the poses took over the West.

Now, millions of people were doing them, and not just your simple downward-facing dogs, chair poses, and reclined cobbler's. There were headstands of all varieties, and handstands, and side crows, and inverted scorpions. Yoga practitioners, especially young ones, were doing complicated poses at a pace and intensity that ancient masters had never meant for the average human. It took Krishnamarcharya a decade to learn 500 poses in a cave. These days, you could get half that in the average retreat weekend. Modern yogis thirsted for experience that was newer, crazier, harder.

The Forbidden Pose wasn't supposed to exist, but if it did, it wasn't meant to be practiced lightly, if at all. In legend, it served as the ultimate test of yogic commitment. The books said your organs would shut down if you practiced The Forbidden Pose for too long, but you'd be so absorbed in its patterns that you wouldn't notice, and would then die. Only yogis at the very peak of the ladder would be able to control their bodies enough to survive.

Renée LaRue hadn't been at the peak of the ladder.

Whether or not he was sober enough to drive, Bolster headed out. It was a straight, if overwrought, shot down Figueroa, right on Sunset. He got to the shala at 3:30, just as the teacher was unlocking the door. Bolster knew this guy. Nate Walker. He'd been doing Ashtanga before Ashtanga was cool, and was still doing it now that Ashtanga wasn't really cool anymore. He was short, 5'6" or so, with a shaved head and about as much body fat as a starving rooster. Nate threw his legs behind his head more times before breakfast on the average Sunday than most people did in a lifetime. He went to bed at 8 p.m. every night and woke up at 3:30 a.m. to practice for three hours. That's probably why he'd been divorced twice.

Bolster approached.

"Hey, Bolster," Nate said. "Been a long time. Ready to rejoin the fold?"

Bolster patted his sore hammy.

"No forward bending for a while," he said. "I'm a little raw."

"There are always adjustments."

"And I ate goat tacos, with extra onions. You don't want me in that room."

"Gotcha," Nate said. "So what do you want?"

"Do you know someone named Renée LaRue?"

"Of course. She used to practice here all the time. Not so much lately, though. Why do you ask?"

"She was found murdered this morning," Bolster said.

Nate staggered back against the door.

"What?"

Bolster got out his cell phone and flipped over to the photo app. He'd taken some shots. But he hadn't posted them to Instagram. Nate looked even more shocked if possible. He unlocked the door.

"Come inside," he said, his voice almost in a whisper. "I've got class in 20."

The studio was hot and damp and dark as an Altadena alley. Ashtanga wasn't Bikram, but its practitioners liked their towels. They measured themselves in sweat volume. No one ever turned on the fan, even during *savasana*.

"*That's The Forbidden Pose*," Nate Walker said.

"You know it?" Bolster said. He leaned in menacingly. "Did you *teach it to her?*"

"Of course not," said Walker. "I would never teach that. I would never even *do* it. Guruji showed us a diagram back in 1991, but he said, 'Forbidden Pose is Death Pose for all but highest masters.'"

Guruji referred to the late Sri K. Patthabi Jois, the founder of Ashtanga Yoga.

Walker continued: "We asked him if he did it himself, and he didn't say much. Which was strange, because Guruji loved to talk. He just said, 'It is not something to do.'"

"Well," Bolster said, "Renée did it. And now she's dead."

"Shiva save us all," said Nate Walker.

"When was the last time she practiced here?" Bolster asked.

"She used to come in every day until about a year ago," Walker said. "Except on moon days, of course."

"Of course," Bolster said.

Ashtangis didn't practice when the moon was full. Maybe they were werewolves. Females didn't have to practice when they were on their periods, a rule considered quite progressive when it was implemented.

"She was advancing very nicely," said Walker. "We were working on third series. Only the most experienced yogis ever get that far."

"I know," Bolster said.

He'd never gotten that far. Not yet. And probably not ever.

"That's why I thought it was strange when she stopped showing up. She seemed frustrated I wasn't moving her on to fourth series, but it was just going to be a few more months. A year at most. She was only 27 years old, she had plenty of time."

"The impatience of youth," Bolster said.

"And then I didn't hear from her again," said Walker. "No one did. Some people tried calling or emailing her, but she was just gone."

"Do you know *anyone* in town who does, or could teach, that pose?"

"No one sane would ever teach that pose," Walker said. "It's just unethical."

So Bolster was looking for someone insane. Great. Typical. There was never a sane yoga murder.

"Poor Renée," Walker said. "We should have a memorial service."

"If you want to make yourself feel better," Bolster said. "She doesn't care either way."

The students had started coming in with their mats, looking deadly serious, the only way to look before an Ashtanga class. You could only consider Ashtanga fun if you had a fetish for the rack. It would wring them out, though, really clear the *samskara*. And then, Bolster thought ruefully, a few years later they could end up dead.

Bolster thanked Nate Walker and went outside, puffing on his G-Pen all the way to his car. He got a text from Martinez. It was an address in Hollywood, on Selma, which included an apartment number. What was that about? Bolster hoped for a poker game, again, but he doubted that highly. Then came another text.

"We found another one," it read.

The second victim's name was Jeremiah Doyle. The cops found him in the exact same pose as Renée LaRue. He lived (or *had* lived) in a multi-unit low-rise, with neighbors who didn't care, so they estimated he'd been in the Foridden Pose for four days or more. Yet the body had no real signs of putrefication, other than a slight musty odor. The Forbidden Pose locked you in place like a statue, or a yoga mummy. It seemed to slow down time.

Martinez had been there for a couple of hours by the time Bolster appeared, his arrival delayed by his refusal to park in anything but a non-metered spot.

Bolster entered the apartment, equally as spartan as Renée LaRue's, but, instead of scratched wood flooring, it had moldy carpet. If you did yoga in L.A. you either lived like a pasha or a slum dweller. Maybe that was the case anywhere. Bolster took one look at Jeremiah Doyle's body, and said, "Great."

"I am so fucking tired of this yoga shit," Martinez said, carefully riffling through Doyle's pathetic selection of books, half of which were about holistic living, all of which had been bought used.

"Tell me about it," Bolster said.

"You got anything for me?"

"I went to a studio where Renée LaRue used to practice. The guy who runs it seemed legitimately shocked. Said she hadn't been by in about a year. Do you have anything for *me*?"

Martinez handed Bolster a pair of surgical gloves.

"Put these on," he said.

"I didn't know you cared," Bolster said.

"Funny," said Martinez. He produced a baggie that contained a card. On one side was an illustration from those yoga *asana* posters that started appearing in the '70s, very old school. It showed a guy in shorts and a wife-beater on his stomach, hands on the tops of his feet. His legs bent forward, actually in half, until the feet were in line with the hips.

"*Bhekasana,*" Bolster said. "Frog pose."

"Read the other side," Martinez said.

It was one word: "Lakshmi."

"Huh," said Bolster.

"What?"

"That's from Indian myth. She was Shiva's partner in the heavens."

"I think someone might be trying to get in touch with you, Bolster."

Bolster was wondering the same thing.

"Maybe," he said. "Either way, it's going to cost you."

"I'll put it on your tab," said Martinez.

Bolster drove home, no easy feat at 4:30 p.m., trying to figure out the connection between frog pose and Lakshmi. None emerged. At his place, he took a couple of bong hits for inspiration. That didn't help, though he did find himself absorbed in a 45-minute restorative practice that involved a stack of three blankets. A nap, a visit to the beach: none of it did anything to stimulate ideas.

A day passed. Then two, and then a week. Martinez called. Another victim had been found, in an apartment at Western and Fountain. Bolster went out. It was a young woman, lean and fit, almost ascetic, and once again drawn up into The Forbidden Pose. And again, someone had left a *bhekasana/* Lakshmi card at the scene. At some point, the press would get wind, and then there'd be a yoga serial killer on the loose. That would mean Bolster could up his rates, but he really didn't need the hassle.

He also couldn't get over that these notes were meant expressly for him. Bolster kept it low and not flashy, but there weren't a lot of yoga detectives in town. Someone was trying to show him up, or contact him, or both.

These weird cards were the only evidence. There were no prints on any of the three bodies, no discernible prints anywhere in the apartments, no sign of struggle, no particular motivation. The only thing that appeared to tie the victims together was they all had intense and at least superficially advanced yoga practices. But you could say that about a lot of people in L.A.

Bolster drove Whitey up Mount Washington. He seemed to spend a lot of time on the east side. *Maybe I should move here*, he thought. Still, he liked the beach. It was 15 degrees cooler in the summer. He had a landlady who didn't seem to exist, and hadn't dealt with a rent hike in years. Give him a real reason to relocate and he'd think about it.

His meditation teacher, Lora Powell, lived up on a hill, in a makeshift *zendo* with a couple of shady pseudo-celibate pseudo-monks who didn't seem to have a lot of disciples but did seem to have a lot of family money. Lora was the only one of the bunch with students, probably why they kept her around. Also, she didn't mind sweeping.

That's what she was doing when Bolster pulled up, running a corn broom along the front stoop.

"Hey, Bolster!" she said. "You come by for a sit?"

He presented her with a nice bud of AK-47. She didn't smoke it herself, but her roommates always enjoyed the present, which kept them from casting suspicious looks Bolster's way.

"Nope," he said. "Just needed to clear my head with some mountain air."

Lora took Bolster inside and gave him some tea. The *zendo* had no furniture, other than some tatami mats in the bedrooms and pillows, lined in front of floor-to-ceiling windows overlooking the less-than-sylvan hills of Lincoln Heights where Bolster had spent more than one unpleasant evening as a cop getting shot at by The Avenues gang. This was a much better vantage point.

Bolster told Lora was what going on.

"See, this is why I meditate," she said. "*Asana* just screws people up. It should come later in the process."

"Agreed," Bolster said. "Or it should just be called exercise and not given this special spiritual status."

But they weren't there to dork out. Bolster needed Lora's help. He showed her the card. She laughed.

"What is that guy doing?" she said.

"*Bhekasana*," Bolster said. "Frog pose."

"That doesn't look like a frog!"

"It's just a name."

She turned the card over.

"Hmmm, Lakshmi," she said. "Shiva's consort."

Bolster almost spit out his tea.

"Wait," he said. "What?"

"His consort. His guide. His partner."

"Hang on," Bolster said.

Something about that word sounded familiar. Why hadn't it occurred to him before? Maybe he should lay off the weed.

Nah.

Bolster got out his phone. There was an app he used that tracked all L.A. street names. It provided their general geolocation. When he'd been a cop he needed a 200-page book, plus another one for the Valley. And another one for the other Valley.

Sure enough, there it was. "Consort Way."

"Look at that," he said.

Lora did.

"It's in Frogtown," she said.

Of course, Bolster thought. Consort Way, in Frogtown, a little area just east of Griffith Park, just north of Elysian Park, somewhere near I-5, the 2 expressway, and the L.A. River. It was all warehouses and art studios, a sooty, concrete-strewn mess about seven years from total gentrification. That's exactly the sort of cheap space where yoga starts to take hold. Bolster knew he needed to go. The clues had been asking for him all along. It was, even with traffic, 15 minutes from his current location.

"I'm heading down," he said.

He wrote down Martinez's number, and gave it to Lora.

"If you don't hear from me in two or three hours, call this guy."

"Which one?" Lora said. "Two, or three?"

"Make it an hour and a half," Bolster said.

"How do you know that's the place?" she said.

"I know," he said.

And he knew who he'd find there, too.

***

Consort Way was a one-block dead end, three clicks down from Riverside Drive, named for god knows what, god knows when. The street, if you could call it that, contained no cars, other than a soot-crusted cement mixer that looked like it hadn't moved in 20 years, no vegetation other than weeds the winds blew over, and no decoration other than a rusty chain-link fence festooned with taco wrappers and plastic bags from before the city ban. The dirt on the curb was half broken glass and a third used condoms. No one wanted this particular patch.

Bolster parked Whitey in front of the only building on the block, a warehouse with bricks painted beige and a back lot, fence topped with curled barbed wire. He peered through the links and saw some half-finished woodworking products and a few large spray-painted paper-maché heads. He figured they were the product of some kind of half-assed Occupy protest, a sure sign that whatever landlord owned this wretched property was renting on the cheap.

In the middle of the building, there was a long metal garage door. Bolster tried to lift it, but it was locked. Down from that was a proper door, painted brown. The number "1080" hung over it auspiciously. Bolster turned the handle. It opened.

Inside, Bolster heard a harmonium playing low. It sounded like a bagpipe on downers. The music was coming from a dark far corner of the warehouse. Light from grease-stained windows occasionally hit the floor like faint spotlights, motes dancing like low-rent dance contestants. Bolster found himself oddly drawn toward the music, like he was moving down a tunnel. He couldn't stop himself from going forward.

There, in a far corner, sat a man, about ten years younger than Bolster. He had a longer beard and longer hair than Bolster remembered, but the ascetic body looked familiar, as did his eerily peaceful gaze as he sat on a cushion in lotus pose, hands on his knees in *jñana mudra,* thumb and forefinger pressed together, the seal of wisdom. Bolster didn't know where the harmonium music was coming from. Maybe the guy had learned how to manifest the sound from the air.

"Barlow," he said.

Andrew Barlow opened his eyes.

"Bolster," he said. "You got my invitation."

Andrew Barlow was one of the world's leading yoga scholars, or at least he had been. He'd gotten his Ph.D. in Sanskrit and Vedic Studies at 26, staggeringly young, and had gotten immediately hired by Tom Hart, the founder of Hart Yoga™, who'd kept him on intellectual retainer and allowed him to continue his studies. Unfortunately, Barlow studied too intensely, and developed various *siddhis,* or extraordinary powers, as outlined in the *Yoga Sutras.* One night, in an act of spontaneous outrage at Hart's sexual mistreatment of his students, Barlow had used those *siddhis,* tearing his boss' heart from his chest using a mystical procedure unknown even to the highest dark masters of yoga. Bolster had caught him, but Barlow had escaped into the Northern California hills, never to be found.

Until now.

"You're not getting off this time, Barlow," Bolster said.

Bolster picked up his phone to call Martinez. Barlow uttered an incantation, raising his hand.

"Uh-uh," he said. "I don't want anyone interrupting our lesson."

Bolster put the phone back in his pocket. He didn't want to, but couldn't help the action. Barlow had extraordinary powers, after all.

"You don't have anything to teach me," Bolster said.

"Maybe I can teach you what I taught those others," Barlow said. "How to let go. How to transcend."

Bolster was frozen to the spot. He clenched his fists.

"Transcending doesn't mean dying," he said.

Barlow wasn't moving, though he finally opened his eyes and raised his chin slightly.

"Doesn't it?" he said. "Is there any greater test for a yogi than to maintain *samadhi*, even in the face of death? If you can learn to not be afraid of death, then you've solved the puzzle of life."

Barlow had a certain perverse logic, Bolster admitted, but yoga was about living in the present moment and accepting the fact that you were going to *eventually* die, not forcing death on young people who overworked their bodies. That was a misappropriation of the guru's role.

"You're just wrong," Bolster said.

Barlow unfolded his legs. He stood and walked over to Bolster, who wanted to hit him but couldn't. Bolster just stood there, mesmerized and angry.

"Maybe you're just afraid to try The Forbidden Pose," Barlow said.

"I don't want to do your fucking Forbidden Pose," said Bolster.

"Don't want? Or can't?"

"Want."

Barlow stood in front of Bolster.

"Inhale deeply," he said.

Bolster did, against his will.

"Now exhale in full."

Bolster did again.

"Focus your gaze, tightly, on a point in front of you, while continuing to breathe."

Bolster knew once he picked a *drishdi,* or gazing point, everything was over. He tried to resist, but did it anyway. His gaze settled on one of the golden strands coming off Barlow's meditation cushion. Then slowly, carefully, Barlow began to draw him toward The Forbidden Pose.

"I...have...an injury," Bolster said.

"Eternity doesn't care about injuries," said Barlow. "They're just signs of deeper healing. Push through them and taste the nectar of eternity."

"That is wrong!" Bolster said.

Barlow put a finger to his lips.

"Shh," he said. "Breathe and gaze."

Bolster did, unbidden.

Next, Barlow told Bolster to bend his right leg, slightly. Bolster did. Then, via instructions, he bent forward, slightly, lifted his left leg, and cradled it gently in his hands, warming up the hip. Bolster could feel the barking of his limpy hamstring attachment. He wanted to stop, but couldn't. Once his hip joint was loose, he picked it up and lifted it over his shoulder, a maneuver which he didn't even know he was capable. The crook of his knee hooked around his neck, his foot brushing his right shoulder. Bolster could feel himself sweat, grunting without thinking.

"Relax," Barlow said. "Concentrate."

Barlow's instructions were pure and accurate, drawn from ancient texts, not half-assed, not made up. He practiced yoga as the scriptures dictated. This made him authoritative and homicidally dangerous.

Soon, Bolster's left arm, almost impossibly, was threading the gap between his knee and his head, and his fingers were spread evenly on the floor. He bent forward and balanced on his arm, hovering over the ground like a mobile. Then, according to Barlow, he lifted his right leg as well, straight in front of him, also flexing his foot, placing his right hand on the knee, hand drawn into *jñana mudra*. And there he had it.

Bolster had entered The Forbidden Pose. His breathing was even, his gaze steady. He barely sweated. Barlow was right. It felt transcendent.

"Isn't it good, Bolster?" he said. "Isn't it the best?"

Bolster didn't respond. He didn't want to, because he didn't want to break the spell of the Forbidden Pose. It seduced.

"I do it myself, of course," said Barlow. "Every day, for four and a half minutes. That's the very outer limit. Most people's systems fail at five minutes. A few can hang on until six. I give you about five-and-a-half."

I don't want to die, Bolster thought, but he didn't really mean it. He was in The Forbidden Pose now. It transcended care of death.

"You're a powerful yogi, Bolster," Barlow said. "You needed to see what it's like."

Bolster knew now. It seduced him like no woman ever could. And as the time drained from his body, each second grew more transcendent than the last. His mind became clear as glass. Even a dingy setting like this one felt like heaven. Every breath, every thought, every speck of dust looked marvelous, a miracle of creation. Light was otherworldly, but also part of him, and of everything. Bolster, his body and his mind, merged with the cosmic tapestry of eternity.

Barlow went back to his cushion and began to meditate, eyes cast slightly downward, riding shotgun on the end of the only lawman in the world able to stop him. But even though Bolster was strong in body and spirit, Barlow had years of study and practice on him. Where Bolster indulged, Barlow abstained. And soon, Barlow was going to live while Bolster died. By Barlow's clock, Bolster only had about a minute and a half left.

Bolster's brain was somewhere beyond this earth. He saw himself moving through the stars, toward a circle of white light. Maybe this was a cliché, maybe it was what eternity really looked like. Either way, Bolster felt the *prana*, the cosmic life force, flood his body at a thousand times the intensity than ever before. He was ready to burst with ecstasy, to lift up beyond himself. No thought crossed his mind. He didn't even remember his name. Bolster launched himself toward the forbidden end.

And then, he felt something, and not something good either. His left hamstring attachment was tearing away from the bone, and quickly. The nerve receptors sent hot shards of pain.

"AHHHHHHHHH!" he shouted, while wincing.

Barlow looked up, surprised. Usually, they just faded away quietly in The Forbidden Pose. Bolster seemed to be fighting the end. Barlow wasn't surprised. But Bolster would succumb. It was inevitable.

Then, Bolster lowered his right leg, until he was standing. He unlooped his left hand. And, gingerly, he unfolded his left leg. He plopped to the floor, gasping, his eyes glazed but alive.

He looked up at Barlow, sweating.

"You almost had me, Andrew," he said.

"I'll get you again," Barlow said.

Bolster stood, but he could barely put weight on his left leg.

"I'm gonna be on the DL for at least six months," he said.

He lurched toward Barlow like a Golem reborn. Barlow stood, lunged, and pushed Bolster in the chest with two hands. He wasn't very strong, not in a brawling sense anyway, but Bolster was only half there and all hurt. He toppled over as Barlow ripped across the warehouse toward the open door.

Bolster fell, but was up quickly, lurching toward the door, which Barlow had left open. The light hit his eyes in a full wash. Barlow was across the street, climbing the chain link. Bolster hit the street, wincing, his leg barely supporting him, as Barlow flipped himself over. It was hard for Bolster to climb, but he did it. On the other side of the fence was a narrow strip of dirt, which quickly emptied out into a outflow wash of the L.A. River, all weeds and concrete and abandoned shopping carts and graffiti from taggers who the LAPD hadn't even tried to catch.

The bottom of the wash was slick from algae and a light trickle of runoff. Barlow was way ahead of Bolster, at this point predicting several weeks of crutches, minimum, and having to replacing his usual round of yoga classes with a series of low-rent motel stakeouts to make money.

Barlow turned, tauntingly.

"You gave up eternity for this, Bolster?" he shouted. "To chase a supposed madman through a ditch?"

"It's better than being dead," Bolster said.

"Is it?" Barlow asked.

Bolster had to sit down. His thigh was burning. Barlow laughed, kept running, turning right at the bend, where he disappeared into some sort of tunnel, a pipe, something.

Bolster's phone was in his pocket, still charged. He got it out to call Martinez. In the distance, he heard a motorcycle revving. That was Barlow's usual mode of transport.

What if I hadn't been hurt? Bolster thought. *I could have caught him.*

But he had been hurt, and that's why he hadn't succumbed to The Forbidden Pose. He'd wanted to; he'd thought about it. Bolster would never forget how it had felt on the edge of eternity. If only he could return. But he knew that he couldn't, he mustn't, that it was a secret he'd carry with him for however long he walked the Earth, practicing and teaching yoga. He'd seen the end, he knew the truth, and he could never pass it along. It was a secret too blissful and terrible to share. Thanks to Bolster's aching hammy, The Forbidden Pose had loosened its deadly grasp. Bolster knew what it was like to transcend reality, and he never wanted to do it again.

He lay on the concrete, parched, dizzy, and pained. Boundless gratitude filled his heart. He loved his life, down to every last raw and ruined muscle. Barlow hadn't known what he was doing, not really, and that's why he was so dangerous. Injury is the only real teacher. Bolster had learned the lesson.

The present moment, now matter how uncomfortable or unpleasant, was good enough for him.

He called Martinez and gave his coordinates, told him to put out an APB for a long-haired yoga teacher on a motorcycle. You'd think that kind of person would be easy to find. But Barlow was more slippery than a mountain salamander. After that, Bolster lay back and waited. He reached into his pocket, pulled out his portable vaporizer, fired it up, and inhaled the sweet here and now.

Cougar Witch Plot

by Richard Rayner

1.

Megan Maloney no longer believed in therapy. Yoga was a
bust, ditto jogging, and, though her rage went on pouring
itself into fantasies of wild revenge, she opted not to buy the
cute little nickel-plated Smith & Wesson that she'd seen online
(and so discounted!) at Sharpshooter.org, but instead fixed a
lunch date with Alice Raskin, usually known simply as Mrs.
Raskin, who, Megan had heard, was some kind of a witch, or
kabbalist, or sorceress, and could take care of the situation
with spells, chants, and whatever.

"I want him to die. Like, *horribly*!" said Megan, surveying
her surroundings in the Urth Café on Main Street in Santa
Monica, the usual hubbub of successful women of a certain
age, lunching and chatting in pairs, and other women, dressed
casually in sweats and looking relaxed and fit, recently
returned from Gold's Gym or Yogaworks. So what if Mrs.
Raskin was a fraud? Megan felt better already. "I want him to
contract testicular cancer and suffer just bucketloads before a
bus slams into him and crushes him."

"He slept with you but he hated you," said Mrs. Raskin,
calmly authoritative, regarding Megan with dark
expressionless eyes. Mrs. Raskin had once been a beauty,
and in many ways she still was. She was tall, slim, and
dressed with oddball elegance in a white lace blouse and
vest of antique velvet. Her smooth pale skin was untouched

by plastic surgery or Botox and seemed preserved by other
means. She was maybe over fifty, maybe even over sixty, but
her exact age was impossible to determine. Those spooky eyes
suggested black infinities of experience. "He mocked you,"
Mrs. Raskin said, peering straight into Megan's thoughts. "He
humiliated you."

"How could I possibly have fallen for him?" said Megan,
gulping her second glass of cabernet. Usually she said no to
booze at lunch. Today, she'd been eager to make an exception.
"Oh grow up, Megan!"

The truth was, of course, Megan knew exactly why she'd
fallen for Fred Gilbert. He was tall, broad, muscular, with
features that belonged on Mount Rushmore or in a comic
book. And that was just the start of it. He drove an Aston
Martin and had properties scattered all over Europe, plus
the house by Richard Neutra in the Palisades. He was *uber*-
handsome and Megan should have guessed all along that if
something seems too good to be true, it *is* too good to be true.
Just a week ago, almost a year into their relationship, she'd
discovered that, along with his other toys and treasures, Fred
Gilbert had a wife and three children he'd omitted to mention.

"I'm thirty-four," she said. "Okay — *as if!* I'm thirty-eight and
he handed me a pretend reality and I so bought it."

A reckless marriage, undertaken in her twenties when
Megan was still in college in Chicago, had predictably gone
down in flames. Out here in L.A., she'd spent ten years with a
cameraman who already had two kids and eventually realized
he didn't want any more, and didn't want Megan either. Since
then her romantic life had been pretty much a procession of
self-inflicted disaster - a monster ego of a director, a bad boy
writer, a couple of nice boys who were boring in the end, a
need junkie, and an actual junkie, after whom had arrived the
seeming miracle of craggy Fred Gilbert. Like an idiot, she'd
viewed him as a keeper. She had only herself to blame, Megan

knew, and that was the cruelest cut of all.

"So what if I'm forty?" Megan said with a sniffle. "He lied to me and then he dumped me like trash. I feel beaten and stupid!"

Mrs. Raskin handed her a napkin.

"I'm so not on the shelf!"

"You're whatever age you want to be!" said Mrs. Raskin. "You're a strong woman! You're famous!"

"Not any more. Not really," said Megan, forcing a smile and brushing her hair away from her face, a gesture she'd played for the camera a hundred times or more. Megan had straight, long hair, ash-blond, and good hands, not feminine hands especially, but with elegant fingers. Her large blue eyes were swift to convey surprise, sorrow, amusement. Eyes, hair, hands, humor: these had been her selling features back in the day. But it had been over three years since she'd landed a part. A new generation of casting directors no longer knew her name. Her agent dropped her calls. People thought she'd died or vanished or gone to live on Maui. "I've pretty much put my acting career on hold. I sell cosmetics and I'm damned good at it."

"Of course you are. And don't short-change yourself. Everybody remembers 'Red Hot Law.'"

"They do?" said Megan, smiling for real now, knowing she was being played but grooving with it.

"It was a *classic.*" The shut doors that were Mrs. Raskin's eyes opened a crack, allowing Megan to glimpse — or was she just imagining that she glimpsed? - sparks and glowing red fires. "It's *criminal* that you're not in multiple new shows. I find it inconceivable."

"You're right!" said Megan, roused. Something about Mrs. Raskin's eyes alarmed and thrilled her. But then Megan saw that a fly had strayed into the dregs of her wine and was spinning there, gorged on sugar, dying no doubt, or dead already, and she felt her heart grow heavy again. "You know what Fred said the last time I went up for a part?"

"He *undermined* you. He pulled the rug from under the feet of a strong woman who *scares* him."

"He said, 'Is the show called 'Desperate Grandmothers?'"

"He *deserves* to be punished."

"He so does," said Megan with a brief gale of laughter. Raising her hand, she signaled to the handsome waiter who looked a lot like Brad Pitt, the young Brad Pitt, the preposterously gorgeous Brad from 'Thelma and Louise,' and who either was actually from Italy or had cultivated an Italian accent with Method-like conviction. "I'll take another glass, please. It's the cabernet."

"At your service, *signorina*," said the waiter, leaning across Megan and brushing her shoulder with the bare, tan skin of his forearm before, with a flourish, he whisked away the glass that had the dead fly in it and made it his ostentatious business to hasten back at once with another glass, fresh and full.

"Well, la-di-da!" said Mrs. Raskin. "That boy likes you. You should fuck his brains out."

Megan spluttered into her wine.

"He's in awe of you," said Mrs. Raskin.

"I'm way older than his mother most likely."

"Forget that nonsense and self pity! He sees a beautiful woman who can teach him about the world."

"The world? It seems to get further away from me on a daily basis." Megan said with a stab of pain as she remembered Fred Gilbert in that room at the Fairmont Hotel, knotting an Armani tie in front of the mirror, saying, "It's over. Get a life." Fred knew about the world alright. He did snazzy things with money. His knack for moving cash and making it grow had only been spurred by the downturn. He was a *superman* of the objective world. "It's a book I used to have that disappeared.

It's floating into the distance and leaving me stranded!"

"Take action! Assert your reality and mean it!" said Mrs. Raskin, reaching into her fringed Jimmy Choo tote for a fountain pen and a Moleskine notebook plastered with day-glo stickers and girlish swirls. The fountain pen was green, Megan observed, and more exotic in appearance than even Mrs. Raskin herself, with a snake-shaped clip of sinuous, curving gold. Mrs. Raskin unscrewed the top and wrote with swift, decisive strokes. "What are you reading in your book group?"

"Jane Austen. It's generally Jane Austen," said Megan. Why did she feel defensive? She unashamedly worshipped Jane Austen and went gaga for those heroines who laughed at the precariousness of their fates and negotiated worlds of rank and money with smarts. With smarts and sex. Or the *promise* of sex. Whatever.

"Jane may save you," said Mrs. Raskin. Her dark eyes gleamed. "But sometimes you need help from beyond. Elves. Fairies. Spirits. *Demons.*"

Mrs. Raskin ripped out the page on which she'd been writing.

"I'll need a possession of Mr. Gilbert's," she said. "An item of clothing would be ideal. If unwashed, so much the better."

Megan inspected the creamy unlined paper into which the cruel nib of Mrs. Raskin's fancy fountain pen had almost carved a 90049 address. The ink was red, with a whiff of vinegar. *Demons!* It had to be a joke. Mrs. Raskin was just a nutty old broad who loitered around the tennis courts and had the hots for young boys.

Still, Megan thought, this was better than sitting at home melting with helpless fury. "Something with his blood on it?" she said gaily. "To make the spell work better?"

"Your faith isn't necessary," said Mrs. Raskin, with that same ominous ability to look straight into Megan's mind. "But don't forget to bring a checkie!"

2.

Two days later Megan was back at the Urth, this time
with Kate Zola and Lily Prendergast, her best friends and
most loyal compadres. They sat by the window, as usual,
in the shade but with a view of the street and the human
traffic. Three identical copies of "Pride and Prejudice" — yet
another new edition, this one handsomely bound in golden
cloth — lay on the table in front of them. But for once they
weren't talking about Darcy or Wickham or Mr. Collins, or
Elizabeth Bennett's self-preserving tactics of wit and irony.

"*How* much?" said Lily, not having to feign astonishment.

"Five thousand," said Megan.

"She wanted five grand?" said Kate, with one of her raucous
laughs. "And you *gave* it to her? This is too sweet!"

Megan answered with a defiant shrug. She had an audience
and a story to tell. She was enjoying herself.

"You don't have that kind of money right now," said Lily,
and she knew, being a CPA and in charge of Megan's taxes.
Lily was fair-haired, pink-faced and remorselessly competent,
while Kate was sharp-featured and hard-boiled, a former
lawyer who blogged for Huffington Post. Lily, a Catholic,
was reserved; Kate had once pranced about in spike heels and
leather mini-skirts to get herself fired from Brackett, Liebler,
Kaufman, Wimbash, McToochney and Toms.

"I put it on a card. The Visa I didn't max out yet," said
Megan. "She's, like, letting me pay in installments."

"No!" said Lily, who paid all her bills on time and monitored
her credit rating on a daily basis. Lily's husband had died in a
car wreck a year ago and she was bringing up two sons solo.
Kate, already into her third marriage, had twin daughters and
didn't mind if she got dirt under her fingernails. Kate's hair
was a tangle of curls; Lily knew what carelessness could do to
the best of your hopes and plans.

"This is so awesome," said Kate. "Where does she live, the old crocodile? Don't tell me — in Beverly Hills, right?"

"Brentwood. She has this totally swag three storey Craftsman with a tennis court and a pool," said Megan, seemingly fated never to have kids of her own while speaking and dressing like the teenagers the other two were trying to raise. Ditziness was Megan's incognito, her stratagem against the mire and fury. "And the same gardener as the guy who created 'The Mentalist.'"

"That figures," said Kate. "Scoring five grand a pop from suckers like you."

"And she's not a crocodile. She's kind of beautiful, in a scary way. Like Annie Hall grown up and gone lulu," Megan said. "You're absolutely *not* allowed to write about this."

Kate held up a hand. "I promise. I make the most solemn of oaths. I double and triple swear. But I'll die if I don't get the scoop — every single grisly detail."

"A woman, posing as a witch, in Brentwood?" said Lily, shaking her head, still trying to get her head around this affront to her orderly world-view. "I guess I shouldn't be surprised. This is the city where it would happen."

"A kabbalist, not a witch," said Megan.

"There's a difference?" said Lily, surprised.

"Her arrangement's not with, like, Satan. She uses signs and symbols, hidden meanings inside the Bible."

"The Torah," said Kate.

"Whatever," said Megan. "Anyway she had these books she was looking at. One of them had this, like, freaky cover and she said it had belonged to some crazy famous old English dude and it was bound in human skin."

"Eeeeuuu!" Kate exclaimed.

"Total grosstown!!" Megan agreed. "This other book she had was, like, normal by comparison except it was the size of a suitcase and she goes, 'This is one of the rarest books in the world. It was printed in Italy in the time of the Medicis,' and

I go, 'Cool!' She goes, 'My mother got it from her grandfather in Budapest,' and I go, 'No, really?' and she goes, 'My mother had the power. In World War Two, she made Hitler invade Russia not Syria.' I'm thinking this lady is seriously *out of control*. But I just go, like, 'Wow!' and she goes, 'These secrets come all the way from Moses. He learned them from an angel in the wilderness,' and I go, 'I so totally didn't know that,' and she looks right through me with those weird eyes she has and she goes, 'You'll see soon enough.' Then the lights dimmed and she summoned her followers and the ceremony began."

"Her *followers*?"

That was Kate again.

"Her helpers, flunkies, whatever. There were three of them. All young guys. One of them was that kid with the mohawk who works behind the cheese counter at Venice Whole Foods."

"I know him," Lily said, a frown creasing the usual frank certainty of her face. "Even I think he's adorable!"

"Is she fucking him?" Kate, again, cutting to the chase.

"My guess is that she's doing all three."

Lily's jaw dropped.

Kate exhaled audibly. "No way!"

"They looked, like, *used*. Just exhausted and wrung-out."

A brief silence fell.

"I know. Go figure," said Megan. "Mrs. Raskin says she can get them a record deal."

"It's so bogus!" Kate said.

"She gives a good show," said Megan, recalling how, after she'd handed over a silk tie that Fred Gilbert had left behind at her place, Mrs. Raskin had put the tie on a cleared area of floor and drawn a circle around it in chalk. "Then she hands each of us — that's me and the three boys — our own stick of chalk and we get down on our knees while she stands there with this plan kind of a deal in her hand, telling us what to draw. Lines and shapes. Tunnels with writing inside them and hands growing out of them. Cool kabbalah shit."

"Oh just get over it," said Kate, actually angry now. "She's a total imposter."

"Whatever," said Megan. "Anyway she tells us to hold hands and the lights go out, like, completely. Out of nowhere, a wind starts to blow. A Santa Ana, or something. Except it's shrill, howling. And Mrs. Raskin has her hands pressed together and she's chanting in some language I never heard. Like her voice wasn't her voice any more."

"She was in a trance?" said Lily.

"Faking it! What a bunch of baloney!" said Kate.

"The room seemed to shiver. The wind drops and Mrs. Raskin opens her eyes and holds her hands up to the height of my eyes. Slowly she pulls them apart and there's something between them — a crystal ball, spinning."

Megan spoke softly now, no longer laughing, as if the intensity of the memory did indeed open a door on some unknown other world.

"She blinks and claps her hands and the lights come back on. The little spinning ball isn't there any more and Fred's tie is totally *gone* from inside the chalk circle."

"One of the young guys took it," Kate said.

"Maybe," said Megan, not believing that. She'd been there, watching every second. None of the others had touched that crystal ball. "Anyway, Mrs. Raskin goes, 'It is done,' and her voice creeps me out — it's still deep and strange, like it just came back from, wherever it had been. And that was it."

"So Fred Gilbert's dead already?" said Kate.

"Well, duh, like, *no.*"

"See? What did I tell ya? It's a total scam!"

In Kate's voice Megan detected, not just amusement now, but rising outrage, Kate being, beneath the tough-girl skepticism, a believer in the possibilities of honor and fair play.

"Let's *expose* this bitch!"

"Mrs. Raskin gave me this." From her bag, Megan took a small box that she placed on the marble table-top beside the Jane Austens. "She said the spell was made but the choice was mine. She goes, 'Open this and he dies.' Then she puts the box in my hand."

In silence, the three women peered at the box, small, brass-hinged, ornately carved, casket-shaped, with mother-of-pearl inlay.

"Kind of fancy, for a box," said Lily.

"It belonged to an Englishwoman from the burning times. That's what Mrs. Raskin called them," said Megan. "The woman died at the stake. The box survived."

"What a bunch of crapola! It's from Pottery Barn," said Kate, reaching out for the box.

Lily stopped Kate's hand. "I don't think we should mess with this."

"Come on! You can't be serious," said Kate, looking from Lily to Megan, who shrugged and threw a glance towards the cool young waiter who looked like Brad Pitt. That morning Megan had put on her favorite pair of faded True Religions and tucked them into a pair of old, tight Dior boots she knew flattered her legs. She felt relaxed and good about herself, with her friends again.

"Kate's got to be right, right?" Megan said "I mean, this is a game. I was, like losing it, and you guys were out of town, and I hated Fred and I still do and I just wasted a shitload of money. But it's way more fun than therapy."

Without further ado, Megan seized the box. A faint whiff of vinegar pinched at her nostrils as soon as she lifted the lid. Inside lay a strip of black paper, coiled like a spring or snake. The paper stirred and writhed as if at the command of a burning hot breeze. It glowed and Megan saw markings, symbols and letters and hieroglyphs, that emerged from the blackness and defined themselves along the moving strip.

"Holy shit," Megan said in a whisper, reaching for the paper, but it slithered and rustled, then rose suddenly, unfurling like a banner, evading Megan's snatching fingers as it flew up in the air and out of the window.

3.

"I mean, I don't even know why I was there," said Megan, late in the afternoon of the following day, sitting on a plump leather sofa in the low-ceilinged living room of Mrs. Raskin's Brentwood Craftsman. Megan already felt tipsy, having drunk most of an apple martini. "It's so totally strange. Like, I don't remember driving there. Like I was drawn or something. *Compelled.*"

Mrs. Raskin's dark shut-down eyes seemed fathomless.

"That was a part of the spell too?" said Megan, guessing the answer, even before seeing the hint of a smile that cut across Mrs. Raskin's cheeks. "I stood there. Defying him to notice me," Megan went on. She'd been at the north-east corner of 4th and Wilshire, across the street from P.F. Chang's, and she'd seen Fred Gilbert come out of the restaurant, talking into his cell and striding with his customary money-whiz confidence. It had been in the middle of the afternoon, just a few hours ago. "But at first he didn't. Like, he *couldn't.*"

That had been because Fred was too busy trying to disentangle himself from the thin black snake of black and red paper that gusted from the sidewalk and wrapped itself around his neck. His hands flapped and failed, clutching at the paper, which, as it was torn, burst into flaming pieces, embers that the wind tossed and swirled away. "He doubled up, yelling and clutching his pants."

"The testicular problem you ordered."

"He was in pain."

"Violent pain," agreed Mrs. Raskin.

"I mean, like — that must have really hurt!"

"But of course!" said Mrs. Raskin.

Megan's hand shook a little as she helped herself to more martini from the bedewed solid silver shaker that Mrs. Raskin had left on the table in front of the sofa.

"And then he *did* see me," Megan said, recalling how the rugged quarterbackiness of Fred's face had been distorted by agony and fret and the dawning of an astonished puzzlement that she couldn't help but find funny. "I'm totally ashamed of myself. Totally. I laughed. He was the one who was looking stupid and terrified, standing there clutching his balls in the middle of Wilshire Boulevard."

Megan gulped at the martini.

"I don't think he even saw the bus," she said. "But he sure was staring at something."

"The demon I sent," said Mrs. Raskin, standing in front of a floor-to-floor to ceiling bookcase in which some of her ancient volumes were arrayed, wearing a diaphanous gown of black silk that floated down to the platformed mules on her feet. On the wall beside the bookcase, Megan saw, was a Picasso print with many noses and eyes. "A fire demon."

"I feel, *like*, so awful about him," Megan said. The Santa Monica Big Blue bus had smashed into Fred Gilbert from behind, tossing his mutilated body into the air.

"Do you?" said Mrs. Raskin. "Do you really feel awful about him?"

"He never stood a chance."

"He got what he deserved."

Megan asked the question that had been nagging at her. "Did we make that happen, really?"

"What do you think?" said Mrs. Raskin.

A tingle rushed upwards from the base of Megan's spine. Was that fear, or just the booze? She swallowed more of the sweet-smelling gin.

Outside, night was coming down. Through the patio doors Megan glimpsed the dying light sparkle on the rippling waters of Mrs. Raskin's pool. Swathes of manicured green rolled towards a tennis court. And only now did Megan see something else: enshadowed and defined by the sun's setting rays were three smaller areas, side-by-side, oblongs where the grass grew long and lush like uncut hair. They could almost be graves, she thought.

"I've been married three times. I loved them all!" said Mrs. Raskin, dark fires burning in the depths of her eyes. Megan heard, or dreamed or imagined she heard, distant moans and screams, as if three souls, or maybe many more souls, were held captive within Mrs. Raskin's skull, trapped and buzzing like flies.

Whoa! said Megan to herself, *I've really gone over to the dark side!*

It was true, what she'd said just a minute ago. She did feel awful about Fred. Well — maybe not *that* awful.

Megan took a deep breath.

The merest nod, or desire, or whim, and it seemed that with Mrs. Raskin's awesome powers the whole slippery cruel world of Los Angeles could be brought to heel. And, like, why not?

She'd better tell Kate and Lily they'd be switching to "Rosemary's Baby" or "The Shining" for the next book group. Had Jane Austen written anything with witches?

Kabbalists.

Whatever!

There was a part she'd heard about, something big in a new thing at Showtime.

Was she, like, totally evil?

She wanted and needed that part.

"La-di-da!" said Mrs. Raskin with a flash of those troubling eyes. "You're perfect for it!"

An Eye For An Eye

by Terry Mixon

If you prick us, do we not bleed? If you tickle us, do we not laugh? If you poison us, do we not die? And if you wrong us, shall we not revenge?

Shylock - William Shakespeare, The Merchant of Venice, act 3, scene 1

And thine eye shall not pity; but life shall go for life, eye for eye, tooth for tooth, hand for hand, foot for foot.

Deuteronomy 19:21 - King James Bible (Cambridge Ed.)

Justice is a poor man's revenge. Never let someone else settle your scores.

Al Blake, blood mage assassin

***

Al Blake tugged his light coat closer against the wind and shouldered his way through the crowd toward the courthouse steps. The afternoon would warm up, but the morning chill still had a bite. He'd need the umbrella, though. L.A. might not have real winters, but it did rain a bit.

He checked his pocket watch. He had a few minutes before the target put in an appearance, but being early never hurt. The client wanted to send a message. Killing the district attorney on the courthouse steps in the middle of a speech about cracking down on organized crime would do just that.

The specific requirements of the job had intrigued him. Blood magic required getting close to his target for the kill—no more than a few dozen feet—despite how the dime store novels made it seem. Yes, a less invasive spell to track someone might work from all the way across the city for a powerful mage, but Al couldn't drop someone from his living room.

Nor would he want to. Al was a professional, an independent contractor. Not some mob thug. He insisted his jobs be done right, and that meant he had to be there to tweak the spell, if necessary. Or abort if something went south.

The press, predictably enough, covered the lower steps. Several photographers stood up front to catch Marcus Parker's good side for the afternoon edition. With all the hoopla surrounding the most recent bootlegging crackdown, his farts got a headline above the fold.

Al could pretty much guarantee he'd get a picture with a full page spread today.

He pulled out a press pass and stuck it in his hatband. The cops probably wouldn't even look at it. He'd attended the last press conference just to be sure. Once the D.A. dropped dead, Al would have a minute or two to make his getaway before they locked down the plaza. He had a "borrowed" car parked at the curb to speed his getaway.

He wondered who wanted the man dead with such public spectacle. If it were the mob, they'd stir up a hornet's nest. If it wasn't, then perhaps the client wanted it to look like the mob was behind the killing.

Someone close to the target had to be in on it, or they

couldn't have gotten the blood-stained handkerchief he'd received with his money. People who made enemies like Parker had were careful about leaving their blood, hair, and fingernail clippings lying about. For obvious reasons.

He gave a mental shrug. He didn't need to know the backstory. Too much curiosity made for a fatal character flaw in a contract killer.

Parker finally came out of the building with his staff at his heels. He looked like a shark with his hair slicked back, his eyes cold as he scanned the reporters from the podium. A well-dressed shark, since that subdued charcoal grey suit had to have cost a pretty penny.

Al ignored the man's opening statement. Blah, blah, blah. Crime, arrests, booze. He'd heard it all before. The jerk probably had his fingers in all the pies up to his elbow.

Instead, Al took a few minutes to admire the well-endowed blonde to the DA's left. She had a sexy little mole over her upper lip that gave her face a lot of character. She also wore a peach sweater that did absolutely nothing to hide her generous figure.

Neither did the skirt she wore. Hemlines had inched upwards for most of the '20s and if they kept going, the decade would go out with a loud whistle, a trend Al heartily approved of.

With more than a hint of genuine regret at getting back to business, he reached into his pocket and found the handkerchief he'd brought. He'd taken the precaution of wrapping it in raw silk to be sure the blood spots on it weren't contaminated. He didn't want mistakes.

He closed his eyes for a moment and invoked his talent. Immediately, he felt the tenuous connection with his target. He allowed his senses to sink into a meditative state. It sped the process and made failure unlikely. No mage ever courted a botched spell if he could help it.

When the mental jigsaw snapped into place, he opened his eyes and invoked the spell. The man kept jabbering along, unaware of his impending demise. Al knew the man's blood pressure would spike in a few seconds and keep going until he had a stroke. Without immediate intervention from a gifted healing mage, he'd die on the steps.

The woman sneezed and stared at her hand. Al saw the blood on it and more on her upper lip. It streamed down her face and onto the peach sweater. The lurid red shocked him.

He killed the spell.

The backlash staggered him. Pain blossomed between his eyes and his vision wavered. He heard more than saw the woman collapse. The crowd came to life with cries of alarm and shouted questions, mixed in with the pop of flash bulbs.

Well, this certainly would make the headlines, but for all the wrong reasons.

He used the confused jostling of the crowd to make his escape. Once away from the press of people, he slid into his getaway car, a sleek A-Model Ford. Black, of course. His vision had returned enough for him to drive. The police hadn't even begun to spread out before he pulled away from the scene.

His thoughts raced as he put distance between him and the debacle. That kind of spell didn't miss. Someone had double-crossed him. He'd almost certainly killed the spell in time to allow the woman to live, but it didn't change the fact that he'd blown it. He needed some aspirin, and then he had to figure out who to hunt down.

He breathed easier once he switched back to his own car. The sharp pain behind his eyes had faded to a dull ache, though his fury had grown to towering proportions. Time to go see the intermediary that had serviced the contract.

The trip to the weasel's office took almost an hour in the heavy traffic. An hour that allowed the hot rage to turn into cold and calculating fury.

The weasel's place occupied a corner of the third floor of a dilapidated office building on Bunker Hill. The grime on the outside hinted at the mess inside. Trash littered the lobby and someone had broken the desk into firewood. The stairwell was, if anything, worse. No wonder the man had wanted to meet at a diner.

The lettering on the scarred wooden door reminded him of the weasel's name: Lenny Craft, Private Investigator. He probably fit the hard drinking and womanizing stereotype, but the man certainly didn't have a heart of gold under his gruff exterior.

The man himself sat at a desk in the front room when Al went in. No secretary for him. That said a lot about his character, too.

Craft looked up from a newspaper with bloodshot eyes. His wardrobe matched the decor: dirty, old, and soaked in booze. Al made a note never to use him again, if he allowed him to survive more than the next few minutes. He'd also have a word with the man who met the clients for him. He should've known better than to make a deal with this loser.

The man put on what he probably thought of as a friendly smile. "What can I do for you, sir? Pull up a chair and tell me your problem. Cheating wife? Lying business partner? I can get to the bottom of it."

Al closed the door behind him and sat in the wooden chair after brushing off the crumbs of someone's lunch. "I hope you can help me get to the bottom of a bad business deal. You see, I took some money to do something and the job wasn't as advertised. Now I need to find out who screwed me."

"I can help. Who set up the deal?"

"You did."

Craft blinked at him stupidly for a moment before he frowned. "Excuse me?"

Al smiled amiably. "You met with an associate of mine yesterday and gave him a substantial sum of money to kill a man." He pulled the handkerchief out of his pocket and tossed it on the desk. "Does that spark your memory?"

The P.I. blanched. "Hold on, now! I didn't double-cross nobody! I did exactly what the client told me."

"And who was this client? A man in his thirties with dark hair?"

"I don't have to tell you squat. You got paid, so get moving before — "

Al casually drew his automatic and leveled it at the P.I. Sometimes even a blood mage assassin needed a more conventional threat. "Normally I'm a big fan of client confidentiality, but not when someone wants to have me kill a woman. Call it a quirk, but that's not my flavor of evil. Someone knew that when they hired you and you're going to tell me, one way or another."

The P.I. started sweating, virtually pouring down his face. "Look, you got it all wrong. Hell, a woman hired me!"

Al considered that. He pulled a pocketknife from his vest and tossed it down beside the bloody handkerchief, which he retrieved and put away. "Cut your thumb and put the blood on something."

"For a blood mage assassin? Do you think I'm stupid?"

"Yes. The question now is how stupid are you? If I don't get my answers, I'll shoot you somewhere painful and take your blood that way. You'll answer my questions before you bleed out." He could do it, but he'd rather conserve his energy. Hopefully, the threat would be enough to get the man to talking.

Craft licked his lips. "You won't kill me if I'm telling the truth?"

"Regretfully, no. If you tell me the truth and haven't double-crossed me, I'll walk out that door and leave you unharmed."

The P.I. hesitantly picked up the knife and pulled a faded handkerchief from his pocket. It looked like he'd blown his nose on it. Many times. Well, it wasn't any skin off Al's nose if the man got an infection. Craft made a shallow cut on his thumb and winced. A few drops of blood beaded up.

Al tried not to sneer as the man wiped the blood on the handkerchief and sucked on his thumb. So much for the hardboiled gumshoe act. This guy was over easy. He took the tattered cloth and held the blood between his thumb and forefinger.

Truth telling was one of the simplest spells in a blood mage's repertoire. He didn't even have to focus to feel the link to the P.I. "Who hired you to retain my services?"

"A real pretty blonde with curves in all the right places, if you know what I mean."

The magic response surprised Al. Craft had told the truth. "She specifically told you she wanted to have District Attorney Parker killed in the manner you passed on to me? Did she give you her name?"

"She wanted it done exactly like I told your guy. She never gave me her name and I didn't ask."

Another truth. "Did you change anything that you passed on to me? Could someone have replaced the handkerchief?"

"No, everything was just as I said."

A lie. "Bull." Al cocked the hammer on his Colt 1911.

Craft held up his hands. "Okay! I kept some of the money! I'll give it to you!"

"You robbed an assassin? If it weren't self-evident, I'd tell you exactly what kind of idiot that made you. Were there any other changes to our deal between when she hired you and when you briefed my guy?"

"No," the sweating man said, the whites of his eyes gleaming. "Nothing else."

True.

"Did the woman have any identifying features? Moles, freckles, birthmarks?"

"She had a little mole over her upper lip. Just a tiny thing. Very hot."

So the woman who'd collapsed this morning was his client — an odd and unexpected turn of events. Al put his pistol away. "You've been mostly honest, so I'll take the money you owe me and leave you alive. Hand it over. All of it."

The man pulled out his wallet and counted out a number of bills. Al picked them up off the desk and tucked them in his pocket with the man's handkerchief. "I'll just hang onto your handkerchief for now. I suggest you carefully consider who you rob in the future."

No one disturbed him on the way out. Thankfully, his car was still in one piece, though some local toughs were eyeing it. They backed off when he gave them a cold look.

He stopped at the corner once he made it to a better neighborhood and passed over a couple of pennies for the afternoon edition of the Herald Examiner. He read the article on the events at the press conference, which didn't make the front page. The police didn't consider it an attack at all. That was a lucky break.

Instead, the news reported that the woman—Darla White—had an unknown medical condition. District Attorney Parker pontificated about how tragic the event was, and how glad he was that his secretary seemed to be recovering well. The hospital they took her to was close to the courthouse.

He found a space in the hospital parking lot and walked around the side of the building. As expected, he found a couple of interns outside smoking. He gave them a nod and headed in through the employee's door they'd so thoughtfully propped open.

It only took him a few minutes to liberate a white coat, clipboard, and stethoscope from someone's office. With his suit, he looked like every other doctor walking the halls. With the aura of authority he'd appropriated, none of the nurses hesitated in helping him locate the room where Darla White recuperated.

He closed the door most of the way behind him and examined the woman in the bed. Her face was significantly paler now, but her breathing seemed regular enough. He'd stopped the spell in time. She'd make a full recovery.

That made him feel better. Not only would killing her have violated his code, killing one's employer—even by accident— wasn't something to put on a resume.

She opened her eyes when he cleared his throat. "Oh, I'm sorry, Doctor. I didn't hear you come in."

He walked over to her bed. "You're looking better than when I last saw you. I'm pleased to tell you that you're going to make a full recovery."

Some of the worry left her eyes. "That's reassuring. Thank you."

"I do, however, have some delicate questions for you. First, I need to know why you wanted to kill your boss."

Her eyes widened and her body stiffened. "What?"

Al smiled. "No need to worry. You see, I'm not your doctor. I'm the man you hired to kill Parker. A job that almost went spectacularly wrong this morning."

Her eyes flicked toward the door.

He nudged it closed. "There, now no one can overhear you. I assure you, I'm not with the police. I know you hired that private dick, Craft. He hired me and provided me with the handkerchief. You see? If I were with the police, I wouldn't need to trick you. I'd just arrest you."

"Perhaps..." She cleared her throat. "Perhaps I'm more concerned that I'm in a room alone with a paid killer."

Al pulled the wooden chair over to the bed and sat. "The key word is paid. You've paid me to complete a job. You have nothing to fear from me. Someone double-crossed both of us."

The woman slumped a little in the bed. "It had to have been Marcus. I don't know how or when, but it had to have been. He's always been tricky like that."

"I normally don't ask, but why do you want him dead? And why so publicly?"

"I suppose it doesn't matter if you know. He and I...well, we had a thing for a while. He made the move, but I didn't resist very much. Anyway, I'm pregnant."

Al's stomach did a slow roll. "I hope the baby is okay."

"The doctor—the real one—said he could still hear a heartbeat. He seemed confident that the baby would be okay. I'll find out in a few months."

A slow rage built inside Al. Parker had almost made him kill a woman and her unborn child. Oh, the man would pay big time.

He kept his face calm only with the strongest effort. She didn't need to see how he felt. It wouldn't be helpful. "Getting pregnant is serious, but not usually enough to warrant killing the man."

She smiled. "No, I suppose not. I told him I was going to have a baby. He demanded I get an abortion. Even if I didn't want to have a child, I wasn't going to do that to a baby. It's illegal and terribly dangerous for me, as well."

Since she hired a hit man, the law wasn't the primary driver in her refusal. "And how did he take your response?"

"Poorly. He told me that if I ever named him as the father, he'd be sure I didn't live to see the next dawn. Then a man almost ran me over outside my apartment."

"Not an accident?"

"He chased me back over the curb. No, the guy wanted me dead. Then someone broke into my apartment while I was out. I'm pretty sure the cut up mattress was a message."

Al nodded. "How long ago was that?"

"Two days. I looked in some of the files to get the names of some men who might know how to hire an assassin. When they referred me to Craft, I paid him enough to get it done fast. After that, I never let Marcus corner me. I stayed at a friend's house last night."

"Why go back to work? Why not call in sick?"

She raised her chin defiantly. "Because I needed to see it happen. He tried to kill my baby and me. I figured that if I'm going to have someone killed, I should see it in all the ugly detail. I just didn't figure I'd get attacked instead."

"And that's why I'm here. The handkerchief had your blood on it, not his."

Her jaw dropped. "That's not possible."

"I assure you it's a certainty. How did you get his blood?"

"He has nosebleeds sometimes. I filched the handkerchief after I found out I was pregnant. I needed to have a blood mage check to be sure he was the father."

If Al wasn't going to judge people for hiring him to kill for them, he wasn't going to judge the woman for sleeping around. "He must've known you'd taken it. Or figured it out later. Would he be aware of your research into hiring me?"

"I told the records clerk the files were for a case, but it's possible Marcus found out."

"You have any ideas how he got your blood?"

She nodded. "He punched me when I slapped him. That had to be it. I took the handkerchief home to wash, but he must've swapped the two somehow."

"He may try again now that he's failed. Can your friend come and stay with you? Or someone else?"

"I'm pretty sure she'll come if I call her."

"Do it. And forget we ever met." He rose to his feet.

"You're going to finish this?" She sounded surprised.

He allowed her a small smile. "You paid for results, so

you'll have them. When the police come calling about it, be shocked. Your alibi will be iron clad. Good luck, Miss White."

Al slipped out of the room. The clock was ticking and he needed a new angle. Without the man's blood, this job had become a lot more challenging. In a way, he approved. If everything went right every time, the job might become boring.

He thought about other angles as he drove away from the hospital. Parker would be on his guard now. Even with the police thinking Miss White's episode was a natural consequence of her condition, Parker knew exactly what had happened. What he didn't know was if Al would try again. Smart money said he'd prepare for a follow up attack, at least until he succeeded in eliminating his inconvenient lover. And possibly her paid assassin.

It took a couple of hours to track down where Parker lived, up in the Los Feliz hills just west of Downtown. The man wouldn't want any riff-raff finding him. Or getting to him. The walled estate made that more difficult. Al figured there were armed guards on the other side of the dark stone. He didn't hear any dogs, but that wouldn't surprise him either.

Al parked up the road and discarded various ideas. A distraction was bad because it would tip Parker off that someone wanted in. He'd undoubtedly warned the guards to look at anyone making a delivery. More likely, they knew all the people that made them. A new face would set off alarms.

There were ways, but they took time. Time that he didn't have to spare.

Actually, he knew one car that would be coming here tonight. Getting into it would be a challenge, though. Still, it made for an exciting evening.

Parker's driver came out the gates just before dark. He was alone, with no other cars following him. Any guards must already be at the courthouse. That made this plan feel right.

He pulled out into traffic and matched the man's pace with a few cars between them. That became easier once he was sure the man was indeed heading for the courthouse.

Hopefully Parker wouldn't be waiting in the lobby. He didn't seem the type to wait around on a lackey, but you never saw all the curve balls.

The driver stopped at the curb almost exactly where Al had parked this morning. Karma, perhaps? A second chance, certainly.

He parked behind the man, walked calmly up to the passenger door, and slid into the front seat. His pistol came out to cover the driver. "Don't make a peep and you get to live. Understand?"

The old man gave a terrified moan. "Please, don't hurt me. I have some money."

"Drive."

The trembling man started the car and pulled into traffic. "I'll give you whatever you want."

"Yes, you will. Turn left."

He directed the man to the commercial district. There were several empty warehouses off Los Angeles Street near Olympic he'd used in the past that would make a good place to stash the man for now.

They pulled up to a wide set of doors and he forced the man out while he opened the lock with his pick. He'd done it enough that he ought to have a key made. He rode the running board inside and pulled the driver out of the car again while he closed the doors.

The man was undoubtedly certain he'd die here. Al put away his gun and shooed him toward the old office. "I said you'd live and you will. I need your car and have to keep you tied up while I do it."

He already had some rope on hand, as well as a handy chair.

The last guy he'd brought here hadn't walked out under his own power, but the driver was an innocent. Being a bad guy didn't mean Al had to be an evil son of a bitch. He took the man's coat and hat, then tied him up.

Once Al had secured the driver, he walked behind him and took out his knife. He found a fleshy part of the man's arm when he rolled up his sleeve. A shallow nick brought out a little blood and a lot of screaming.

Al touched the blood and reached through it to the man. "Calm down and hear the truth of my words. I'm not going to harm you. I swear it." His prisoner sighed and stopped making any noise. The bond that bound them together showed him the truth. He would know on an almost instinctual level if Al lied.

"Your employer offended a very dangerous man. I'm going to kill him tonight, but you will be released unharmed."

Al took a clean handkerchief from his pocket and soaked up the old man's blood. What he intended to do wasn't easy magic. In fact, it was extremely difficult and draining, always a last resort for a blood mage. The single plus this method had was no one would expect it, since it was one of the powers that never seemed to make it into the public consciousness because people like him had good reason to keep the spell secret.

First, though, he needed to deal with the driver. Leaving him tied up was cruel. Leaving him with a good description of the man who kidnapped him was dangerous. Neither of those choices were acceptable to Al. Frankly, the ropes were just there to keep the man still while the blood mage performed the ritual.

He popped a handkerchief into the man's mouth to keep him quiet, too. Better safe than sorry.

Al opened the locked cabinet at the back of the office. He touched the quartz stone beside the door and deactivated the booby trap. If someone else broke in, the contents of the cabinet would burst into flames. And so would the would-be thief.

He took the roll of leather to the desk and laid it out. Multicolored stones worth a small fortune gleamed and winked in the light streaming through the window.

Most blood magic was simple enough to perform on the fly, but the most powerful workings required concentration and focus. They also required speed the stones allowed. When activated, each stone released a powerful spell segment that could be loaded in advance. That allowed him to cast a spell that would normally knock a mage out from exertion.

Al arranged the stones in the proper order and began the spell, the bloody handkerchief clutched in his hand.

Ten minutes later, he sat back in the chair, covered in sweat. He felt the same, but he knew how to test the efficacy of the spell. He walked on shaky legs to stand in front of the driver, gently pulling the gag from his mouth.

The old man stared up at him in shock and fear. "What have you done? You look like...me."

Al smiled and touched the man's forehead with his bloody handkerchief. "Sleep. Wake when I snap my fingers." He forced his will on the man, who slumped in his chair. That drained him a little, but he'd gladly pay the price to avoid killing the man.

He untied the man and laid him gently down on the beat up couch in the corner. He'd sleep until woken, or wake up in about six without intervention. If things went as planned, Al would plant some false memories to match the events yet to come when he woke him. With everything that had happened, the man would want to remember anything else.

If the man awoke on his own, Al wouldn't be in a position to care.

Al took his workbag out of the cabinet and secured his

magical gear. He shrugged into the old man's coat. It was a little tight, but workable. With the glamour in place, Parker shouldn't be able to tell anything was wrong. The hat fit perfectly.

The bag went into the trunk. The return trip to the courthouse took longer than he'd have liked, but that couldn't be helped. He swung around so he would come in from the appropriate direction.

A visibly irritated Parker stood near the curb with two men that screamed bodyguard. He allowed one of them to open the rear door for him and slid inside. The guard followed him while his companion sat up front.

Parker glared at Al. "Where have you been? I've been waiting ten minutes."

Al put on a contrite expression. "My apologies, sir. The car stalled and it took me a few minutes to get it running again." That kind of thing was all too common, even with the newer models like this one.

The District Attorney grudgingly nodded. "Fine. Take me home, then. Dinner will be waiting."

Al said nothing else. The more he spoke or drew attention to himself, the greater the chances the glamour would fail. He drove straight back to Parker's home and let everyone out at the front door. They didn't give him a second glance as they went in.

He parked the car in the garage, got his bag, and went into the kitchen through the back door. An older black woman gave him the stink eye. Perhaps the chauffeur wasn't allowed in the house. Or the man was an ass. On the other hand, she might just be that kind of person. No matter.

The assassin smiled, nodded his head, and kept going. Parker might be downstairs, but Al put his money the man of the house was upstairs changing into something else. He found a good corner to watch the stairs.

"Jacob?"

Al turned to find an improbably tall man dressed in a butler's formal clothing behind him. He made a curious noise, since he had no idea of the man's name or even if Jacob used it.

The butler frowned. "Can I do something for you?"

Ah, so the driver wasn't usually in the house. Al gave him the same smile he'd given the cook. "Mister Parker said he might need the car at a moment's notice. I'm to wait for him until dinner."

"Wait in the parlor, then. It's unseemly to have you lurking about." The man walked past Al with a sniff of distain.

Al had no idea where the parlor was, so he just moved to a different room with a view of the stairs. If the man came back, he could shoo Al to another one.

Parker came down the stairs only a few minutes later, much to Al's relief. He waited a few minutes and then headed up the stairs.

The master bedroom wasn't hard to find. Expensive-looking carved oak furnishings filled the space. Dozens of expensive suits filled the closet and pictures of Parker glad-handing various celebrities and politicians hung on the walls. Since Al knew Parker wasn't married, it was his room and unlikely to have anyone else come in at this hour.

He slipped into the bathroom to wait. And snoop, of course. The bath was even more ostentatious then the bedroom. Marble floors, a huge claw foot tube, and an enormous gold plated cheval mirror. The towels looked thick enough to sleep on. He made a mental note of the maker. One could never have enough good towels.

The next thing he looked for was the man's hair brush. Hair wasn't as good as blood, but it might work. Instead, he found a toothbrush. It used a strip of cloth rather than bristles, which still hadn't caught on yet since they tended to tear up a man's mouth. Many people didn't brush because of that.

Apparently, Parker wanted his teeth to shine.

Excellent. He could use it much more readily than hair.

He settled into the closet across from the tub and waited. Killing people required patience and Al could wait for hours with only his thoughts to keep him company.

Good thing, since Parker took his sweet time coming to the bedroom, and then he listened to the radio for an hour. Al waited for an extra hour after the radio went off for the man to fall asleep. That would make his task much simpler.

When he finally allowed himself to move back into the bedroom, Parker lay under the covers snoring softly. Al held the toothbrush cloth in his hand and focused on the target. He felt the link and smiled. *Got you, you son of a bitch.*

He focused his will and sent Parker deeper into sleep. When Al was certain he wouldn't wake, he set the bag on the bed and touched the sleeping man on the cheek.

Parker didn't even twitch.

Al opened the bag and pulled out a bottle of gin. The stuff was awful. It had obviously been made in a bathtub. He'd never touch it himself. It could kill a man.

Next, he brought out a coil of rubber hose and a funnel. The hose went down the man's throat. He wiggled when it triggered his gag reflect, but Al suppressed the feeling in him. Then he poured almost the entire bottle down his throat.

If this had been a dime-store novel, he'd have woken him to explain why he had to die. Luckily, Al was too pragmatic for that stupidity. He poured a little on the man's chin and set the bottle on the nightstand.

Parker's breathing slowed and eventually stopped. Al held a finger to his throat to be sure. Then he pinched the man's nostrils closed. He didn't react at all to having his air supply closed off. He was dead.

Al put the hose into the bag and slipped out of the bedroom. He moved extra cautiously and froze when he heard voices at the foot of the stairs. Two women spoke in hushed tones and started up.

He retreated to the hall closet and slipped inside before they made it to the second floor. He calmed his racing heart and waited for them to go by. After a few minutes of quiet, he slipped out and down the stairs. The kitchen was quiet now, so no one bothered him on his way back to the car.

The only hitch on the way out was a guard at the gate who waved him down. "Where you going?"

"Mister Parker gave me the night off and let me use the car."

The man didn't look convinced, but he let Al drive away. That was good enough.

A feeling of elation filled Al as he drove back to the warehouse. He'd carried it off. The irony of a district attorney known for cracking down on booze being found dead of drink would get all the right kind of attention. The press would love it and wouldn't be looking for holes.

The police might be suspicious, but their mages wouldn't be able to find a magical cause of death, no matter how hard they looked. The spell he'd used wouldn't be detectable by morning. The client was in the clear.

He loaded the sleeping driver into the car and drove him to the courthouse. He put his coat back on him and put him into the front seat. He stood outside the driver's door with the handkerchief stained in the man's blood in his fist. He snapped his fingers and made the link to the man.

Jacob woke, but still looked glassy eyed. Al focused his will into the man. "You've been on a drive. Mister Parker gave you the night off and let you use his car. Go do something fun and forget you ever saw me. Be back at Parker's house in the morning. Understand?"

The man nodded and started the car. Al watched him drive away without a backwards glance.

Al would lay low tomorrow and keep tuned to what the radio

had to say. This job had tickled his fancy. It felt good to walk on the side of the angels. Well, as close as his kind ever got.

What really made him smile was getting his own revenge for the setup. No one crossed Al Blake and lived to tell of it. An eye for an eye, indeed.

ALMOST ANGELS

BY BRENT NICHOLS

Los Angeles, 1947

Bright sunlight makes the darkest shadows.

I had to squint as I got out of my car and wormed my way through the ring of gawkers and the inner ring of grim-faced cops. The body lay sprawled where grass gave way to gravel, a dozen feet from the water's edge. The late-morning sunshine glittered on the surface of the Silver Lake reservoir. It's one of the prettiest spots in L.A., and I'd had the thought in the back of my mind for months that I ought to come by and spend an afternoon.

Not any more.

Noonan was the lead detective, and he stood beside me, chewing a toothpick in stolid silence while I stared down at a fan of bleached hair spread across the gravel. It took me a minute to work up enough nerve to look at the rest of the body.

It was a young woman, eyes half open, staring past me at the sky. I couldn't tell if she'd been pretty in life, but she likely was. L.A. draws the pretty ones from all across the country, with the same allure and the same dangers as a candle drawing moths in the night.

When you're stuck in some nowhere town watching the years trickle past, L.A. can start to look like heaven. The movie stars are angels, beautiful and aloof, and you wonder if maybe you could be one. Young dreamers pour into the city by the thousands.

The lucky ones wise up in a few months and go back to the sticks. Sometimes, I think the worst thing that can happen to a girl when she gets to Hollywood is to be discovered and get some work, because then she stays.

And when prey gathers in large numbers, the predators show up.

She was nude, lying on her back with one arm to the side, the other hand curled over her stomach as if to hide what had been done to her. It wasn't enough. Her stomach and chest had been carved with exquisite and awful precision. There was real artistry, for all that it made me want to lose my breakfast. Whirls and circles and curves and sudden sharp corners, at first glance a jumble of shapes all drawn over top of each other. But if you looked closely, you could see it was all one unbroken line.

"Well," said Noonan, "what do you think?"

I drew him apart from the nearest cops. I wanted to be clear of the faint whiff of corruption coming from the corpse, and I wanted the others out of earshot. At the best of times, Noonan isn't sure if he believes in magic, despite the things he's seen. With his fellow cops around, he feels the need to throw his skepticism in my face.

"It's no amateur," I said. "It's a real pro, draining magical power from a soul at the moment of death." He quirked an eyebrow at me. "That's what the symbols on her stomach are," I told him. "It's the equivalent of a siphon stuck in your gas tank."

The toothpick moved up and down as he considered that.

"You remember Diaz," I said. It wasn't a question. No one who'd seen the body of Jesus Diaz would ever forget it. His lover had butchered him in a frenzy, then cut a pentagram into his stomach to divert suspicion to the growing occult community.

Noonan nodded, and I continued. "This is different. I wouldn't bother looking for a boyfriend this time. This is a serious sorcerer, not a disgruntled lover. This one is much worse than Diaz."

His eyebrows rose, the equivalent of a shout of surprise from a normal person. "Worse than Diaz? How?"

"This guy's had practice."

"Practice, eh?" He looked skeptical, but with Noonan that doesn't mean much. He'd have doubts if you told him the sky was blue, a cop's occupational hazard. "Then where's the other bodies?"

"Well, he may have burned them up."

There was amusement mixed with his disbelief now. "Really?"

"The amount of magic you can get from a human soul at the moment of death is fantastic. You can burn the corpse to ashes and have plenty left over."

"Right." He was grinning, not even pretending to take me seriously. "So why isn't this one burned up?"

I shrugged. "Either he couldn't harvest the magic, or he got interrupted."

"Of course."

"Look," I snapped. "Take a good close look at those cuts. It's precise work. It's not the kind of thing a jealous lover would do in a rage."

He nodded, conceding the point. Unfortunately I couldn't tell him much more than that. I brooded over it all afternoon, sitting at my typewriter and not writing a single word of my thesis on magical cults in eighteenth-century California. I slept badly that night, seeing the blonde girl standing before me, her eyes staring past me, and a host of shadowy figures behind her. I knew somehow they were the other victims, the ones the sorcerer had practiced on. And the future victims as well. There was no way this guy was done.

I was working my way through coffee and toast the next morning when the phone rang. It was Noonan, sounding smug. "We got the guy. I thought you'd want to know."

My exhaustion fell away. "Already? That's fast work." It never hurts to flatter a client.

"It was the janitor in her building," he told me, his voice a bit cooler. You can't butter up a born cynic. "We picked him up this morning."

I spent the next hour or two trying to concentrate on my thesis before packing it in. I knew from the morning papers the victim's name was Marcie Jackson. She was fresh-faced and pretty in her head shot, but it was the pallid face and unseeing eyes from the reservoir that I saw every time I blinked my eyes. I finally decided that she was going to keep on pestering me until I went to see the man who killed her.

I ran up to my room and took a little silver ring from my bedside table. It seemed to be a series of interlocked rings, some round, some angled, but if you looked closely you could see that it was one unbroken silver wire. It was a bit gaudy for my tastes, but I would need it for this errand.

Noonan was out when I got to the precinct house, but the desk sergeant recognized me and had a freckle-faced rookie take me back to the cells.

The janitor's name was Quinlan. I found him huddled in the back corner of a narrow cell, staring at his shoes and hugging himself. He was pudgy, middle-aged, thoroughly ordinary. I looked at the top of his head for a while, fingering my silver ring, which was at room temperature. Then I said, "Mr. Quinlan?"

He twitched, but didn't look up.

"Mr. Quinlan? Hey, Quinlan!"

He looked up, his eyes wide and frightened. There was a strange slackness around his mouth, his voice was thick as he said, "I done it. I done what they said. I done it."

The freckled rookie kept up an indignant monologue all the way back to the front desk. "We should be locking up all the half-wits, not waiting for them to kill somebody first. That girl might still be alive."

I did my best to tune him out, thanked him, and left. Then I sat behind the wheel of my car, telling myself it was none of my business. If he was innocent, and he was, it would come out at his trial. Probably. I told myself it had nothing to do with me.

It didn't work.

I knew from the papers that the victim had lived in Boyle Heights. The phone book told me there was only one building with a Jackson and a Quinlan. The building, when I found it, was nicer than I expected. Rents were dropping in the Heights. A lot of Japanese live there. They used to bring a certain elegant dignity to the neighborhood. Now they just bring hooligans who want to punish someone for Pearl Harbor and Okinawa.

I buzzed 306. There were two names by the buzzer, Jackson and Vaughn. I assumed it was Vaughn who answered, her voice tinny over the speaker. "Yes?"

"I'm an investigator, ma'am. I'd like to come up and speak to you."

She let me in after a long pause, and I took the stairs to the third floor. She had the chain across the door. All I could see was one brown eye framed by auburn hair. Her voice was a low contralto. "Show me your badge, officer."

"I'm not a police officer, ma'am. I'm a consultant. I don't have a badge."

She looked me up and down. "Turn around. Let Mrs. Nagoya have a good look at you."

I turned. The door across the hall was open a crack, and a wizened brown eye was peering out at me. I tipped my hat

and smiled, and the door clicked shut. The door to 306 closed
as well, and I heard the rattle of the chain. The door swung
open. "I guess you'd better come in."

Vaughn was slim, maybe thirty years old, wearing a
long brown dress and low heels. She led the way into her
apartment, sat in a chair, and gestured me toward her couch.
"What can I do for you, Mr. Consultant?"

"My name is Tom McBain," I said.

"Tara Vaughn."

"Thank you for speaking with me, Ms. Vaughn. I'm very
sorry for your loss."

"What's all this about, Mr. McBain?" Her voice was cold, her
posture stiff in the chair.

"Just Tom, please. The police arrested your janitor this
morning."

She nodded.

"I don't think he did it."

Her eyebrows rose. "Why not?"

"Let me guess," I said. "Quinlan made you uncomfortable,
didn't he? He didn't quite know how to behave. Maybe
he stared every time he saw a pretty girl?" She didn't say
anything, but I could see the truth of it in her face. "The cops
came by, spoke to you, spoke to everyone in the building. And
Quinlan's name kept coming up. So the cops picked him up,
maybe they slapped him around a little, and pretty soon he
confessed to whatever they wanted him to confess to."

She gazed at me for a long time. At last she said, "It doesn't
mean he's innocent."

"Marcie Jackson was killed by a sorcerer," I said. "Quinlan
hasn't got a scrap of magic in him."

I gazed into her eyes, waiting for disbelief, for scorn. Instead,
she furrowed her eyebrows. "I heard about the… marks, on
her body. That was for magic?"

I nodded. "Did Marcie know anyone who dabbled in the

occult?"

Tara shook her head.

"Did she have any new friends? Did she do anything different or meet any new people in the last few days?"

Tara's lips tightened. She was annoyed, and I wondered what had triggered it. "No," she said. "Was there anything else?" It was a pretty clear dismissal, and I stood.

"I'm sorry to have bothered you," I said, picking up my hat. "Thank you for seeing me."

I was in the hallway, heading for the stairs, when I heard her voice behind me. "Mr. McBain? Tom?"

I stopped and turned, and she came down the hallway to me, then led me a little farther from Mrs. Nagoya's door. "There is something," she said. "I didn't tell the police. They were so rude, and then when they are arrested Mr. Quinlan, I thought it didn't matter." She bit her lip, then took a deep breath and looked me in the eye.

"Marcie had a new boyfriend. He was some sort of gangster." She scowled at the memory. "She thought it was exciting. It made her feel like she was that much farther from her boring hometown, you know? Life in the big city." Tara shook her head. "His name was Dirk. She met him about a week before she... before she died."

"You know his last name? Or where he lives?"

Tara shook her head again. "I can tell you where to find him, though. Marcie told me, the first time she went to meet him. She wasn't supposed to tell anyone, but she didn't entirely trust him. It's a warehouse in Alhambra." There was exasperation in her face. "She thought it was so romantic, having a boyfriend with a hideout."

I scribbled down the address and a description of Dirk. "Thank you, Ms Vaughn."

"Tara," she said. "Call me Tara." She smiled. "You're welcome. That's more than those detectives ever said."

Her brow furrowed, and I waited, knowing there was more. At last she looked up at me, her face earnest. "I should have told them about Dirk, shouldn't I? I knew he was bad news. But they were so rude. They were bullies, and I didn't want to help them."

Noonan could be abrasive, and then some. "It's all right," I told her. "You've told me. And it was already too late for Marcie. You didn't do anything wrong."

Her face drooped, and the grief that had always been below the surface finally showed through. "She was always looking out for me, you know? I'm older, and I've been in the city longer, but she was the one who was worried about me." Her hand went to her throat, and she drew out a silver locket. "She gave me this. She said it would keep me safe." There was pleading in her eyes as she looked up at me. "I should have made her keep it. She was the one who needed it."

I reached out a fingertip and touched the locket. I felt nothing, not from my fingertip, not from my ring. "It's just a locket," I said. "It's not magic. It wouldn't have helped."

She nodded, gave me a tight-lipped smile and breathed deeply, composing herself. Her voice barely quavered when she spoke again. "Will you tell me what you find out? I really want to know."

"Of course."

"I work afternoons at the Matinee Coffee House. It's two blocks south on Palm Street. I'm there until five." Then she turned and walked briskly back to her apartment. I tipped my hat to Mrs. Nagoya and headed for the stairs.

My car was an oven, and I drove to Alhambra with the windows down. Music drifted in from the street, along with the honking of traffic and the occasional shouts of children. The city sparkled and thrummed with life. It seemed impossible that I was on my way to see a sorcerer who devoured dreams and snuffed out lives.

L.A. is all about illusion. It's our primary export. We package glamour and dreams and ship it around the world. In L.A., the girls are always pretty, the men are ruggedly handsome, and those who do evil get their just desserts by the final reel.

Sometimes I think the biggest illusion of all is the city itself. It's darkness and shadow, with a layer of brilliant sunshine to help you ignore what's really going on. It made me think of Marcie Jackson, lying on a table, the cuts covered by her best dress, with a mortician applying a delicate layer of makeup to put a healthy blush back into her pallid cheeks. The sunshine and palm trees were no more real than rouge on a corpse.

The warehouse was a narrow property jammed between a second-hand store and a greasy spoon restaurant. The paint was peeling, and the little strip of grass in front was dead and brown. The lack of pretence was almost refreshing. I parked in front and spent a moment staring at the middle finger of my left hand. The ring was cool to the touch, and there was nobody in sight. That meant one of two things. Either the warehouse contained a sorcerer of remarkable power, or I was imagining things.

Well, I couldn't go to Noonan until I was sure, and there was only one way to be certain. I got out of my car, walked to the front of the warehouse, and opened the door.

I caught a quick glimpse of a dusty reception area. A bell tinkled above the door, a man came through a door on the far side of the room, and the ring turned to ice on my finger.

I took my hat off and smiled into the face of the most powerful magic user I had ever encountered. He was in his thirties, his hair as black as soil in a graveyard, his skin strangely pale for California. His eyes were tight with suspicion, his mouth set in a sullen frown. I tried to see what Marcie had seen in him, and failed. This guy was bad luck and trouble.

"Whaddaya want?"

The door swung open behind him, and two more people came in. There was a big, slope-shouldered guy with sunken knuckles and scar tissue around his eyes, and a slim brunette who looked like she'd eaten a lemon. The big guy crossed his arms and flared his chest muscles, glaring at me. The girl went over to stand beside Dirk.

"I'm looking for Wilson Exports," I said, trying to sound puzzled and innocent. "Bob Wilson? Does he work here?"

"Get lost," said Dirk, and I shrugged.

"Maybe it's the next street over." I gave them all a vague smile and turned, reaching for the doorknob. I heard a floorboard creak behind me, and I fought the urge to turn, still trying to look innocent. Then something slammed into the side of my neck and the world exploded in pain. I felt the impact of the floor against my knees, then a swirling disorientation. I was on my back, not quite unconscious, but I couldn't see, couldn't move.

Hands ran over my body, patting my pockets. I felt my wallet slide out. After a moment it landed on my chest. "No badge," said Dirk. "No gun."

"He's some kind of cop," said the girl. "I can smell it on him."

"Look at this," said Dirk, and I heard the rustle of paper. "My name, and the address of the warehouse." More paper rustled. "And here's Marcie's address."

Damn it. They had my notebook.

"Who the hell are you?" A toe prodded my ribs. "You a reporter?" He kicked me. "Who gave you my name?" Another kick. "Was it the other broad?" Kick. "Was it Tara?"

"Never mind that," said the girl. "We have to clear out of here."

"I'll meet you at Joe's place," Dirk said, his voice ugly. "There's someone I need to talk to first. I don't like little birds who sing songs in too many ears."

Somebody groaned. I didn't think it was me, but I was the

only likely suspect. Something crashed into my head, and I spent a little while floating in a dark red sea of pain.

I found that if I took slow, shallow breaths the pain wasn't too bad, so I focused on that for a while. Then I started to cough, which sent waves of pain through my head. The coughing got worse and worse, until finally I brought my hands up to cradle my head and made myself open my eyes.

I saw flames. They were no more than a foot away from my head, and I stared, trying to make sense of it. I was hot, feverish, my elbow closest to the flames was starting to sting, and there was so much smoke in the room I could barely breathe. That seems like enough information to put it all together, but it still took me thirty long seconds to figure out that the building was on fire.

I tell people that I crawled because the air was clearer close to the floor. The truth is, I couldn't stand. I crawled in a straight line until my head bumped the wall, and then I followed the wall for a ways. I was coughing with every breath, and it hurt like hell, but it seemed to be clearing my head.

My eyes stung, and I couldn't see very far through the smoke, so I left them closed. I found the door by touch. It was locked, so I hung onto the doorknob and used it to drag myself to my feet. My plan was to kick the door open, but I was too shaky on my feet. The smoke had me completely blinded, so I ran my hands over the walls, looking for a window. Instead, I found a fire extinguisher on a rack. I lugged it back to the door and used it as a battering ram, slamming it into the doorknob.

I swung again and again, my body wracked by coughs, my eyes blinded by tears. The room seemed to swim around me, and finally I collapsed onto my knees. I sagged forward until my forehead was resting on the tank of the extinguisher.

It didn't look like I was going to make it. Marcie Jackson

would go unavenged. Worse, Dirk would find another girl, and another one after that.

No, it was even worse than that. Dirk was going after Tara. Because of me.

The air was a bit better down by the floor. My dizziness was gone, and the coughing was less. I took a deep breath and held it, rose to my feet, and slammed the fire extinguisher into the doorknob with everything I had. I swung in a frenzy, over and over, and then one of my swings met no resistance and I went stumbling forward.

I landed on my knees in the alley behind the warehouse, coughing and crying while smoke billowed out of the doorway behind me. When I stopped coughing, I got up and took off at a stumbling run for my car.

By the time I slid behind the wheel, I was thinking more clearly. Tara worked afternoons in a coffee shop. She wasn't in immediate danger. I drove back to Boyle Heights at a sensible pace, not dawdling but not running any red lights, either. I found the Matinee Coffee House easily enough, and a weight of tension left me when I peered through the glass and saw Tara wiping down a table.

She smiled when I walked in. Then the smile froze on her face, and I looked down at myself, wondering just how bad I looked.

"Oh my God, Tom, what happened?"

I grinned at her. I couldn't help it. The concern in her voice was as good as a week of bed rest for making me feel better. "Nothing a good cup of coffee won't fix. I take it black."

I must have looked even worse than I thought, because she brought me the coffee with cream and sugar stirred in. The place was pretty quiet, and she dropped into the chair across from me. "What happened?"

I thought about sugar-coating it, but everything I knew about Tara told me she was a sensible girl who could face things head-on.

"You should have gone to a hospital," she said. "There are phones, you know." Her forehead puckered in thought. "That gives me an idea. Wait here."

I sipped my coffee and watched her walk to a pay phone in the corner. She made a short call, then came back and resumed her seat. "I've never heard Mrs. Nagoya so excited," she said. "There's a man in my apartment."

I phoned the station and got lucky, catching Noonan at his desk. He was not a man for small talk, and I didn't give him any of my own. "You got the wrong man," I told him. "I have good news, though. The real killer is in the victim's apartment, waiting for her roommate to come home."

Noonan was understandably skeptical, but a prowler in the girl's apartment was enough to get him to act. I returned to the table, smiling. The case was practically wrapped up.

"Detective Noonan will be joining us here after he makes the arrest," I told Tara. "I told him he'll have to improve his manners."

"You'll stay until he gets here?"

"Of course. It's my new favorite coffee shop."

"I didn't like this place when I first came here," she said.

"L.A.?"

"No, I loved L.A." She gestured around her. "I mean the coffee shop. I didn't come all this way to clean tables and serve coffee." She put her chin in her hand. "It felt like failure, you know? If I had to work here to pay the bills, then I was failing as an actress."

I said, "But now?"

She smiled. "Now it's the best part of my week. The auditions were exciting at first. Terrifying and exciting. I would spend so much time getting my hair and makeup just right." She examined the tip of her right finger, using her thumb to trace the outline of a chip in the nail. "I didn't even want to wash

my own dishes, because I wanted my nails to be perfect."
She gave me a self-deprecating grin. "I was all about my
appearance. So were all the other girls around me. Sometimes
I think Los Angeles might be the shallowest place on Earth."

She leaned back in her chair and smiled. "I still do auditions
sometimes. But I tell people I'm a waitress, not an actress.
Waitresses are actually good for something."

I smiled back, liking her wry honesty. Then the smile froze
on my face as my ring went cold. I twisted around in my
chair. There was a yellow Buick out front, and I watched as
the passenger door swung open and the brunette from the
warehouse got out.

"What's the matter?" said Tara.

"Dirk is in that car," I said, "and his girlfriend is coming in."
I thought furiously. "Listen, if you get a chance, slip out the
back. Go to the lobby of your building. There should be cops
all over the place."

The door to the café creaked open and the brunette scanned
the room, stopping when she got to me. She strolled over to
our table, cool as you please, and sat down. The ring was so
cold my finger ached. It had to be the boxer who was waiting
in Tara's apartment. Dirk was in the car, and he'd sent the girl
in to lure one or both of us outside.

"I must say, you look like hell." There was a contemptuous
curl to her lip. "Still, you look better than I expected."

I turned my chair, trying to keep the car in my peripheral
vision. Dirk was the real threat. "What do you want?"

"Now, don't be like that, Tom." She managed to make a fake
pout without losing the sour twist to her lips. "We never got a
chance to finish our conversation. I want to know why you're
sticking your nose where it doesn't belong."

"I'm an academic," I told her. "We can't help ourselves." I
wondered how long it would take for Noonan to arrive. I
would have to tip him off about the Buick without spooking

Dirk.

"Oh, you'll tell me," she said. "You'll tell me everything."

The absolute confidence in her voice brought me up short. I gave her my undivided attention for the first time, and her eyes bored into me. There was something in the depths, something I couldn't quite define, but it drew me in. The room seemed to fade away. I could hear Tara calling my name, but it didn't seem important.

Tires squealed in the street outside, the brunette turned to look, and I was suddenly myself again. I whipped my head around. The Buick tore away from the curb and a siren howled as a police car gave chase. I sprang up and ran to the window, but both vehicles were out of sight by the time I got there. Dirk was gone.

It took me a moment to realize that the ring was still icy cold. Realization hit me like a punch to the gut, and I spun around. The table was empty. The brunette was gone, and so was Tara.

There was a woman behind the counter, her mouth still open in surprise, staring toward the back of the cafe. I dashed around the counter and burst out the back door.

Tara lay on her stomach in the alley, the brunette above her with a knee in her back and a fist in her hair, pulling her head back. The brunette looked up when the door banged open, letting go of Tara's hair and turning to face me.

"She's in the alley," I yelled, pretending there was someone to hear me. Then I took a deep breath and walked toward her. "This will go easier if..."

Her hand stretched toward me, and I leaned back. Most magic requires a touch. I started to bring my arm around, planning to knock her arm aside and belt her across the jaw. I never got the chance. Her fingers glowed blue, and a spark shot from her fingertips to my solar plexus. It felt as if the biggest fist in the world slammed into me, and I crashed onto my back in the alley.

I stared up at a ribbon of blue sky visible between the buildings, my brain screaming urgent commands that my limbs ignored. I couldn't move, couldn't breathe, couldn't even move my eyeballs.

The brunette stepped into my field of vision, smirking down at me. One hand pushed her jacket back, and I saw a little silver-handled knife sheathed at her belt. "I'd like to take my time with you," she said, "but I'll have to take what I can get."

"Get away from her, you bitch."

The brunette turned, and I found I could roll my eyes just far enough to see Tara rising to her feet, an empty milk bottle in her hand.

"Oh, please." The brunette gave a derisive snicker. "You're not even worth harvesting." Then Tara stepped close, bringing her arm back for the swing, the brunette's fingers glowed blue, and a fat spark shot toward Tara's heart.

Just before it touched her, the spark changed direction, shooting upward. Tara's locket glowed blue as it absorbed the spark, and I saw the brunette's jaw drop in astonishment an instant before the milk bottle slammed into her head.

In the movies, the bottle always breaks. This one didn't. There was a hollow thump, the woman's head snapped to the side, and her legs folded like matchbook covers. Her knees crunched into the gravel of the alley and she shook her head slowly from side to side.

"Again," I croaked.

Tara nodded, wound up like Babe Ruth, and clocked her a good one on the side of the head. The brunette flopped onto her face and didn't move.

I could see flashing police lights at the end of the alley coming closer, as Tara knelt beside me and brushed the hair back from my forehead. It felt nice. It felt better than nice.

"Are you okay?"

"I'll live," I admitted, "but don't let that discourage you from what you're doing."

She smiled at that, then frowned. "How come my locket worked? You said it wasn't magic."

I tried to shrug, but it hurt too much. "I think Marcie was a natural witch," I said. "They're pretty rare. I can't detect that kind of magic." I looked at the sorceress face down in the gravel. "She wouldn't have been able to harvest any energy from Marcie, either."

Tara's mouth drooped. "She died for nothing, then."

"Well, she frustrated this bitch here, and she indirectly saved you. That's not nothing."

Tara gave me a sad smile. "That's how I'll remember her. Not as a victim. As my guardian angel." Her hand caressed my cheek. "You too, of course. You're my other guardian angel."

Noonan's face appeared above her shoulder. "He's nothing of the sort," he said. "He's a devil, punishing me for my sins. Do you know how much paperwork you've caused me, McBain?"

"Do you still have those silver handcuffs I gave you? You're going to need them."

He nodded. "How long?"

"A couple of hours," I told him. "After that she should be safe enough. Just don't let her do any more ritual sacrifices and you should be fine."

"I think we can manage that," he said dryly. "Do you need an ambulance?"

I probably did, but I didn't want anything interfering with the care I was currently receiving. "I'm fine," I told him. "I'm just faking it, for obvious reasons."

That brought a ghost of a smile to Noonan's face, and a mock scowl to Tara's. She didn't stop stroking my forehead, though. Noonan took charge of the prisoner, and I let Tara help me to my feet. We walked together through the coffee shop, out the front door, and back into the sunshine.

Sign of the Times

by Michael Ashleigh Finn

"Dig."

I lobbed a shovel at her, making sure the talisman in my left hand never wavered. It was the only thing keeping the dame from ripping into my jugular.

It always starts with a dame, doesn't it? All good stories begin with one in trouble, or causing it. In this case, it was literal... Dame Mara Hawkes, O.B.E. A large part of me doubted her credentials; as corrupt as the British government might be, I couldn't see them knighting this particular woman.

"Pick up the shovel," I said evenly, drawing a small vial of her blood from my vest pocket. "And dig."

She pouted at me, long legs cocked at the hip.,. She bent over and picked it up by the wooden handle...then proceeded to take a swing at me with the metal end. I danced back, hissing a curse, and almost tripped over the heavy chains piled by my feet.

The talisman flared to life, a flash of white and an afterimage of indigo; she screamed and dropped the shovel, hands clawing at her head. She fell to her knees as the blood began to trickle from her scalp, through the auburn locks.

"Let's try this again." The wind picked up, bringing the promise of rain in a few hours. "Pick up the shovel and dig."

She glared up at me in the fading autumn light. "You can't kill me."

I lifted an eyebrow. "I know what you are, sweetheart. In about five years, you'll wish I could have killed you." I nodded at the ground beneath her feet. "Spade to dirt. Now. Under the L, if you please. I don't trust the other side of the sign; some idiot drove his car through the H last year. Right here should be good."

She hissed something in another language—sounded like Sanskrit—and the blade of the shovel bit into the glorified dust that passes for dirt in Los Angeles.

She was a grifter from Europe; the English part was likely true enough, given her accent. My guess is that she'd spent time in India, picked up enough resources to forge credentials as a recipient of the Order of the Star or some such...but also picked up a Mara demon, one of the Indian spirits of corruption and temptation. It wouldn't be too hard for such a creature to lure her into allowing it into her body, given her profession.

The name was a bit of a stupid giveaway, though. Mara demons are often clever as hell, but not always bright enough to resist the temptation of their own fancies. Your average joe wouldn't catch it, of course, but did she really think America was devoid of practitioners? That she'd be the only one out here using her mojo on the populace? This was Hollywood, after all. Between here and Washington, America may have more demons than Hell itself.

Next to those chains sat a metal tile, engraved with various sigils that would form the second ward. It was the cap to her prison, a headstone of sorts to be buried with her. Keeping the talisman trained on her while she worked, I spilled a drop of her blood from the vial onto the metal and felt the magic stir.

About a foot down into Mount Lee, she paused and took a breath. "So how did you find me, Wormwood?"

"I wasn't looking for you, Hawkes. That studio exec you tried to swindle? He keeps me on retainer. He's learned from past experience with some of his starlets and their deals with demons. He knows just enough to know he should have an expert around, just in case. Keep digging."

Her perfectly shaped eyebrows, slightly marred with blood, shot up. She let out a surprised bark of a laugh. "You don't remember me."

I squinted at her in the dying light of the day. "You're wearing that poor woman like a meat cocktail dress. How the hell would I recognize you?"

She let out that short, sharp laugh again, and leaned on the shovel. "Same dress, different party."

I motioned with the talisman, pointing like one would with the barrel of a gun. "You're stalling. No breaks."

She sighed and started moving dirt again. "It wasn't that long ago, for us. This dress was pretty new at the time, though."

Alright, so she hadn't picked up the Mara in India. Unless....

"You're wearing Jonas Smythe's little girl, aren't you?" Smythe had hired me to deal with a Panis demon that was messing with his crew. When I'd banished it from the East India Company camp, we thought it had gone after his family. I got his wife back, but we never found the daughter. Now I was wondering if the Panis was just a distraction, a turn, and this Mara the real trick.

A wry grin cracked her face. "Not wearing. Coexisting." The shovel hit a stone, and she scowled.

Something wasn't right. Classically, Mara demons tended to take over their host completely. They didn't share. She was trying to con me. "That was during the Sepoy Rebellion. You're looking awfully good for someone pushing a hundred. Especially in this climate." She didn't look a day over thirty, and Mara hosts often aged quickly from the stress.

She grunted as she levered the rock out of the dirt. "And how old are you, Wormwood? What name are you using these days? Nick?"

"Special case. I'm of the blood of..." Then I got it. "Smythe wasn't just a practitioner; he was a magus of some sort. It was in his blood?"

She rolled her eyes. "I love men. They're always so focused on the models they build up in their tiny little minds. No, not him. It was the mother who had the line of Zoroaster in her blood. I was after her as a host; I was only using her daughter as leverage. When you sprang the mother, the girl and I worked out a deal." She twisted the shovel under the rock, prying at it. "She was just old enough to know what she was doing." With a sudden flick of the handle, she flung the rock up in the air, straight towards me.

It wasn't a real attack; there was no power behind it. Just a small act of defiance that caused me to sidestep to the left, away from the chains. I moved back before she had a chance to make a grab for them. "Hey, now," I admonished.

She shrugged and grudgingly went back to work. By now, the dirt had ruined her evening dress. It was never going to be her Friday night best, ever again. Not that she'd be going out much after this. "So we have a time-share arrangement. Works beautifully for both of us. Magic from her mother, raised by one of the East India Company's most underhanded executives, plus my centuries of experience in seduction of the mind."

I was badly craving a cigarette at this point, but I couldn't let go of the talisman to light it. "Working so beautifully for you right now, isn't it?"

She shrugged again, and kept digging, as if she was digging my grave and not hers. "A girl gets by."

"So you created the ultimate grifter by combining talents, rather than dominating her."

She snorted. "Grifting's such a common term. We're so much more than that. What's that German word? Gestapo?"

"Gestalt. More like her bloodline made her too strong for

you to corrupt outright, so you were forced to strike a deal."

"Perceptive. Yes, there is that. Some people I can't just outright take because of who and what they are." She waggled her brows meaningfully at me.

I wasn't sure which meaning of the word "take" she had implied, but neither were on the dance card for that evening. "Stalling again. You'll want to stop that."

"Or what? You'll haul me out into the hills and bury me in an unmarked grave?" She looked around her, by way of proving her point.

"Oh, sweetheart, you have the best grave marker in the world," I said lifting my chin up at the HOLLYWOODLAND sign towering above. "But you and I both know you're not dying tonight." I tapped the chains with the toe of my boot. "But I'll tell you what: if you stop stretching this out and just make the hole already, I won't toss this here talisman in with you to keep you company while you whittle away the centuries."

I opened the vial and let a drop of her blood slide onto the chains, which stirred like a waking serpent. Her eyes widened, then narrowed. She lost her attitude and got back to work.

I'd thought I'd won. I figured she'd given up. When she was silenced and covered with dirt, and the capstone and yet more dirt, I locked those wards in place using the letters of the sign, finally lit up a cigarette, and walked away.

When my client died a year later, I left for greener pastures. If I'd stuck around, I would have been up on local events. As it was, I lived in blissful ignorance.

Until the day I saw a postcard of a sign that said Hollywood on a mountaintop. It looked odd to me, and I stared at it for a full five minutes before the light dawned.

Oh crap.

An hour later, I had booked a flight on Pan Am back to America.

***

So here I am, digging. I hate digging. Ground's either too dry or too wet. Nothing worth digging for is ever in the right kind of dirt for a spade. "Quit whingeing," I tell myself, coughing in the arid dust I'm kicking up. "It's your own damn fault."

See, I should have paid attention to her gestalt comment. You think it was an accident that a few years later the city agreed to a renovation of the sign? No. That LAND was removed as part of the deal between the Parks Department and the Hollywood Chamber of Commerce. The anchor of of the wards I'd placed around her burial site was in that giant L. In the years since, the sign was getting more and more dilapidated, a reflection of the town below. Hell, her mere presence probably caused the vowels to fall apart faster than they should have.

Infernal woman really did become greater than the sum of her parts when she mixed with the Mara. I was being played the whole damn time. That wasn't the demon in there talking to me, and it wasn't Smythe, neither. It was the damn gestalt thing, that mix of mage and demon. I'd call it an abomination, but that cuts a little too close to home for me. Oh, don't get me wrong, I'm in charge of this suit I'm driving around. The mage who gave it to me a few hundred years ago didn't need it any more, largely due to a noble sacrifice that required my assistance. (No, not like that. It was his plan and he needed my help. It really was a noble act on his part. My payment was to get his body, which he didn't need any more. Win-win.) But I have my own little hybrid situation going on; we just didn't meld souls.

But this isn't about me, it's about her.

Back in the '40's, when I'd cornered her with that talisman,. I had her pinned, and she knew it. So she played me. She knew that she was more powerful than the juju I put in those chains; they were designed to bind a Mara, not what she had become. Oh, sure, they'd hold her body, but her influence, overlooking a town where dreams were made? That's downright biblical stuff right there, the demon on the mountaintop, tainting the valley below. Alright, it's barely more than a hill, and Hollywood's just a neighborhood with delusions of grandeur, but you get the point. Mama Corruption's been having a field day here the past thirty years, and it's my doing. I aim to fix that with a new bag of tricks.

There's a problem, though. I swear I'm digging deeper than she ever did. I'm neck deep, and I'm taller than she is. I should be hitting that metal cap by now. It doesn't help that the sides of the hole are so dry that with every spade of dirt I toss out, more crumble down onto my feet. I look up and around, outside the hole. Maybe I'm off a foot or two? Hard to tell with the L missing....

There's a sharp smell of hot metal on stone and the stars brighten for the briefest of moments, then the whole world smashes down on the top of my head. Through the Technicolor haze of pain, I see a large square metal tile careen into the ground in front of the hole, something dark staining a corner. I hear a throaty, feminine laugh and some quick shuffling steps behind me. I try to turn, but the horizon tilts and the hole starts to swallows me.

As if to add insult to injury, that's when the chains fall on me. Yes, those chains. The ones I'd been expecting to find under my shovel, under the cap plate I put on her prison. The cap plate that likely just hit me on the back of the head and is lying a couple of feet away, which I now see is speckled with blood.

My blood.

Oh, crap.

I try to scramble out of the hole, but my arms aren't working too well and I'm getting blood in my eyes. I realize the blood is about to fall on the chains, and I abandon my attempt to extricate myself in favor of getting those damn things off me before it's too late.

"Oh, you're already caught, little fly," she says, in velvety tones. I see equestrian boots halt at the edge of the hole, then the Mara-thing squats down, just out of reach. I sigh and lean back, feeling the first ward start to activate as the chains react to my blood. "Mara. Those boots look pretty good on you."

A lopsided grin crosses her features. "And I like this look on you. You should wear it more often."

"How long have you been out?"

"Oh, ages. When I heard you were back in town, I figured you'd come check on me. Took you a week to come visit? I'm hurt."

I try a shrug. It doesn't work very well, the motion making the chains slither and tighten. Once my blood had hit the chains, the spell had activated. "Ow." I go for a nonchalant look, instead. This is hard to do when covered in sweat, dirt, and your own blood. "You know how it is. I wanted to to look good for you. How did you know when I arrived?"

She snorts. A hand waves in the direction behind me, towards Old Tinseltown below. "This is my town, now. No one of any consequence comes or goes without my knowing about it."

"Aw, thanks, Mara. It's nice to be loved."

Her face hardens. "I was stuck in that hole for years. Couldn't move. Couldn't eat. Couldn't breathe. Couldn't *scream*."

"Couldn't happen to a nicer girl." Good one, Wormwood. Go ahead, taunt the woman who holds all the cards.

Her hand snakes down to snag the handle of my shovel; I try to lunge for her, but the chains pull me down into a fetal position. If I close one eye, I can see straight up out of the hole. She straightens, looking down her nose at me, chin raised in an almost picturesque expression of gloating. "So I just relaxed and bided my time." The shovel starts to toss dirt down in the hole. Down on *me*.

"My corruption seeped into the mountain and into the town below. Those wards were meant for me in my demon form, not for what I'd become. They may have bound me here physically, but they couldn't stop my influence. Not like you'd intended." More dirt falls on me. She isn't being efficient about this, oh no. She's taking her time. "I figured in fifty years, I'd be able to get out and have that town all ready to make me its queen."

"You weren't even down there half that," I manage. "Someone dig you up?"

She laughs. It's one of those slow whispers of a laugh, barely audible over the scrape of the shovel through the dirt. "Hell, no. That town has turned out to be a power source for me. Instead of corrupting it, I just drank from its well of petty desires and rotten deals until I was able to break your bonds all by myself. But I saved them for you." This time, the dirt falls on my face, obscuring my vision somewhat.

"This can't kill me, you know," I manage to cough out.

"Oh, sweetheart," she purrs, "Of course it won't. Where would be the fun in that?"

I feel the second ward kick in as she tosses the metal tile onto my hip, then she begins to fill in the grave in earnest.

All good stories start with a dame. I'd forgotten that most of the tragic ones end with one as well.

I relax and settle in to my new prison sentence. She expected me to be here a while; I didn't have access to her special happy trough of backstabbing lust in the valley below. But these chains weren't meant for me; I'd be able to worm my way out of them. She was being sloppy with her wards, just tossing them in with no careful alignment. I should be able to circumvent them. She thought she was damning me to the prison I'd intended for her. Given her nature, she probably figures on coming by to taunt me every few years, to corrupt me to her side while pretending she might let me out early for good behavior.

Screw that. I'm going to see if I can beat her record as an escape artist.

Jonesing for a cigarette right now. Kinda hard to smoke without the use of your hands. Or, you know, air. It's weird though.

I haven't wanted one in years.

THAT OLD HELL MAGIC

BY JUSTIN MACUMBER

As soon as her rose petal lips parted and the first warm jazz note slid into the air, I knew she was the one. Every fiber of my being pulled me toward the stage she shared with a quartet of musician droids, and, when her hands lightly grasped the microphone stand, I wished it was me. She was the most beautiful woman I'd ever seen: soft blue eyes above a gently curved nose that barely cast a shadow on a mouth that looked plump and sweet, all framed by nanite-enhanced hair that slowly changed from red to violet to blue and back again as the music swelled around her. She was tall, with skin kissed by the sun until it was the color of honey, and clad in a sparkling blue dress curved in all the right places, her slowly swaying hips tapering down to reveal just a hint of leg. My heart hammered behind lungs that could barely draw breath. She was the one, the person I'd been searching for. I was instantly in love, and I knew every other man in the club — not to mention more than a few women — felt the same way.

The fact that she was a demon seemed almost beside the point.

No, I told myself, clenching my fists hard enough to make my knuckles pop and bring me back to reality. *That's **precisely** the point.*

In spite of the carnal desires of my nether region, my

brain — aided by magically enhanced eyes — was right. The woman on the stage was gorgeous with a voice to match, but it was a lie. Tawny skin and whiskey vapor contralto might be all the rest of the club's occupants knew about, but not me. I saw the horns peaking up from her hair, the tail that swished in the opposite motion of her hips. She was an unholy creature spawned in the pits of Hell, and because of her more than a dozen innocent people had lost their souls. I wasn't going to be another name in her coal black ledger.

As if hearing my thoughts, the singer glanced away from a man sitting at a table just in front of the stage and focused on me. Her eyes glimmered in the glow of a spotlight hovering overhead, and for a moment I would have sworn she stared straight into my head. Given her hellish nature, she probably did.

Fearing she might have indeed read my thoughts, I reached up and tugged my old fedora lower on my head. A spell had been cast on it to protect me from telepaths years ago by a Manchu shaman, and it saved my bacon more than once. As soon as the felt brim settled above my eyebrows, the singer frowned before shifting her sultry gaze elsewhere.

"This isn't a free concert, asshole," a voice said behind me.

I turned to find a skinny guy in a tight black button-up shirt and red tie standing behind the bar I was leaning against. On the right side of his scrawny chest was a nametag — Azriel. On the left side was embroidered "Perdition" in optical fiber shimmering like fire. He was white as a ghost, but, unlike the singing demon, his paleness came from too many hours spent in basements cutting himself to the latest goth music. Various occult tattoos littered his hands and neck, but they were strictly civilian. The bartender didn't have even the faintest whiff of magic about him.

"You better order something, man," he said, thin lips slipping into a scowl. "Two drink minimum. Otherwise I call *them* over and they'll throw you out." He tilted his head toward two bruisers covered in short fur standing at the other end of the bar.

Fucking werewolves. At least they weren't fully turned, otherwise the stink would have emptied the club.

"And when I say throw you out," the goth kid continued, "I mean in pieces. *Chewed on* pieces."

The bartender's smirk was meant to frighten me, but it didn't. I'd tangled with worse in my time. But there wasn't a point in causing trouble, so I nodded and said, "I'll take a vodka. Double."

Satisfied that I'd been properly cowed, Azriel grabbed a glass, snatched up a clear bottle covered with Cyrillic writing, and poured two fingers worth of vodka. When he handed the half-full glass to me, I pressed my palm against the pay pad embedded into the bar. A green light flashed a second later. His work now done, the skinny goth shook his head and walked to the next thirsty patron.

I turned back to the stage, raising the vodka glass as I moved, but, before the alcohol could touch my lips, I whispered a brief spell that turned the vodka into water. Dressed in plain clothes though I was — brown hat, tan slacks, blue shirt, brown jacket — it wouldn't do for an LAPD detective to be found drinking on the job. Being part of the Supernatural Crimes Department was hard enough without giving my non-magically inclined fellow officers another reason to hate me. Like it was *my* fault the nether world had decided to break through the dimensional barrier and crash our party on that chilly January night back in 2026. Like it or not, the supernatural was now mingling with the plain old natural, and someone had to police them. Lucky me, I was born with an affinity for magic and a keen nose for sniffing out the things that went bump in the night.

The beauty on stage ended her song to thunderous applause.

Everyone was on their feet, clapping and whistling as though Heaven's own choir had come down to play for them. Wrong end of the metaphysical metaphor or not, the singer smiled and bowed before the musician bots behind her struck up another song. Seconds later, her voice washed over the audience once more.

"What's her name?" I asked the bartender when he passed close enough to hear me. I made sure my voice was airy and filled with love.

The goth raised a thrice-pierced eyebrow. "Shira. Not that it'll do you any good."

I almost laughed. *Shira* was Hebrew for *song*. Not exactly imaginative. At least it wasn't Melody.

"Why do you say that?"

"'Cause Shira has champagne tastes, man, and you're obviously on a beer budget. Do yourself a favor and leave now before you embarrass yourself."

Irritation dug into my chest with cat claws, but I tried to not let it show on my face. "I have to meet her," I said as I gulped the last of my drink and set the glass on the bar. "She's amazing. I'll die if I don't get to at least talk to her."

"You might die if you do," Azriel replied under his breath. The words were ominous, but the smirk on his pasty face said he wished I would. "If you're determined to look like an idiot, leave the way you came in and head around to the right. Her dressing room has a door that opens out the back of the club. Sometimes she meets and greets fans that way. But if you're going, you better soon, 'cause there's always a line and it's always long."

I gave him my best *golly gee thanks* look and pushed away to meld into the crowd. The club entrance was ten meters behind me, but I wasn't heading that way. I fully intended to meet Shira, but I wasn't going to wait in line like some schmuck. No, I had other ways to go where I wanted, and, by magic or mayhem, I was getting there.

The Perdition Club was like half a dozen other bars that sprung up on L.A.'s Sunset Boulevard after the other side broke through to Earth and made pests of themselves. The old standbys like the Whiskey A-Go-Go and the Viper Room were still around, but they were steadily losing business to the newer joints that catered to guests with decidedly more mystical needs, like brimstone suppression sprinklers and UV blocking windows. My job had me in and out of nearly every club on the strip, but this was my first time here. Despite the demon on stage and the two mangy mutts working security, I kinda liked it. Jazz was America's only true musical art form.

Slowly but surely, I worked my way through the crowd standing beyond the seated guests arrayed before the stage. Shira's smoky vocals followed me everywhere, almost like she was sitting on my shoulder, promising me all the things I could ever want, top of which being her. A dozen protective glyphs were tattooed along my arms and back, each one meant to keep me safe from one spell or another, and, as I surveyed the joint, I felt an itch between my shoulders where my anti-persuasion tattoo was located. The itch grew worse with every word Shira sang. It wasn't enough for me to pull out my gun and arrest the singing demon on the spot, but it was enough to give me just cause to dig deeper. She was obviously a succubus, and that meant trouble.

Perdition's security was substantial, if a little heavy on the hellborn. Besides the two werewolves, I spied four vampires standing in dark corners, bald heads surveying the club like albino cameras, and a pair of wraiths drifting just above the lights of the stage, most likely to protect the demon from fans who fell too far under her spell and decided they had to have her there and then.

The real muscle, though, was reserved for one person in particular — Nikko Alvarez — the owner of Perdition and

L.A.'s fastest rising member of the millionaire club. Mr.
Alvarez had a box seat on the same level as the balcony above
the back quarter of the club, far enough away that he didn't
have to smell the stink of the people who made him rich.
He was sitting there at the very moment, the king of all he
surveyed. Given his wealth and dark good looks, I couldn't
blame him. A bottle-blonde bimbo sat next to him, her face
buried in the crook of his neck and her hands God only knew
where, while two shades stood at the back of the box. The
ethereal guardians were hard to see, their bodies shadows
against shadows, but the occasional flicker of fire where eyes
should have been and the gleam of metallic claws let me know
they were there. I'd never tangled with shades before, and I
hoped that run of good luck would last me through the night.
If everything went as planned, I'd have Shira in custody before
anyone knew they had trouble in their midst.

By the time the singing demon sang her last note, it was
all I could do not to rip off my jacket and beg one of the
werewolves to scratch the protection sigil off my back. As she
bowed, the audience broke into thunderous applause, and
roses flew toward the stage like they were fired from cannons.
She caught several in the air and drew them to her face, the
red blooms so bright and cheerful against her tanned skin. As
she stepped back and bowed again, she damn near had to kick
the flowers out of her way.

"Encore!" a slew of voices shouted. "Encore!"

Shira smiled and mouthed a silent, "Thank you," but didn't
return to the microphone. When she turned and exited the
stage, her blue dress joining the darkness beyond the hovering
spotlight's reach, the crowd clapped and called out to her even
louder. I stuck around for a minute to see if she came back,
but she didn't, so I eased my way around the club toward the
stage as her adoring fans slowly gathered their things and
exited in a slow trickle.

I reached the stage without much trouble, but the two wraiths drifting lazily overhead stopped me in my tracks. Wraiths are tricky bastards, and I didn't want to tangle with them if I didn't have to, but I had a job to do. So, knowing I had to find another way to skin this particular cat, I risked a quick grab for one of the roses left on the stage, one that she'd touched and still had her aura wafting around it. The wraiths hissed, which alone was enough to send ice racing down my back, but I had a rose in hand and was walking away before they could do anything else.

A sign on the wall to my left read "Restrooms" and had an arrow pointing down a hallway. Once I was through the door marked "Men" and made sure the bathroom was empty, I went into a stall. The toilet was clean, a minor miracle for a club on the Sunset Strip, but I didn't sit down. Instead, I held the rose in my left hand and waved my right over the flushed petals. Several auras clung to the flower, but by far the strongest was Shira's. Unlike the vaguely pink glow humans produced, the demon's aura was like smoke turning the rose's red petals into blood splatters.

Mingling my aura with it wasn't what I'd call a recipe for a good time, but I didn't have much choice. I placed my fingers into the murky glow. Instantly my hand went cold, then I said, "Energy black and cold as night, join my soul and aid my sight."

Responding to my spell, the demon's aura leapt from the rose and twirled up my arm until the haze blended with my own spirit's glow. A chill settled over my skin, but after a minute it went away and I felt normal again. I wasn't fooled though. The demon's taint would have to be exorcised as soon as the case was done, because, as long as it was part of me, I risked corruption and eventual damnation. It was just one of the risks of being a cop walking the hellfire beat.

With my senses now attuned to her, I exited the bathroom.

A large crowd still milled around the exit doors, their love-struck hearts beating together like one massive coronary. Security was busy making sure they all made their way out of the building, so I used the distraction and let my magically-enhanced senses guide me to my quarry.

The hallway extended down to my right. Waiters and waitresses walked back and forth like robots or zombies — which a few actually were — their trays loaded with dirty dishes. None of them looked my way as they went about their jobs. My eyes, though, were drawn to the right like a magnet sensing the pull of its other half, so I turned that way and put my tan loafers in motion. I stuck close to the wall to further reduce my presence.

Magical energy wafted through the hall like glowing smoke as I passed by one unmarked door after another. A pretty blonde waitress stumbled and spilled her tray, sending half a dozen wine glasses tumbling to the thinly carpeted floor. Instinctively, I reached out to help her, but all that would have done was delay me and get unwanted attention, so I kept my hands to myself and went on following Shira's aura. Her energy crackled against my skin, the snap of it sharper with every step, and, in spite of myself, I looked forward to finding her. Demon or not, she was a beauty, and who didn't need a little extra beauty in their life, even if it was only there long enough to read them their Miranda rights.

The hall turned left, and, as I stepped around the corner, my skin went numb. Shira's energy suddenly felt far away. To my right was another set of bathroom doors, and another army of waitstaff milled through the area. I kept my eyes low and breezed past them just as I had the earlier group. Soon enough, I was passing yet more unmarked doors, and Shira's pull strengthened again.

Flump! Tink! Tink! Splash!

I glanced up. Ahead of me another blond waitress spilled

her tray on the floor. Six empty wine glasses rolled across wet carpet.

What the hell? Did Perdition have a monopoly on clumsy blondes? And just how big *was* this damn club? The hallway seemed to go on forever. As strange as the moment felt, though, the increasing pull of Shira's aura drew my attention and feet onward through the thickening magical energy choking the hallway.

My skin itched from the demonic aura swirling around me as she once again drew close, but as I turned to follow the hallway left, she pulled away again. I shook my head to clear it, thinking that perhaps all the magical energy was clouding my senses. That was when I noticed the bathroom doors on my right and the crowd of waitstaff hustling around. With a sinking feeling in my gut I looked over my shoulder. Behind me were the exit doors and patrons walking through them.

Goddammit. I wasn't stuck in an extremely long hallway. It was a magic loop. Thanks to my clouded senses and preoccupation, I'd wasted time and shoe leather, not to mention been made to look like a first-year sorcery cadet. How in the hell had I missed it?

I had excuses aplenty, but now wasn't the time. Instead, I focused on what I could do. Angry, I stormed down the hallway without a wit of care for what attention I got, my senses taking in the nearness of Shira and the building magic in the hall. A minute later, I passed a blonde waitress with a tray full of wine glasses.

"Watch your step," I told her as I passed by.

Seconds later, she chirped a cry of surprise. *Flump! Tink! Tink! Splash!*

When I neared the twice-taken left turn, I stopped and studied the thick magical haze that marked the boundary of the loop spell. To the untrained eye, the hallway corner looked like any other bend of carpet and sheetrock, but, as I opened my third eye wider, it quickly became apparent it was anything but. Magical energy swirled wall to wall and ceiling to floor, and, within its whirls, the world twisted upon itself. Someone with intelligence far beyond my meager thinking would probably call it a wormhole, and they wouldn't be wrong, but for us magic folk it was a loop, and a spell that powerful was usually used for only one thing — hiding something valuable. Or some*one*.

Now that I knew it was there, the problem became getting past it. Loop spells took a lot of magical energy to create, and even more to maintain. Luckily, like any other bump in the road, once you saw it, you just had to go around it. I pressed my hands together and imagined they were wedges tapering down to points so sharp they could split atoms, and then I pushed them toward a point where the hallway wall met the loop's energy. Bursts of electricity snapped at my fingers, sending jolts of pain down my arms. I gritted my teeth and whispered a strengthening incantation to give my hands more power. The pain of the loop fighting me was enough to make me hiss and bare my teeth, and I could smell the small hairs on my hands as well as the fabric of my shirt cuff burning, but I didn't give up. I pushed harder and harder, leaning forward as though fighting a gale, the loop pushing back every inch of the way. But, after nearly a minute of struggle, my hands pierced the boundary. Spreading my hands, the opening widened until it was large enough for me to step through, which I did immediately. The loop snapped back into place with a boom that shook the hallway and sent dust falling from wall sconces. Victory washed over my shoulders in warm waves, brightening my mood, but, when I saw the goons staring at me from up ahead, the feeling was short lived.

"Who the fuck are you?" He talked around a snout full of fangs, his clawed hand reaching for a nasty blade strapped to his waist. Chapped leather clothing protected most of his body, dark fur covering what was left.

Hellhounds were nasty business.

The second goon wrapped his rough knuckles around two daggers and pulled them up in backhanded grips. He looked more than eager to plunge them into my chest.

"I don't give a shit who you are," he grumbled, drool dripping from his sharp teeth in thick strings. "Take one more step and I'll eat your liver after I carve it out of ya."

I didn't doubt his culinary ability one bit, but this wasn't my first dance with devil dogs. Between the two creatures was a door much like every other door in the club, but this one shone in my eyes with a red glow, and beyond it was a heart that beat in time with mine.

"I'm gonna let that threat slide," I replied as I reached under my coat and pulled out my badge. "My name is Detective Darcy Winters. I figure you know why I'm here. Step away from the door and leave without a fuss, and I won't send you back to Hell with your tails on fire."

The nearest hellhound barked a short laugh that hit the air like a whip. "Fuck you, cop."

"Really?" I asked him before shifting my gaze to his partner. "Is that how you want to do this?"

"You're in Perdition, asshole," the second hellhound replied. "Now you learn what Hell is all about."

I sighed and put my badge back in my shirt breast pocket. "Okay. Don't say I didn't warn you."

The hellhounds snarled, both eager to taste my blood, and the one closest to me ran like a sprinter out of the blocks. His speed was incredible, and, for a split second, I was too shocked to move. That split second nearly killed me.

Shaking off my awe, my hand reached into an inner coat pocket and pulled out a short length of rope. The hellhound was close enough to smell the stench of his breath and fur, but there was just enough distance for me to snap the rope at him.

The fibers of the short rope shimmered and then lengthened toward the hellhound like it was a living thing, snaking around him and binding his arms to his sides, bringing him up short. He started to tip forward, but before he could fall I grabbed him by the shoulders and pitched him toward the loop's boundary behind me. As soon as his body hit the spell, he disappeared to the other side.

Unfortunately, the other hellhound was a dark glimmer in my eyes and I was still in plenty of danger. He now knew what I was capable of, and he wouldn't be as foolish as his friend.

Great.

"You can still walk away," I said, hoping he'd listen but knowing he wouldn't.

"Now I don't have to share your innards." His claws clicked against each other, sending sparks into the air. He advanced toward me slowly, his every sense trained on me, thick cords of muscle trembling as he readied himself for action.

As dangerous as the hellhound was, I didn't want to kill it if I didn't have to. The paperwork alone was murder, and Hell's lawyers made earthly attorneys seem like fuzzy little kittens. I would be up to my sweaty armpits in reports and deposition requests before his body cooled. So, hoping to avoid all that, I searched for a way to deal with him that wouldn't result with him exploding, crumbling to ash, or bleeding out on my loafers.

The hellhound swiped at me with a wickedly clawed paw before I could get my thoughts in order, and out of instinct I leapt back and shouted, "Betty!" My right hand instantly felt heavy as a short sword appeared in it. Betty was the sword's name. It was also the name of my mother. Both had a sharp edge and cut deep.

The hellhound's claws scraped against the blade's flat side, and he shuffled backward in surprise. "Nice trick, too bad it
—"

I didn't let him finish. Betty sang as she sliced the air in front of the hellhound's face, driving him back further. He took two steps, then ducked and lunged at me. I raised my right leg and kicked him beneath his snout, but not before his claws raked through my jacket and sliced the cheap fabric to ribbons. I hated seeing that — on my salary even cheap clothing was precious — but better that than my even more precious skin.

"You're too slow, pig," the hellhound said with a huff and a puff. "That shiny sword of yours is only delaying the inevitable."

Dammit, I hated to admit it, but he was right. As far as sorcerers went, I was a fair hand with a blade, but I was still only human. If I wanted to survive the fight and do it without killing the hellhound, I'd have to think of something and quickly.

The hellhound rushed me again, from a low stance. I stopped his first swipe with a slash at his shaggy forearms, but he powered through the cuts and took two more swings at me. The first only ruined more of my coat, but the second tore across my abdomen, sending waves of white-hot pain through my body. With blood now in the air, I knew it would send the beast into a frenzy, so I cast a fire spell that sent him tumbling backward.

For a couple of seconds, I dared to hope he would tumble into the loop spell and disappear, but he dug his claws into the hallway carpet and caught himself before he could roll that far.

I chanced a quick glance at my stomach. Four red lines stretched across my skin in ragged lines, but luckily the wounds appeared only skin deep. My jacket, though, was a total loss. Moving quickly, I shrugged it off my shoulders and slid it down my arms. By the time I drew it over my left hand and started to drag it over the sword in my right — I wasn't about to drop Betty — the hellhound came for me again. I was just about to drop the garment when an idea struck me.

Moving as fast as I could, I rubbed the jacket over my abdomen and wiped blood across the tan fibers. It hurt like crazy, but, once it was as bloody, I threw the jacket at the hellhound. Out of animal instinct he leapt for it, drawn to the blood like a fly to a car's windshield. I waved my free hand at the flying garment and whispered, "Enrapture."

The hellhound was too focused on the smell of human blood to notice the coat increase in size and flare open like a bird of prey coming in for the kill. Not that it would have mattered even if he had. He was already launched into the air after it. That is what poker players call *pot committed*. As soon as he touched the red soaked fabric, the enlarged coat wrapped around him. He hit the carpet a second later like the world's worst sausage link.

"What was that you were saying?" I asked, unable to keep a satisfied smirk from curling my lips.

Muffled growls rumbled up and the coat twitched on the carpet, but that was the hellhound's only reply.

"I thought so. Now it's time for you to go. And thank your Dark Lord you're still alive. If another cop had come here, you wouldn't be so lucky. And if I ever see your god-awful face again, you'll wish I hadn't."

I flicked my wrist, and a wave of energy lifted the rolled up coat and sent it flying toward the loop magic. He disappeared much like his partner had minutes earlier. I instantly felt better. It wasn't until I turned around that I remembered my night was far from over.

The door didn't have a name written on it or on a plaque next to it, but I knew who was behind it. Her aura tingled my skin like heat from a fission furnace. I checked my sidearm — not that my silver bullets with iron cores would do much against a demon — and walked to the doorway. After a quick prayer of purification, I pulled a rosary from my left pant pocket, wrapped it around my hand, drew my gun with the other, raised my fingers to the door panel, and hit the "Open" button.

As soon as the door opened wide enough for me pass through, I rushed in with my badge held up in my left hand, and the rosary next to it. "Under the authority of the Darda'il Council and the LAPD, I—"

I'm not really sure what I expected to find on the other side of the door. There could have been anything from a dark cave straight out of Hell to a flaming pit. It was a demon's lair after all, and the few brushes I'd had with them had taught me they liked to bring a bit of the old homestead with them to our plane. But what I found beyond the door's threshold stopped me cold — it was a dressing room.

Sitting on a white chair in front of a brightly lit vanity, Shira looked at me through her mirror with a mildly annoyed expression on her beautiful tawny face. A rainbow of dresses hung from wall racks, enough flowers to start a garden filled vases, and a fat, white Persian cat lounged on a creamy-colored chaise along the left wall. I cast a true sight spell to reveal hidden dangers, but, aside from Shira, nothing changed. Not even the cat. I was stunned beyond words.

"Oh, it's you," Shira said as she ran a brush through her kaleidoscopic hair. Again I saw black horns poking up from her forehead, and her tail dangled through an opening at the base of her chair. The shiny leather wings folded against her back were new though.

"I'm…" I was too flummoxed to say anything more. This was not how I'd pictured her arrest going down. Some fire for sure, maybe the screams of her damned victims, but not *this*.

Shira put her brush down and picked up a small cotton pad. "Not where you should be?"

"What?" I shook my head and grunted. Expected or not, this was happening and I knew I had to accept it before she launched at me and tried to tear my head off.

The demon sighed and cleaned off the last of her makeup, then put the used cotton pad back on the vanity top. "Listen, whoever you are, no offense, but you should get out of here. I'm not signing autographs tonight."

"Autographs?" My world tipped further under my feet. "I'm not here to get your autograph, demon. I'm here to arrest you."

Laughter was the last thing I expected, but that was exactly what I got. Once she stopped chuckling, she said, "Oh, honey, then you are *definitely* in the wrong place."

"I don't think so, sister." I shoved my gun and rosary at her, done with being off kilter. I had a job to do, and goddammit I was going to do it. "Several men have come forward saying they had their souls stolen by a glitzy demon, and, after fending off that seduction spell you were casting on stage, you fit the bill. So, you can surrender and make this easy, or I can start exorcising your ass and make it extremely unpleasant. Your call, demon."

The cat hissed at me, but Shira didn't lift an eyebrow.

"Then I guess you better start chanting," she said, barely dignifying me with a glance before she reached between her wings and grabbed the zipper at the top of her dress with taloned fingers. "Believe me, I'd love nothing more than to get out of this shithole, but it *isn't* my call."

"Oh, yeah?" I asked, cursing myself for not having a snappier comeback. "Then whose is it?"

Shira pulled the zipper all the way down, and her dress fell away as if it were wine pouring off a statue. Her honeyed skin glowed in the dressing room's light, and a wave of jasmine with just a hint of sulfur washed over me. A black strapless bra and panties were all that saved her modesty — not that she had any. In spite of my knowledge of what she was, and all my protections against her magic, there wasn't anything that could save me from the simple human lust her body and demeanor created. It was her most powerful weapon, and her most simple. I guess that was why I didn't hear the door open behind me.

"That would be *my* call, officer," a voice said.

I whirled around to face the newcomer. To my surprise, Nikko Alvarez stood in the doorway, his blonde date nowhere in sight. Behind him floated his shade bodyguards, all shadow and fiery eyes.

"Mr. Alvarez, I didn't –"

"Of course you didn't," he interrupted, waving at my gun and rosary as though they were trifles. He then looked at my badge hanging from my shirt pocket. "I try not to make a habit of killing cops, Detective Winters. It's bad for business. I'm sure you understand. That's why I grease all the appropriate hands, including the police. So, I'm going to stand aside and let you walk on out of here with your juicy bits intact. That way, everyone's happy. Understand?"

Not even a little. I shuffled to the left so I could keep both the demon and Alvarez in sight. "Mr. Alvarez, I don't know what sort of business you have here, but that demon is stealing souls, and it's my job to bring that to an end. You can either stand aside and let me do that or you can be arrested too. *Understand?*"

"You really are dumb, aren't you?" The succubus turned in her chair to face me. "I'm not stealing souls, you moron. He is. I'm just the middle gal stuck between a rock and a devil's trap."

I wasn't the quickest CPU in the core, but even I could catch a clue when it was tossed in my lap. So this was how Alvarez had risen to fame and fortune so quickly. Nothing in this dimension or any other had as much value as a soul, and a person could get a lot of those if he had a succubus under his control. It was a masterful scheme. It was also evil as Hell and against the law. Over half a dozen, actually.

"Then that means both of you are under arrest. Don't make this harder than it has to be."

Alvarez smirked and shook his head, but the demon shoved herself to her feet and bared her fangs. "Why am I in trouble?" she asked, her wings unfurling behind her like black sails. "I'm the victim here!"

"Tell that to the men whose souls you've taken," I replied, my rosary held up in front of me.

"I didn't want to take them!" She then pointed a long, dark claw at Alvarez. "That son of a bitch made me do it."

Now it was my turn to smirk. "*Made* you take their souls. A succubus. Yeah, I'm sure he really had to compel you."

If looks could kill, the glare Shira gave me would have stopped my heart cold. "You racist bastard."

Once again I was brought up short, but, before I could begin to process her words, Alvarez sighed in a heavy gust and stepped away from the door.

"This is charming and all," he said. "But my pet demon and I still have business to conduct tonight. Detective, I wish it didn't have to end this way, but I can see you won't be reasonable. Don't let it be said I didn't try. Shades, don't leave a mess on the carpet."

The words were barely out of his mouth before the two angry spirits in the hallway drifted into the room toward me. In the dancing flames of their eyes, I could see their hunger to consume my body and soul. I only had seconds to react, so I holstered my gun and tore open the front of my shirt to expose a two-inch long crystal pendant. When the ambient light in the room hit it, the facets took it in, magnified it, and released it in a bright flood. It wasn't enough to destroy the shades, but it pushed them out of the room and down the hallway.

"Cute," Alvarez said. "But crystals are fragile, and so is your mind." He raised his right hand and drew a figure in the air, then in a loud voice said, "DESTROY THE TALISMAN."

The persuasion ward on my back burned as his spell tried to take control of me, but he was just as unsuccessful as Shira had been earlier. I reached for my rope to bind him, but remembered I'd already used it on one of the hellhounds. Thinking quickly, I grabbed my tie and yanked it from my collar, then tossed it at Alvarez. "Enrapture!"

My tie lengthened as it flew toward the club owner, and, for a moment, it looked like it would be just as good a constrictor as my enchanted rope, but suddenly a blade sliced through the fabric, shredding it to ribbons fluttering uselessly to the floor.

"You're not too bad a caster," Alvarez said, the compliment tumbling from his mouth like a stone. "But I'm betting your sword fighting skills aren't as robust. Let's find out."

He came at me like someone out of one of those old black and white 2D movies you had to watch on an actual screen, his body and sword acting as one. I yelled, "Betty!" just in time to swat aside his first attack. He came at me again, then again, both strikes barely blocked. His third strike was too fast for me to parry, and his blade cut my left side just above my belt. The pain was immediate and intense. I stumbled backward and looked down to see blood seeping from the cut.

"And so we bring this to an end," Alvarez said in self-satisfied tones. "I promise the next cut will — OW!"

When I looked up, Alvarez had his arms up in front of his eyes, the light of my crystal pendant shining directly at him. I took advantage of his distraction and scrambled toward him. Even blinded, he managed to put up an impressive defense, but I knew I had him, so I pressed in close to finish him. At that moment, he reopened his eyes and saw the crystal bounce on my chest, then he sidestepped me and smashed the pommel of his sword against the talisman. Its light went out in a bright flash, and more pain shot through me as dozens of crystal shards sliced into my skin and stayed there like some kind of new piercing. I cursed, but what was done was done. When I turned to find where he'd gone, I found him leaning against Shira's vanity catching his breath. His shirt had several long slashes cut through it, but, aside from some strange markings on his chest, I didn't see any blood or wounds.

Suddenly Shira hissed and glared at her master with blood-red eyes. "Ah, there it is! Now I see why you never took your pleasure of me!"

Alvarez glanced down at his chest, then clutched the shredded shirt together. "Back away, beast! Harm me and you die!"

Tumblers whirled in my head, each one trying to unlock the mystery of Perdition. Shira was a succubus, and the desire of all succubi was to seduce men into giving up their souls in exchange for carnal pleasure. But if Alvarez was the one who had possession of the souls, that meant Shira had given them to him. The next question was why a demon would do that. The only answer, which the succubus had mentioned earlier without me really understanding, was Alvarez had her ensnared in a devil's trap, which made her his to command. Normally those were painted on the ground and meant for temporary use, but, if Alvarez wanted to control her over a long period of time, then he'd want the trap less obvious, somewhere he could protect at all times.

Alvarez had carved the devil's trap into his own skin.

"You're right," the demon said, spit flicking from her fangs to land on Alvarez's face. "I can't harm you." She then turned to look at me. "But he can."

Alvarez followed her gaze, and, for the first time that night, he looked afraid.

"Cut him," she said, her red eyes locked on mine. "Break the trap, and I'll end this for you."

Alvarez shuffled away from the demon toward the door, but, in the blink of an eye, Shira teleported ahead of him and closed it, then smashed the lock panel with a casual flick of her hand. Sparks sputtered from the ruined electronics

"Dammit, stop!" The club owner's bronze face was now pale and covered in sweat. "I command you to open that door!"

The demon shook her head. "You only command me for souls. Everything else is your fucking concern."

"You goddam bitch! Then I command you to take his soul!" The finger Alvarez pointed my way was as unsteady as a dingy in the middle of the deep blue sea.

"No can do," Shira replied. "He's warded against my charms. No charm, no seduction, no deal. Sorry." She didn't sound the least bit.

Alvarez was frantic as he looked for options. He looked at me again, this time with fear and just a little hope. "Detective, I apologize for how this got out of hand. Please, let me make it up to you. Exorcise this demon back to Hell, and I will shower upon you all the wealth you could possible imagine."

"I don't know," I replied, another old movie flashing through my mind. "I can imagine quite a bit."

"It will be yours," he said, now pleading. "I promise. End her!"

I entertained the idea. Who couldn't use that kind of money? As a detective, I made barely enough to keep me out of poverty. Alvarez's promise would mean I'd never have to want for anything ever again. And, if his earlier comments were to be believed — and I did — every other cop and politician was already on the take. All I had to do was exorcise a demon, which was my job anyway. Where was the downside? Who would be hurt by it?

The answer to that was easy — I would. I didn't become a cop because I wanted to be rich, or because I thought the easy way was the right way. No, I was a cop because I believed in doing what was just, and because I was all that stood between the people of Earth and the nightmares waiting in the dark. Just because this nightmare wore a human face didn't make it any less evil.

"Like the lady said," I replied. "No can do."

Before he could try and stop me, I magically grabbed the crystal shards embedded in my chest and flung them at his. He swung his sword to swipe them out of the air, but there were too many. Red blossomed across his chest as the shards tore into this skin. The devil's trap carved in his flesh flared for a moment, then turned to ash.

Shira laughed. "You could have known my love," she said as she advanced on the club owner, her wings beating the air behind her hard enough to buffet my hair. "Now you'll know my wrath."

I looked away as she leapt on him. I could have tried to stop her, but perhaps even demons deserved a little justice. She howled behind me, and Alvarez screamed until his throat gave out, the sound of splashing and breaking bones enough to force bile up my throat. But I held it down. Barely. A minute later it was over.

"A squeamish cop?" she said. "You might want to get over that if you intend on dealing with my kind much longer."

I turned around and tried to ignore the carnage spread across the floor and walls. The white cat now looked pink. In her fury, the demon's underclothes had somehow been removed. Seeing her naked glory would have probably dropped me to my knees if it hadn't been for the blood and bits of torn flesh clinging to her.

"I should still take you in, you know," I said, unsure if I meant it or not.

Shira snapped her fingers, and above her hand appeared a thick sheaf of papers. She snapped her fingers again, and the pages went up in a puff of smoke. "All the souls I took for that asshole are now back where they belong. No harm, no foul. Right?"

She was half right, but in that moment half was good enough. I was done with Perdition. I nodded. "Just make sure I never see you again, Shira. You got me?"

The demon laughed, and, as the sound flittered into the air, her body turned from tawny to the sort of bluish-pale you'd find only in the highlands of Scotland, and her hair turned a glorious shade of brown. A few seconds more and she was dressed in a simple peasant's skirt and blouse. Now she looked nothing like the woman who'd sung on stage. The transformation was as stunning as it was quick.

"Like you would even know if you did see me," she replied with a wink of her now green eyes. "But yes, I got your meaning."

Unsure if I could trust the word of a demon but even more sure I didn't have it in me to care, I nodded again. "Then get going, and don't let the door hit you on the way out."

Shira chuckled and stooped down to pick up the cat. Like her, it had been cleaned, but it was still the fluffy white Persian I'd first seen. Once it was in her arms, she turned and gave her ass a seductive shake. "Guys always hate to see me go," she said over her shoulder, "but they love to watch me leave. Tata, Detective." And with that she was gone, disappearing as though she'd never existed. The air popped from the sudden vacuum.

"I bet they do," I said to myself with a laugh.

With one last glance at the slaughterhouse of the room, I grabbed my badge and held it in a tight grip. In a few minutes, CSI guys would be crawling all over it, as would half a dozen attorneys looking for a victim, but for now I was done with the place. I still had to type up a report, but, after that, I had a date with a bathtub and a scrub brush. Magic couldn't be washed off, but blood could. For that I was grateful.

"Get me out of here," I said.

The badge warmed in my hand, and slowly the bloody room dissolved into a dark haze. It was as wonderful a sight as I could have hoped for.

The Hounds of Tartarus

by Patrick Scaffido

"L.A. never stays the same. I've pulled jobs here since the '80s and it's always different. Darker skies, cleaner cars, brave new public transportation that nobody uses. Some love this town: lights, flashy people, constantly changing landscapes of faces indistinguishable from one another. Over the decades trends keep shifting. That's why I hate L.A. It's a massive monument to forgetting what's important to chase the glittering distractions of the moment. If I had to die somewhere, I'm glad I died here."

Charles Parker pushed the pliers deeper into his torso, digging for bullets without flinching as he hated poetical on my city. His skin snapped like layers of dry phyllo dough as he excavated rusty bullets covered in a crust of blood, then held them up for inspection. "I could help with that." I said. "Be a little gentler with what's left of your body."

"Doesn't hurt. So why do you stay in L.A., Hess?"

I laughed. "Jose. Hoe-say. If you say my name, say it right."

"I've been calling you Hess for fifteen years. Too late to change now." He dug another bullet out with a crackling crunch and dropped it in a metal tray. "Seriously. I hate this city. I don't remember many Mexicans around. Why do you stay?"

I grabbed the pliers from his hands and took over, checking each of the seven bullet holes in his torso to make sure nothing else was stuck in him. "We've always been here. Maybe you just never noticed before." I teased the last of the bullets from his body, dropped it in the tray, then cleaned the salt and seaweed from the brittle wound before beginning the tedious process of sewing them shut.

"I'm serious, Hess. You could live anywhere." He was so deep in his rant he didn't flinch when I finished sewing and sprayed antiseptic on the wounds.

"Hey," I interrupted, "It's home." That shut him up. A man like Chuck could never argue with home. It wasn't in his nature. Dogged champions of tradition were weak for the classics: loyalty, tradition, history. And nothing was more classic than home.

I shrugged. I wasn't worried about him believing me about L.A. I needed him to believe in the warehouse, the surgery, our friendship. Luckily, he was distracted by the stitches. He fingered them, feeling nothing.

"I'm lucky you stayed. I've been walking around with these untreated for... a while. It was a long walk to L.A. These look the same as when I crawled out of the ocean. I can't believe they don't hurt."

"Well, you died. That changes things, eh? Here let me do the bandages."

"I can do it myself." He tried unsuccessfully to wrap one around his stomach.

"Maybe you aren't as limber after getting shot." I grabbed the gauze and helped him cover his torso. "Most people don't try to bandage their own wounds. You're supposed to lie on your back not screaming to prove your manhood while I do amateur surgery without anesthetic."

"Vince had the decency to shoot me in the front when he stabbed me in the back. I barely felt it."

"You've always been tough," I said as I taped bandages to him.

"Not that tough."

"You never needed a doctor before."

"I've never been shot before."

"Only because you shoot first."

He rolled his eyes, then studied the bullets in the tray, dented from impact and covered with his dried blood. "He really wanted me to stay dead when he shot me."

"I guessed that after the sixth bullet we pulled from you. You should be dead."

He looked down at his half-bandaged chest. The skin was torn up, a lawn ripped to shreds by a dog hunting buried bones. Chuck had just pushed the pliers in and pulled anything close to the mark. I shivered. I hated violence like that right in front of me. "I should have felt something when I did that. I'm really dead, aren't I?"

"As dead as a horse beaten with a doornail. Lucky for you, your body is mostly intact. Don't expect it to get much better than this, though. Take care of it. Now move so I can finish up." I rolled gauze under his shoulder and taped it off. "You don't have to worry about changing this often. Dead skin doesn't heal."

"You don't seem all that bothered, Hess."

"In my business, you see all sorts of things. I'm just glad you came to me first." Really glad. If he'd gone straight to hunting Vince, I'd have a bloodbath on the streets. Instead, I could finesse this, keep it contained. As long as Chuck kept trusting me, maybe I could even talk him down, find a nice non-violent way of dealing with his return from the grave.

He stretched. "Well that takes care of one thing. Now I need to go after Vince and get my money back."

"And Lucy?" I asked, watching his eyes.

His face blackened a bit as he said, "I guess I should have a little chat with her too. And I need a gun. M1911, good condition."

"Afraid I don't have one." I pulled a dusty tool box from a cabinet. Lifting the top tray and flipping a switch, I folded out the bottom to reveal a small collection of semi-automatic pistols.

"Here's the selection, Chuck."

"It's Charles. Chuck's what the football girl calls the bald kid in 'Peanuts.'" Peanuts. He comes back from the dead and he remembers the Peanuts. Humans have strange minds.

He rummaged through the box. "These are all.. What is this, plastic?"

"Polymer frame. Much lighter, easier to conceal, same..." He shied away from the gun as I handed it to him.

"No way. Guns should be metal. Hard. Plastic just doesn't feel right."

"You're an antique, Chuck."

"Charles," he said.

"Whatever. You're still an antique. Polymer frames are more durable. Proven by tests and studies and research. You know, stuff you don't trust."

"Damn right. What have you got in steel? I don't want a child's toy." I tossed him one which he held awkwardly. "It's light."

"Beretta M9. This is the gun the army replaced your beloved M1911 with. It's army strong."

"I hate that slogan. Be all that you can be was a good slogan. They never should have changed it."

"The world keeps spinning even when you're dead."

He sighted down the grip and noticed a few nicks in the metal. "It's scratched."

"It happens. Aluminum frame. Bruniton coating, whatever that means. Sounds cool, eh? Don't bother returning it. You'll hate it, but it should be hefty enough to smash someone's head in when you run out of bullets."

He frowned. "It'll do."

"Look, Charles, you've found a gun before you found shoes. That's not like you. You're walking around with a torn shirt and oily hair. This isn't you."

He nodded. "Of course it isn't me. I died when Vince shot me. So I'm not me. I just look like me. I'm really a spirit of divine vengeance."

"Don't kid yourself. You could put a bullet in Vince's head, and Lucy's too, seconds after they beg for forgiveness and not a thing would change. You'll still be a broken man. Going after them guns blazing won't get you anywhere. Look, let me get your part of the money. I can go through channels. I know a guy. We could fleece Vince for the cash and you could be out of town before he has any idea you're back. I know you hate this place."

"Sure, I hate L.A. I think everyone does, even the people who live here. But this isn't about money or vengeance. You're missing the point, Hess. It's about loyalty. It's about honesty." He pulled a waterlogged photo from his shirt pocket and waved it in my face.

"This is a photo of the three of us, from the day I married Lucy. There's a hole in it. Tell me why."

I shrugged. "I don't know."

He grabbed me. I could hear the rustling of his dead skin around his wounds. "You know why. Tell me why. Why is there a hole in a photo from my wedding day? Tell me!"

I sighed. "The best man at your wedding shot you point blank in the chest then ran off with your wife and your money and you were sappy enough to be carrying a sentimental picture of the people who betrayed you the moment they turned on you."

"Maybe you can forget stuff like that. God knows what you've been up to since I've been out of the picture. But it doesn't matter what it costs me or who I have to go through. I can't give up. I can't forget. I remember their faces, their friendship, and I'm going to show them something they never understood. Loyalty isn't some abstract concept. Loyalty is a physical force like gravity or gasoline or love. They'll see, they'll understand. That's the only way this thing ends."

As he spoke his thoughts and reason gave way to raw emotion, his body burning with it, the tips of his fingers glowed orange with heat pouring from the hand gripping my shoulder. I had to push him away to avoid singeing my suit. I didn't want to explain mystic undead burn marks to my tailor again.

"You're my friend, Hess. You should want to help me, do what's right. You're not one of them. You're a better man than that."

Was I? I didn't think so. I wasn't much more man than he was and he had no idea why I was helping him. "This is a bad plan. You'll end up hurting yourself more than they ever hurt you." I looked him in the eyes, trying to stare him down. "You don't know people, Chuck. They're not what you do. You're good at scaring people, but you aren't good at seeing people. You don't have the skill set for what you want to do. You're set up for failure, but you have the option to skip all this drama. Let me handle it. I can set you up elsewhere, a new life. You can relax and let go. No need for this mess. Drop the vendetta, accept reality, and move on."

I could tell he was buying it. I'd managed to make his argument explode in his face. Just a little more. Believe me, Chuck. Accept your death. Accept what I'm telling you. It's hard, but it'll make death easier for both of us. It could be over painlessly if only you could let go.

He was almost nodding. I was waiting, hoping, but then he stopped. "What then?" he asked. "You've got something better? A better reason I came crawling out of the grave? Look at me! I'm barely alive!" He ripped the gauze off his wounds, then ripped into them, fingers black with the oxidized blood, no healing despite how long his flesh sat there. "I don't scab. I don't bleed. I don't even breath! I'm a dead man." He stuck his fingers deeper into one of the sewn up wounds, reopening the unscarred flesh and flinging bits of himself to my warehouse floor. "Nothing! There's nothing! You want me to what, start a new life? Only the living get new lives. I don't. I've got nothing but vengeance!"

I shrugged. "Fine. Go kill everyone you ever knew. That makes sense. The only path to your redemption has to be a trail of blood and bodies. Nothing else could possibly make sense."

"Good. You get it." He had a crazed smile, his teeth grinding into his lower lip.

"No, that was sarcasm." I pointed at his mouth. "Don't chew your lip. It won't heal."

"Doesn't matter."

"Fine. Look, go get yourself cleaned up so you can interact with polite society and I'll do some digging. Vince rotates between a bunch of different properties." I handed him a cell phone. He held it with two fingers, like the body of cockroach, at a distance. "I'll let you know when I find him."

He stuffed the cell into his torn pocket trying not to think about it. "Just one last thing." He took the photograph and set it leaning against a shelf. Standing just a few feet away, he drew a bead through the sights of his new gun and pulled the trigger. The first shot missed, hitting a wall. The second hit Lucy right where Vince's arm was draped over her, hugging the couple from behind and grinning. The photo had two holes now, one in his ex-wife and one in his former best fried. The only person in the photo left to destroy was Charles and then he'd have complete vengeance on the three people who'd ruined his life.

"This gun... it'll do."

I watched him stumble out of the warehouse clutching the

ruined photograph and failing to cry. His tear ducts had dried up months ago, salted by his time spent adrift in the River Styx. This wasn't going to be easy for him. Killing people would be, but dealing with consequences wouldn't. To convince himself of his cause, he'd needed to reopen his wounds and leave bits of his soul laying all over my warehouse floor. But he'd see things my way.

"Keep in touch, Chuck. I'll be watching you."

In life, it wouldn't have been hard for Chuck to swipe a wallet or two and, in death, people seemed to take even less notice of him. As the hours passed, he used and abandoned stolen credit cards before cashiers ever began to wonder if they should have asked for his ID. As Alex or Gladys, he'd pay for a large American breakfast or the familiar feel of an off-the-rack suit from J.C. Penny's. A shave, a shower, a shampoo, and a hair cut- the last oddly quick as if his hair hadn't grown an inch since his dip in the River Styx- and his transformation from dead man to businessman was complete.

He didn't feel like a new man. Or like anything at all. He combed his hair in mirrors and checked clean teeth for traces of stray food. He popped a mint from a tin of Altoids into his mouth, then placed it in his jacket pocket next to the ruined photograph. He had a watch on his wrist that said quality, but didn't say it loudly. Charles showed the world a face that was respectable, not flashy.

Feelings were set low, a flame on simmer, barely noticeable. He stood disconnected, even from the hurt that drove him. I waited till he finished putting on his man costume to text him. It was a moment before he rang my phone.

"You know I hate texting."

I was not going to have this argument. "Did you read the message?"

"Of course not."

"I've got a lead. John Stedman, Vince's partner, works out of an office. The address in my text."

"I'm ready to write it down now."

I shook my head. "Read the message. Find a place to sleep tonight and we'll meet to dress him down tomorrow."

"I know John. I can handle him. Besides, I'm not tired."

"Well, if you're brave enough to try some mad science, there's an app on the phone that you can use to pay for a taxi." I doubted he'd use it but I was hoping for at least a little experimental open-mindedness.

"Nah, I'll figure something out," he said.

"You could still drop this, Chuck. I'm serious. Move on. This only ends bad."

"Sorry. That argument was over this morning and you lost."

"Have it your way."

I hung up. The conversation had made it real for me; he was a revenant now. There would be no stopping him with reason or logic. His head was solid brick. I had to admire him for his strength of will if nothing else. Getting into his memory, becoming a part of his life, had been hard. He didn't take inconsistencies casually. He noticed them and doggedly questioned them unless they fed his need for memories of loyalty and tradition. He'd been a hard case to connect to. I couldn't just be a trusted friend. I'd needed to be an old trusted friend with a history of us looking out for each other.

So that's me. That's how I operate. While Chuck hates visiting L.A., I do a booming business in helping the dead realize they're dead and make a little cash on the side. I'm Jose Fairfax, angel of death to the stars.

Chuck was a special case. My brothers would have chased him, constantly attacking his weak points, spurring him to greater desperation 'til he collapsed and moved on. But Chuck didn't need the unbridled wrath of the Hounds of Tartarus to rip his life apart. Men had already done that and now he was the demon. It was like that Tim Robbins movie from the

'90s. He didn't need more demons; he needed an angel. And a therapist. And a chill pill.

My brothers wouldn't have bothered. They would have torn him apart 'til desperation devoured him, but I liked the guy. Plus I'd get a bonus if he went to the grave willingly. So I played the slow game, certain he'd wake up one day and want peace. No need to get my hands dirty. If that took him killing Vince, then, well, too bad. Besides, I had a few more cards left to play. Maybe beating some sense into a thug like Stedman would beat some sense into Charles as well.

I pitied him, loved him, was him in a way. When he looks in a mirror, I look back. As long as he was in denial, there was no way I could take him in a direct confrontation. I'd tried this morning and he'd been willing to rip his body to pieces to make a point. I'd needed him to be emotional, on the edge, at the end of his rope, bleeding in the backseat of a car with no idea how to fix the mess his life had become before he'd even consider letting me win. There would have to be quite a bit of collateral damage before he was that desperate. So let the pain begin.

John Stedman's office wasn't run down. That was the nicest thing you could say about it. The small two story office building on La Cienega near West Adams had a keypad to keep out intruders, but some accountant on a coffee run held the door for Chuck without even asking any questions, then promptly forgot about it. If the cops were to come later, looking for who had assaulted or killed John Stedman, I doubt the accountant would even remember the plain looking businessman he had met in passing. That's the funny thing about death. Unless Chuck grabbed you and forced you to be aware of his presence, he'd probably fall from your memory without a trace. He was so hard into his denial that life itself seemed to deny his existence.

The building was squat and ugly, but well maintained.

Charles took the stairs to the second floor and found
Stedman's unmarked door. It was unlocked, the furniture
Office Depot wholesale, and Stedman was snapping pencils
in frustration as he tried to do math on a yellow pad of
paper. One thing John and Chuck had in common was their
mutual dislike for computers. Unlike Chuck, Stedman didn't
have the natural patience that would make up for not having
a document search function. His desk was a mess of piled
notes, to-do items on stickies, death threats, and counterfeit
bills. Photos of John doing neon-colored nightclub shots with
various low rent celebrities hung on walls where he could
stare at them when work gave him a headache.

Charles took in the room. "Looks like you've moved up in
the world, Stedman. Your own office in the middle of urban
wasteland, California."

Stedman looked up from breaking his pencils and nearly
leapt over his desk to give Charles an exuberant hug. "Parker!
I haven't seen you in, what, five years? It's good to see you!"

Charles pushed the younger man off gently and smiled in
genuine surprise. I guess enthusiastic friendliness isn't the
expected greeting when on a mission of blood vengeance.
"You haven't changed a bit, Parker! Same suit! Same
hair! Same watch! It's still running? You must keep ten
replacements or take ridiculous care of that antique."

"It's not an antique. Bought it yesterday."

"You can still buy analogue watches? Strange world. Good to
see you back in town!"

Charles shrugged. "Well, I'm not exactly the same." He
attempted to return the compliment. "Looks like you've
got a new tailor." Last time Chuck had seen Stedman, John
had been a young punk and not much of one. I won't stay
Stedman had style now, but at least he had enough flash to
cover for his lack of sense. His button down blazer glittered
in the light, more suited to the clubs in his photos than his

bland office. Stedman had stepped back slightly after the hug, but was still close enough to Charles to accidentally spit in his face every time he spoke.

"The organization pays better than I'm used to, though I'm still learning the ropes. I miss a spot of the old violence, like old times. It made more sense getting money from a register, but Vince keeps saying the boss calls it bad business." It was. When you're running an illegal operation, the last thing you want to do is get attention from the cops.

Charles's face read unpleasant thoughts. So this was the replacement. The upgrade Vince had chosen after shooting Chuck and kicking him into the ocean to drift away, dead and alive at the same time. The smile dropped from Charles's face. "Stedman, I'm looking for Vince."

Stedman walked to the far side of his desk and lit a cigarette. "Way to rush to business talk after so long. Have a smoke with me, man."

"I've quit." Parker opened his tin of mints and popped one in his mouth. "Should you be smoking in here? Don't they have laws about that now?"

"There's always some flexibility in the law. Anyway, I can't just tell you where Vince is." He flicked ash into an ashtray next to a pile of paper. "I'm paid to keep people away and you are people."

"Not exactly."

"You know," he said, spitting and spreading ash as he gestured, "he never told me what happened, but I'm not so sure he'd be happy to see you. Unless you're trying to make nice, get back in bed with him again. But where does that leave me?"

"You aren't blond enough to be in bed with Vince." Charles decided to try a lie. "I'm just in town for a little business and I thought I'd look him up."

Stedman turned cold quick. "Thing is, Charles, no." He sat

back down in his chair, kicking his feet on to the desk to make sure Charles noticed his stylish sepia wingtips. "Plus, I think maybe I don't believe you. You breeze back into town for the first time in a long time, what with Vince making good, working for the organization, and maybe you want a piece of his pie. Maybe you want to be partners again. But see." He leveled his eyes with Parker. "He has a partner. A good one. Me. He doesn't need some guy like you who vanishes and leaves friends hanging with no idea where he's gone. You should have been dead, but, instead, you're here like time hasn't left you behind. Well, Vince, he doesn't need an antique like you." Stedman's words were confident but his eyes were fear, not fire. Anyone could tell Parker was an operator, confident even under stress, and John was just a thug in tight pants. If Vince had an ounce of intelligence, he'd know he had traded down when he'd replaced Parker. Stedman certainly knew. Stedman worked out, Stedman practiced math, and Stedman raced to be half as useful as Parker had ever been to Vince, so he was having none of the diplomacy.

"Here, I'll give you a tip, for an old friend who used to have my back." Stedman bent over to rummage in his desk and came up waving the cold black steel frame of an M1911 handgun in Charles's face, brushing against his hard nose and promising violence. "Get out of here, get out of L.A., and leave Vince alone before I kill ya. It's a favor to the old Charles that used to post my bail that I don't pull this trigger right now."

With his left, Charles grabbed John's hand and squeezed as snapping sounds came from the fingers holding the gun. He slammed John's hand down on the table hard, denting the wood. With his other hand, he pulled the M9 I'd given him and shoved its barrel lengthwise into John's mouth hard, knocking teeth past his gums and leaving scratch marks and blood on the aluminum frame of the gun. "Gee, that looks painful, John. Is Vince corporate enough to provide dental insurance now?"

With his left hand firmly around John's, Chuck began turning the wrist slowly, putting pressure on joints that weren't ready for the torture. John's fingers let go of his gun and grasped for anything. "Now, don't move or I shoot you. I have enough old friends to kill today and I'd hate to add you to the list." Chuck picked up a half-smoked cigarette from the ash tray and it lit suddenly in his hands as his fingers touched the tip. He held the cigarette to John's mouth. "Have a smoke. It'll dull the pain for a bit."

John hesitated, then took a puff and screamed as smoke crawled across the open wounds in his gums. He coughed and spat out blood and teeth. Charles smiled cruel. "I lied. But this isn't a lie. I don't want to have a battle of wits with you and it looks to me like you're helping me already. See, I hate this gun I've got and you've started using my favorite. I'm excited, see, since we're going to trade. It's very kind of you and has me in a good mood. I'm in a good enough mood that I'm not going to test out your gun on your stomach just to make sure I like the feel. I'm going to take it on faith as a gift from an old friend. So, I'm thinking of putting out this cigarette using your skin as an ash tray. Instead, make life easy and just tell me where Vince is?"

John struggled trying to break free, but couldn't begin to move under Charles's iron grip. His eyes turned wide as he stared down at Charles' fingertips. Flame danced on his fingertips as they dug into Stedman's hand. When Stedman finally broke, Chuck dropped the cigarette on a pile of papers on Stedman's desk where it began to smolder.

"Now let's be clear. It wouldn't be healthy for you to tell Vince I'm coming to see him. He'll really enjoy the surprise and if you ruin it for him, I'm going to come back here and kill you. Stay out of the way and I won't hurt you. You used to be a friend and I believe you. I don't think you helped him out with what he did to me. In fact ..." Charles stuffed a stolen wallet with some cash and a credit card in John's flashy jacket breast pocket. "I suggest you take a small trip. Make yourself scarce for a few days. My good friend Gladys here, she wants you to, on her dime. If you hurry, they probably won't even have canceled the credit cards."

On his way out of the building, Charles stopped to wash his hands in the men's room. He figured he had a few moments since Stedman was busy putting out the small cigarette fire on his desk. The M1911 he'd taken from John felt good in his hand. He felt a little bit more like himself. He straightened his jacket and checked his chin in the mirror. He still didn't need a shave. He stared for a bit, certain five o'clock should be bringing a shadow to his face soon, then turned away, dropping the question as quickly as he'd forgotten he'd never asked how he'd come back from the dead.

He called me soon after. "You were right. Stedman was quite helpful. I've got a location. Funny thing, Vince has all his men using M1911s. Maybe he misses me. Now I just need to find Lucy. You don't have a line on her, do you?"

"Actually, I do. I'll pick you up." Truth was, I knew exactly where Lucy was. But Charles needed a little more than the truth if I was going to break through his headstrong denial. An hour later found us in front of a closed bookstore in West Hollywood as the sun fell below the horizon. I smiled at Charles's puzzled face. "You need information, you go to a bookstore," I told him.

"I thought you preferred the internet. Anyway this place looks shut down."

"It is." I pushed the door open and walked in, Charles on my tail. "Erica, where are you girl?"

A skinny, disheveled brunette with large glasses pushed from behind a stack of books that leaned tentatively on the side of a cardboard box. Most of the shelves were empty and the entire store was filled with boxes. "Jose! Good to see you! You're late! I guess he decided not to take the cab." She smiled a sweet Texan smile, refreshing like lemonade.

"Nope. Erica, honey, you really should keep the door locked."

She laughed. "Don't you worry yourself. I'll be gone long before anyone tries to break into this old place. Besides, the lock won't stop them when they really try."

I looked at the door's metal deadbolts and hard glass. "Whatever you say. You're the all-knowing."

"Oh stop. So... introduce me to your friend already."

I pushed him forward. "Chuck, this is Erica Llewellyn. She's the owner of this fine establishment and one of the best informants I know. Erica, Chuck."

"Hi, Charles. It's my pleasure. Nice to meet you. So sorry about everything. Jose tells me you're looking for.."

Chuck interrupted. "I'm looking for my ex-wife. She owes me some money."

She curled her nose in puzzlement. "Are you sure? I read something different." She laughed. "Well, no matter. I can still help. Sorry for the mess. I'm moving because of the earthquake."

"Earthquake?" Chuck said, looking around.

"There's an earthquake next week and I don't feel like cleaning up after. You'll have to look me up in my new location. It'll be a hoot. I'm guessing I'll be Atlanta, but the outlook is cloudy."

Charles looked at me. "Your master informant is a magic 8-ball?"

"She sees the future. A mystic."

Charles nodded slowly. "Right. Perhaps we should enlist Uri Geller to help me after this."

"Dead men don't get to be skeptics about the supernatural," I said.

"Sure we do. I'll believe what I see."

"Oh don't worry, Charles. I have it right here!" Erica had been shuffling through a pile of books on her counter. "I was keeping it close at hand since I knew you'd ask and didn't want you to get scared off before I got to give it to you. I mean, some people find the prospect of seeing their imminent future poised over them about to fall and crush them like a collapsing tidal wave a little intimidating and I was worried... I'm babbling aren't I? It's OK. Tell me. Anyway, here it is."

She handed Chuck a book and he looked at the title. "*On Grief and Grieving*. By Elisabeth Kubler-Ross? What is this, a joke?"

She shook her head enthusiastically. "Nope! That's the information you need. Hold on to it. This book is better than anything else I could give you! But I know you probably want to learn things the hard way, so I put your wife..."

"Ex-wife."

"Actually, no. You were never formally divorced. Anyway, I put your wife's address inside the front cover in pencil. If you decide not to visit her, which I highly recommend, you can just erase it and move on."

"If you see the future, you know I'm not going to do that."

"A girl can hope." She smiled. Charles opened the book and saw an address in Westwood on the cover, along with a note saying "Seriously, Charles, read the book. It'll help." There was a smiley face and a heart and a signature from Erica. He shut it and tucked it under his arm. "So how much do I owe you?"

She grabbed his hands and held them, letting the warm tingle in his fingertips spread. "It's a gift, Charles. Grief is a gift. You'll understand someday. Do me a favor and try." He nodded, shaking his hands free, and looked uncomfortably at the door.

"Erica, you're scaring my friend with all your mystic insight. So, do you need any other help? I've got the driver and truck scheduled for later tonight."

"Nope! That's perfect. Thanks so much, Jose." She gave me a chaste kiss on the cheek. "Everything's here and I'm all ready."

Charles looked around. "All you're bringing are books?"

"What else would I need?"

He sighed and we left.

As I followed the automated GPS voice to Lucy's address, Charlie tried reading the first few pages of the book, but kept getting bleary eyed and turning back to start over. He barely paid attention to complaining about recent changes in the Century City skyline.

"You know," he said, "Maybe we shouldn't go."

"What? Why not?"

"I could skip seeing her. Just go straight to Vince and get the money. Call it a day. Maybe there are parts of the past I don't have to dig up."

"Too bad I have the car keys. You called me, you had me check my sources, and we're committed now." He was primed. He was ready. One good push would get him past denial and into something. Nothing would push him like seeing Lucy's current state.

He snapped the book shut. "Fine. But if she starts yelling or something, we leave. I don't want to have to deal with that right now. Or if she cries. Especially if she cries."

I glanced over at him in the passenger seat, once more re-reading the same passage in the book, and said, "Sure, especially if she cries."

The GPS led us to one of those gated fields with permanently tended grass and rows of gray stone slabs identifying the inhabitants. We parked and Charles looked around at the buildings nearby. "We parked this far for a reason? None of these buildings look like something she'd want to live in anyway."

"Actually, the address is here." I pointed to gated field.

We got out of the car. Charles was whispering something to

himself and, when I asked him what he'd said, he said, "The first stage of grief helps us survive the loss."

"What was that?"

"Something from that book. I forgot everything I read except that bit." He looked out over the grass field. "If this is the address…" He trailed off. I tossed him a flashlight and opened the gate.

It didn't take us long to find a grave marked Lucy Parker. No epithets, no beloved wife or daughter. Just a name. Not even any dates. "I crawled out of the grave to get revenge on her, only to find out she followed me. I should be angry." He was chewing on his lip again.

"Yes. You should."

"I don't feel anything, Hess. Not a thing." His voice was flat.

"They don't call it denial for nothing."

"You knew, didn't you?"

"Yes. I was hoping Erica might give you something that would help. I know this isn't what you came for." This part was tenuous. He might turn on me here if his denial broke, focusing the resulting rage.

"I should be mad at you, too. I'm not. I'm just.."

"Yeah," I said.

"She's dead, Hess."

"Yeah."

"I don't think I can do it. Kill Vince. Maybe I'll just get the money. Let him live. Run away. Like you said."

"I can give you money," I said. "You don't have to take him on."

"I don't want your money. I want my money. And I need to talk to Vince. Did he do this? Did he kill her?"

I shrugged. "Police reports say suicide by drug overdose. Last I heard, she wasn't taking losing you very well."

That hit the spot nicely. A touch of self-loathing, something to spark him into needing a target. "Maybe she shouldn't have misplaced me."

I could see the anger starting to spread, not just the tips of his fingers glowing now. Flames slowly filtered through his veins, lighting up his whole hand. He didn't notice. Anger was progress, progress I could use. A hole in him was nothing, but this? This was something. "I could have helped manage her habit, you know. Controlled her access."

I had to be delicate. Push him, but push him at Vince. Get him feeling hate without feeling it for me. First, a sprinkle of truth. "Your marriage wasn't perfect, Charles."

"Now I'll never know why she.. This is stupid. This isn't how it's supposed to go. I come back, she begs forgiveness, then I walk away, breaking her heart. I had a plan."

"Well you don't get your plan, dream-boy. She'd dead. You want to know why, don't you? You want to know whose fault it is, right?" Step two, help him pick a feasible target.

"No. I know who to blame. I don't know why, but Vince... he should have done better. He should have protected her."

"You still could give up," I said. I could see it on him now, his soul was leaking out. Since our argument earlier and the crushing blow of Lucy's death, he'd weakened. He'd need something fresh to keep going. This anger might not be the acceptance I needed from him, but it was progress. I'd take it.

"She was so jealous, you know. Of her sister. She couldn't ever take that Billie and I were friends. She'd get so mad that I kept driving for Billie after we got married." Open minded thought, considering the possibilities.

"Well, whose idea was that? Yours? I seem to recall Vince encouraging you to keep on despite Lucy's protests." A simple twist of truth to help get him thinking on the right track.

"Billie was family. Like a sister. I wanted her out of the business. If I couldn't get her to stop, I'd at least look after her."

"Sounds like Vince's logic to me."

"You're saying Vince had been... that he... he set this whole thing up? That he manipulated Billie, Lucy, and I?"

I raised my hands and moved to put the gravestone between us. "I'm not claiming anything. I just think it's suspicious that the guy who ran off with your wife encouraged you to do stuff that made her jealous." I moved slowly, rubbing my fingers along the gravestone, coaxing the hatred out of him.

"That doesn't make any sense." Of course it didn't. That was the stuff of paranoid delusional self talk. But men back from the dead don't need sense, they need fuel, and I could see his thoughts tipping over the edge, imagining the possibilities. It was just enough. The fire of jealous rage burned up his arms, the cuts on his lip glowed orange, then vanished. Success. It was just a little bit, but he'd moved on to anger and I knew that would be enough to propel him all the way to the end, all the way to accepting his fate.

He ripped open his button-down shirt and pulled the bandages off his chest. The bullet wounds he had torn at this morning were now glowing orange and sealing themselves. "What? They're disappearing." We stood together in the gravelight as every last bit of damaged flesh erased itself in anger. "How?"

"You're moving on, Charles. You're angry. That's the first thing you've felt today, eh?"

"It's the first time I've really felt something since I was shot."

"Then you're ready. So quit whining about running off and a new life that you'd never accept. I'm sorry about any secrets I kept from you, but you needed the rage. I bet you know who to blame now."

He checked the magazine of his M1911, fully loaded. "Oh yes. I know." He turned to face me. "I wanted to hurt you for a moment there. You know, you and Billie are the only friends of mine I've never hurt."

"You haven't hurt Vince."

"No. But that's changes tonight." He looked away from Lucy's grave, unsure if he should spit or send flowers, then walked away. Things were in motion now; I hope I'd played him right. If I had, he'd be well on his way to the afterlife before the sun came up.

We pulled up to Vince's current hideout, not too far from the graveyard. He had four or five apartments in gated communities around the city and rotated between them to keep himself from getting caught, but the precaution wasn't going to keep him safe tonight. Chuck sat in my passenger seat, book tossed aside and forgotten as he checked and rechecked his gun.

"You know, I thought for sure I'd feel something if she was dead. Like guilt or something. In my soul."

"What do you feel?"

"A bullet in Vince's skull."

"You see the future now, Chuck?"

"This ain't magic. This is payback."

I watched him step out of the car, gun in hand, shirt still torn. He'd forgotten the wedding photo, it lying in the recently vacated car seat. I tucked it inside his book in the hopes he'd return relatively intact.

As he climbed the condo stairs, the moment felt empty of anything but anger. He knew it was all Vince's fault, as much as he could know anything. Denial had failed to protect him from the pain of Lucy's death, so anger had filled in as a buffer. He whispered as he walked, "This is all Vince's fault. He didn't take care of Lucy and now she's dead. He double-crossed me and I'm dead too. But I've got him tonight." He approached the door to the unit Vince rented and paused, touching the doorknob. "You can do this. It's not like last time. This time, you're going to be the one blindsiding him."

He touched the door and it quietly slid open, no barrier to a herald of vengeance like Charles. There was loud pop music playing from a far corner of the apartment and Charles followed it to a master bedroom adjoined to a steam-filled jacuzzi bath. A woman laying impatiently in the bed looked wide eyed as he slipped through the door and showed her his gun, whispering, "Get dressed and get out. Now." She hadn't bothered to get dressed. Vince was soaking in the bath, ignoring the hot young thing waiting for him.

Charles stepped into the steam of the bathroom where he could hear Vince squeaking along to the lyrics of Justin Timberlake. "I just wanna love you baby.. Girl.." Neither Charles nor I bought it. Vince obviously had other priorities than loving the ladies. Charles crept up and tapped the barrel of the M1911 on the back of Vince's head. "Baby, hold on, I'm soaking," Vince whined.

"Baby, I just can't wait," Charles said in harsh voice. Vince froze. "Good boy. Don't move. I don't know how you've gotten sloppy enough to let me get this far, but your girl is gone."

He relaxed into the bath and rested the back of his short spiky hair against the gun. "Charles. You're dead."

"Yeah. Surprised to see me?"

"Stedman called, but I didn't believe him."

"I told him I'd kill him if he did that."

"Well, I should have trusted the man."

"Don't worry. You won't regret it long."

"I should have known better. I never did trust enough. Especially you. Thought you were as smart as me. I was so certain Fairfax was going to bring you into the organization instead of me after that last job."

"Fairfax? What is this your deathbed confession?"

"Nah, it's my bathtub confession. I don't think you'll let me live to see the bed. I've worked my whole life to get out from under the control of people, just to end up a flunky to some spic crime lord. I'm no more to him than Stedman is to me. That's what killing you brought me. I was so certain you were going to abandon me, your partner, and move up the ladder.

Fairfax liked you, you know. Called you reliable. Me, he calls unscrupulous. He's like you, thinking crime is about all this samurai yakuza bullshit."

"Whoever this Fairfax is, whatever job he would have offered us, I would have demanded you be along. You were my friend, Vince."

"I get that now. It's funny. I kill you to buy my way into a crime syndicate that you would have gotten me into anyway. Now he double crosses me."

"I'm not working for anyone."

"Well, someone fished you out of the water and set you on my trail. If it wasn't Fairfax, I don't know who else could. I shot you seven times, Chuck. Seven bullets in your chest. There has to be damn good reason you're not dead."

"You're wrong. Turn around." Vince slowly turned in the bath. The unbroken skin on Charles's chest grabbed his attention.

"Look," said Chuck. "No wounds. No scars. Nothing. Not even bandages. I'm a whole man."

Vince reached trembling fingers out to touch the dead torso but stopped, remembering the gun pointed at him. "Not possible. I shot you. You can't..."

"I saw Lucy. You should have taken better care of her. If you're going to steal a man's wife, you should at least treat her right." Vince shook as a smile spread across Charles' face.

"So I'm pretty darn angry. I'm trying to decide if I'm going to kill you or every single person in your organization. I was sad for a second. Just a second. But then I remembered what you did to my wife."

"You don't get it. She left me. She thought you were cheating on her with Billie. The whole thing was her idea. I should never have gone along with it. I knew you weren't like that. I've been a dead man since the day I shot you. I can't even please a woman."

Charles laughed. "Oh? How many times did you fuck my wife, Vince? How many times?" His fingers were starting to glow red on the trigger.

"Once. Just once. She said you were better and left that night. She didn't want anything to do with me after that."

"So, what you're saying is, it's her fault? It's easy to blame the dead, isn't it? As a dead man, I find that prejudice offensive. So... where's my money?"

"I don't have your money."

"Liar."

"Jose Fairfax. My boss. I can bring him to you."

"Bullshit. Jose Fairfax is the last friend I have left. And if you've got no money, how do you afford all this?" Chuck gestured at the elaborate bathroom.

"I'm not lying. I'm just a rookie. An idiot. Fairfax is careful with the purse strings, so no one can do what I did to you. Do what you want to me, but if you want the money, I don't have it. I don't want to be a part of this anymore. We work like nine to fivers. This isn't crime, Charlie. This isn't money. This isn't pulling off heists. I'm stuck with an organization that's turned me into a corporate executive. I just want to go back to where we were. And I can't. Ever."

"No. I guess you can't. Your fate was sealed when you shot me and ran off with my wife. Being a sick bastard who drowns in a bathtub is the perfect coda for your pathetic life."

"Drowns? Wait, no, you can't..." He struggled for awhile as Charles held his head below the water's surface, but Vince never had a hope of escaping retribution. Chuck's whole hand burned red as he held the man down and caused the bathwater to steam around Vince's head. When the body floated to the surface of the large jacuzzi tub, the cops would find a dead man's fingerprints in the burn marks where Charles had grabbed him.

As he walked out of the house, Charles's muscles pulsed with electricity, charged with anger from the brutal act of killing. His face, however, was flat. It wasn't the climactic battle of ex-friends he'd wanted. It was quick, brutal, dirty.

I watched him come back down the stairs and slide into my passenger seat. He stared silently at the floor of the car.

"I got you a Slurpee." I had two: blue raspberry and cherry coke. "Dead men don't need to worry about calories."

Chuck grabbed the blue raspberry. "I just killed a man I used to call a friend. I'd prefer whiskey."

"We each pick our poisons. I like money and sugar, you like vengeance and liquor. So, do you feel better?"

We sat for a second then he said, "I'm tired, Hess. Especially tired of friendship. There had to have been an easier way to killing Vince than getting me to do it. I mean, I don't see the point. I'm dead. Lucy's dead. Vince's dead. I just want to get my money and leave. You have it, right?"

"What if I say no? You kill me?"

He shrugged. "I don't know. Probably. Maybe. Would you stay dead?"

"Well, you don't have to worry about that. I have a bag in the trunk that should cover what Vince owed you. But you didn't answer. Do you feel better?"

"Like shit. I came back for vengeance and gunfights. Instead, I find my wife dead, Vince just pathetic, and you're the crime boss he crossed me for. Death sucks."

"Well if you're ready to be dead, I could arrange a nice ceremony for you. Least I could do."

"No, thanks. Part of me wants to go back and snap every bone in Vince's body and part of me wants to sit here sipping Slurpees forever. I can't get a brainfreeze, so I have no idea what I want."

"Well I do. See, there's something I didn't tell you about Lucy. Her grave is empty. Her body vanished before we buried her. She's become like you."

"She's alive?"

"No, quite dead, but walking. She's out east and it's past time for her to come home. I think it'd be kind of sweet for you to be the one to bring her home."

"What do you mean?"

I handed him a business card with the words Jose Fairfax, Angel of Death on it. "I look out for lost souls. Like you. I help them find their final rest."

"So this whole time..."

"I tried to talk you into moving on remember? You weren't ready. So I made sure he was easy for you to find."

"You want to put me to rest, but you're helping me?"

"Well, I'm a busy man and, unlike you, I love L.A. If you're not ready to play dead, then maybe we can bargain. Come work for me, go find your lost love, and spend a little more time. When you're done, come back and I'll find you and see how things stand."

"You're saying I get another chance to see my wife."

"All you have to do is help her move on to the next life."

"Do I have to hurt her?"

"Hell no. I just need her to accept her own death"

"Can I?"

I blanched. "You're sick, Chuck."

"Not sick, just a little angry."

"Well, this job is a little different from your usual. I don't think you'll be able to strong-arm your way to success. So what do you think? I may not be who you thought I was, but I'm still your friend."

He sighed and sipped the Slurpee again. "Yeah. I'd like to see her again. I don't know what I'll do when I find her but... I'd like to see her again."

That's how it's done. Sure, my brothers like their violent game of pursuit, but you can't argue with my results. Denial, Anger, Depression, Bargaining- four stages of grief in one day. He's well on his way to Acceptance and might even help me bring another of my wayward charges in. I handed him his book with the picture still tucked inside.

"Wish granted. Welcome to the Hounds of Tartarus, Chuck. See? Death isn't so bad. At least you get to leave L.A."

Call It Intuition

by Jeff Leyco

I had two new gifts from Roger that night—a metal bracelet, given as an apology from our last fight, and a brand new black eye. He hated seeing me talking to anyone after shows, or hell, between sets. He especially hated it when he saw me hanging around Billy.

Roger couldn't wait to tell me Billy was dead when he barged into the dressing room. He knew because he worked vice for the LAPD. Billy's case fell into his lap earlier today.

"Damndest thing," Roger said.

"What's that?" I asked, staring at a corner of the mirror in front of me, trying to hide any sign of emotion.

"I read the coroner's report on Billy Boy."

I rolled my eyes. Roger talked about coroner's reports a lot. "And?"

"His hand was gone. Not like it was cut off when he died; like it was never there to begin with. His service record said he lost a hand in Belgium."

I perked up. A lock of blonde fell across my eye. I pushed it back up and tried to stick it in place. Ten minutes until the first set started.

"That's funny," I said.

"Did I ask for your opinion?"

I looked away from my reflection, at the bracelet sitting on the vanity. Roger said it was his great grandma's, but it came from Ireland sometime way before the Great Famine. I thought he found it at the bottom of a cereal box.

I continued doing my makeup.

He walked up behind me and leaned over, kissing me on the neck, his chin itching me with his five o'clock shadow.

"I'm sorry," he said casually.

I looked to my side, to the other side of the dressing room. Black smoke danced with wispy tendrils, and I realized I was looking at a table. Two shadows drinking something. Wine, I thought. One leaned in to the other for a kiss.

I could smell another woman's perfume.

This sort of thing happened. The shadows came out to play whenever someone got too close, or whenever I started feeling something strongly. I was the only one who could see it, too. I couldn't pin it down, seemingly random. I considered going to see a doctor about it years ago, but I figured I'd probably just get laughed out of the room.

"Keep going," I said quietly. Moments like this, it usually helped to ignore it.

"Right," Roger said, sneaking a not-too-subtle glance down my dress from his position. "He lost it the day after Christmas, 1944. Battle of the Bulge. Kraut artillery obliterated it. They even had a picture and everything."

I scrunched my face, trying not to think about it.

"He never told me about that."

"Negroes don't talk about lots of things."

I ignored the comment. "How'd he die?"

"Suffocation, looks like."

"What, someone put a bag over his head?"

"That'd make things easier."

"So what then?"

"Looks like foul play. At the same time, it doesn't," Roger admitted. He sounded disappointed. "He was playing his trumpet real loud. Neighbors complained. Suddenly he wasn't. His roommate, that piano player Thomas, found him dead this morning with the trumpet still in his mouth."

"He forget to take a breath?"

"Your guess is as good as mine."

I looked at myself in the mirror again. I hated the way the lights made me look paler than I actually was. I looked like a goddamn ghost, and the green silk I wore wasn't doing anything to help.

"So why'd they call you in on it?"

"Because no one else knew what to do."

"Do you?"

Roger shrugged. "I don't care. He's a Negro. Trumpet players like him are a dime a dozen. Not like anyone's gonna miss him."

Billy Carter wasn't just another trumpet player. Boys like Billy, they didn't drop dead out of the blue. They bought you presents on Christmas. Told you how beautiful you were without wanting anything. Promised you nice things, like getting you out of LA, or getting you the biggest mansion money could buy. They told you comforting things when someone else hit you. Never laid a hand on you unless you wanted.

Hand.

He lost his hand in the war?

Even completely naked, he looked intact to me.

Olivia's, the club I played at, was a dying breed. You couldn't find big bands out anymore. The music was changing; everything was changing. The hopping clubs were the ones that bopped instead. Olivia's was a classic, though. When it got a good band, it was always hot, even when no one came.

We had the usuals, at least. The guys with money, they'd sit up front real close to the dance floor at tiny round tables with red velvet cloth and shining white candles. Kyle was there, smiling his perfectly white, charming smile. He had three houses in Beverly Hills, each one bigger than the last. Sometimes he was accompanied by beautiful women, actresses or models. Tonight, he just had his chauffeur at his side, a hulking, ugly, hairy-headed beast of a man named Took. I couldn't look at him for too long. I hated how he stared at me.

Greg Malone was there, too, in a deep blue three-piece suit and a gold tie. His shoes were so spotlessly white you could see your reflection in them. Malone ran the local mob. He also owned the damn place. Whenever Roger came out, he'd sit as far away as possible.

We had smaller and smaller bands playing these nights - players could be more expensive than they were worth, and jazz players who still played our way were getting rarer.

Tonight we had a full set, though. Seventeen pieces— *seventeen*. Trumpets, trombones, all kinds of saxophones. Four guys on rhythm, including Thomas on the keys, a plaid-suited gentleman who rolled into town about six months ago and set up shop on the eighty-eights.

When we finished our last set, Roger took off. He kissed me one more time. He tried to go for the lips. I turned aside and he got my cheek instead.

"You're too good for him," Thomas told me after Roger left. The same thing Billy would've said. He offered a cigarette, along with a roguish smile.

There are two things I take from men: jewelry, and fine wine. I passed on the cigarette, shaking my head.

"He treats me nice enough."

"Sure. Need some ice for the eye?"

I looked away. A couple moments passed, with just the hum of the crowd around us.

"You found Billy, right?"

The shadows emerged from the floor, from all around. I saw

the outlines of Billy and Thomas's small apartment, smoky and wispy. The door opened and Thomas stepped through.

Billy's corpse lay there twisted, contorted like he died struggling. Roger didn't mention that. The trumpet rested in his mouth.

The smoke went away.

Thomas let a long puff go. Not even a second had passed. "Yeah. I'm looking for a new place now. You know any?"

"What do you think? About him missing a hand?"

He shrugged. He had nothing else to say.

I worked the crowd a bit after that. Whatever vision I had of Billy's death, it didn't look normal, not one bit. Maybe someone had an answer for me. But after the shrugs and non-answers I got from the band, I was wasting my time.

I stared at the stage after the drummer finally packed his stuff and headed out. Most of the crowd had left for the other clubs still open along Central Avenue. Malone was gone, but I recognized a couple of his goons starting a game of cards.

A wine glass appeared in my hand.

"A drink, for the beautiful singer," Kyle said, caressing my arm with soft, smooth fingers. A pleasant tingling danced through my body.

I smiled faintly without saying a word.

"My little songbird seems upset tonight. Come, sit with me." He offered his arm.

I took a sip from the wine and joined my other arm to his. Kyle spent thousands a night in the club. He always came back millions richer. I never knew how he did it.

We took a seat in a leather-backed booth. The chauffeur Took stood nearby. I could feel him staring at me. I couldn't put a finger on Took or where he came from. Every time I wanted to look at him, I looked away instead.

"What happened to your eye?" This was hardly the conversation I wanted. "Let me see it," he said softly, inching toward me. He placed his hand on mine. Warm. The room spun.

We locked eyes for a while. I don't know how much time passed, but it seemed longer than a minute and shorter than a blink.

"A favor for a favor?"

I scrunched my nose, suddenly able to move again. "Of course," I said shakily. I tried to smile.

"A kiss on the cheek, and I will make your little misfortune go away."

I couldn't stifle the laugh. I shook my head. Roger wasn't around to see us, but it still felt awkward.

"I'm serious, dear."

"You're a bit of a creep, you know that?"

"Oh, I do. And how I do. It's unfortunate, really."

I rolled my eyes. What the hell. I leaned over and kissed him lightly on the cheek, just a light peck. Kyle giggled and smiled his own beautiful, charming smile. He brought his hand to my face and rubbed his palm over my eye. It stung for a minute. Then it didn't.

Again, he smiled. "You'll be fine, little songbird."

"What did you do?"

Kyle simply winked. And that was all.

Billy was buried two days later at Angelus-Rosedale, the only decent place in town that would accept Negroes. I hitched a ride with Thomas, whose creaky used coupe smelled like he'd left a dead rat under the seat and forgot about it.

I burned up in the blistering summer sun, and the veiled wide-brimmed hat on my head only made it hotter. Black was not the best color to wear in this heat. Thomas was sweating bullets in his cheap suit.

"You know, Billy Boy was something of a war hero," Thomas whispered while Billy was lowered into the ground.

I nodded. "He told me he saved a nurse's life in Belgium. I liked that story."

"He tell you about her zingers?"

I sighed. Thomas chuckled, then changed the subject.

"I invited him to jam with me and a couple others last week."

"Yeah?"

"Never showed up. Said he hated the cool shit we were trying." I knew what he was talking about. Couldn't say I cared much fort it either. More and more players were heading in the direction of the newer sound. Swing was dead, or it would be soon.

I recognized a couple of the mourners' faces. Jazz players, the guys Billy normally practiced with. I even saw a few of Malone's guys hanging around. The card players from last night. I raised an eyebrow.

"Why are Malone's goons here?"

Thomas looked in the same direction I did. Besides me and him, they were the only other white guys.

Thomas shrugged. "Why don't you ask them? Dinner says they're bankrolling this whole thing. You see Billy Boy's casket? Or his headstone?"

"You couldn't *afford* to buy me dinner."

But Thomas was right. Billy couldn't buy stuff like this when he was alive, much less now that he was dead. Where'd that money come from?

I went to the source.

The tallest of Malone's goons saw me coming first. Despite the black suit, he wore a deep crimson tie, solid-colored and bold. He was slim and lanky, the kind of guy who didn't stand a chance at being physically intimidating. I noticed the pistol bulge underneath his suit jacket. That was intimidating enough.

The other two boys smiled. One looked a bit like a bird, nose like a beak, and the other had a face like a squat tomato. The tall guy talked first.

"Dame T-Two Shots, right?" he said, his voice on the tenor side.

I frowned. That name again. Of course that's how Malone's people referred to me.

"Margaret will do," I said, offering my gloved hand. He looked at it, confused for a moment, then realized what he was supposed to do. He took my hand, leaning down to kiss it. He dropped it awkwardly.

This was going to be too easy.

"I'm P-Peter."

"Charmed. What are you handsome boys doing in a dreary place like this?"

"P-Paying our respects, of course."

"Didn't know you were friends with the departed."

The other two spoke up simultaneously.

"We wasn't that close,—"

"We was *very* close!"

Wide-eyed, they looked at each other, then to me, then to Peter.

I looked at Peter, too. "Which is it?"

"We were close in the p-p-professional sort of way."

"Tell me how close."

Everything got dark all of a sudden, and for a moment I thought storm clouds had gathered above.

It was happening again.

Shadows danced around, coyly. Four silhouettes jumped to life nearby, beside a palm tree standing high and mighty above us. They all had pistols in their hands. I couldn't see their faces at first, but the features sharpened and I realized it was Peter and the other two. And Billy.

Billy? What the hell was he doing with these guys?

Echoes of police sirens sounded somewhere in the distance.

The light returned and the shadows slipped away. Peter

stammered something again.

"I, um, uh—"

"Let me talk to Malone, will you?"

Peter took a tentative step back. He quivered and bit his lip. I saw a single drop of sweat drip down from his forehead and trail off the side of his cheek.

"I'll—uh—I'll set it up."

Two days later, I had a date with Malone at the Cocoanut Grove, inside the Ambassador Hotel. Years ago, the first time I heard that name, I didn't take it seriously. Then I stepped foot in it.

The Cocoanut was bigger and better than Olivia's could ever be. The drinks were stronger, the crowd was crazier, and the damn place even had real coconut trees inside it. I dreamed about singing here. Some day.

One of Malone's boys picked me up, escorting me there in a fancy car with leather seats. I figured there were two reasons why Malone would want to meet here instead of Olivia's: either he didn't do his dirty business in his own club, or he was scouting for ideas. Maybe both.

The music had already started. A pulsing Cuban beat flowed through the air, the horns singing a wild melody. Latin nights like these were one of the dwindling few times you could justify getting a band that big anymore. Some girl with a bunch of fruit on her head danced on the stage.

I made my way over to Malone's box. He greeted me, trademark dark blue still visible in the table's dim candlelight. He stood up and swayed a little, steadying himself briefly. He took my hand and kissed it. I took the seat beside him, a faint smile peeking from the corner of my lips. Malone made no reaction, just blinked a few times and plopped down beside me. He returned his attention to the band. If he was at all taken by my presence, he didn't show it.

"You're awful curious about Billy Boy," he said. "What's a dead Negro to you?"

"Dead Negro was a good trumpet player," I said.

"There's others out there."

"And I got a hunch."

"Women's intuition?"

"You can call it what you want. Boys like Billy don't just drop dead."

"When did you start playing detective? Since you started taking L.A.'s finest to bed?"

His hand clumsily caressed my arm, cold to the touch. I recoiled immediately.

"Touch me again and I'll drop you like I dropped your brother."

A shadow moved somewhere. I looked to the side, saw a wispy silhouette fire a gun at another shadow point blank. I closed my eyes and it went away.

Malone grinned. "Dame Two Shots comes out to play, huh?"

His brother got a little too friendly backstage after one of my first gigs singing at Olivia's. I grabbed his gun, and two shots later he was dead. It wasn't exactly self-defense, more along the lines of manslaughter. Malone was practically *thanking* me for months afterwards. They tried running the town together, messed-up brothers messing up the scheme. Now Malone didn't have to share.

That was the first night I met Roger. He said he'd keep the heat off me if I sang for him every night. What a hero.

I pressed on.

"Billy worked for you," I said, recalling whatever vision I had when I talked to Peter. Women's intuition. Sure.

"So?"

"You bankrolled his funeral."

"I pay to put lots of people in the ground."

"You liked Billy."

"When he didn't screw up, yeah."

"He wasn't the criminal type." He was the nice type. The type that called you on the weekends, that you'd want to bring home to your mother, if your mother wouldn't be absolutely horrified you were on his arm.

Malone shrugged. "You're not the killing type."

"I didn't have a choice."

"Neither did he."

There was alcohol on Malone's breath. I'd been so distracted by my own purposes I didn't realize he was drunk. Or *how* drunk he was. If you lit a match by his mouth, you'd probably set the whole room on fire.

I gathered two things: Malone had been sitting here for a while, whether or not he was waiting for me to show up. And something had gone wrong. Bosses like Malone weren't *allowed* to look even remotely unprofessional. He was being too honest with me. What was going on?

"B-b-boss," a voice said from behind.

We both turned to the entrance to the box. Peter stood there, sweaty as a pig. It was dark, but I could still see the stain of blood on his white shirt.

Malone got up and knocked his chair over. The band below was playing so loud no one noticed.

"What happened?" he demanded. The singer started singing something boisterously melodic in Spanish. I had to strain to hear Malone and Peter.

"It-it went wrong," Peter stammered over the music. "Royce bit it, and Carlo's shot in the gut. W-we're in your suite."

"You brought him *here*?"

"Didn't know where else to g-go!"

Malone may have been drunk, but he socked Peter square in the nose with more precision than a boxer. Peter yelped, nearly collapsing to the ground.

"Call the healer," Malone ordered as he stormed away.

Peter watched as Malone left, then looked at me. I'd already taken off my heels.

I passed Peter without so much as an acknowledgement and followed Malone. He walked fast, his long legs helping him. Every one of his strides was worth two of mine.

When we got to his suite on the top floor, he kicked the door open. I came in behind him and closed it, my hand almost slipping off the knob. I looked down at my fingers, slick to the touch. Blood. Lots of it.

"I didn't tell you to come with me," Malone said.

"You didn't tell me not to."

Carlo, the one with the beak-like nose from the funeral, lay there. His chest moved faintly, almost dead. He held a hand over his stomach, near his kidney or his liver. Roger told me about gunshots like those before, usually with the excitement of a teenage boy. Those kinds of shots were fatal.

Malone dropped to his knees beside Carlo.

"What happened?"

"They knew …. we was coming."

"Who knew?" I asked.

"What's … the dame … doing here?"

"Minding her own business," Malone spat, shooting a glance back at me.

Shadows crept into the room. I looked away from Carlo and Malone, and the wisps of smoke and shadow playfully danced before me.

Three silhouettes emerged. One was Peter, one was Carlo, so the other must've been Royce. Another shadow took shape, big and boxy. I realized it was an armored truck, the kind they used to transport money to the bank.

The silhouettes stalked toward it, guns raised, ready to fire. Suddenly, the back doors swung open and another shadow emerged from the truck. The next thing I saw, Royce was down on the ground. Peter and Carlo started shooting.

And that was it.

Light flooded back around me. Hardly more than a second had passed.

"You were pulling a heist," I whispered.

"Would've been … easier with … four guys," Carlo wheezed.

The door barged open. Peter came in with an older gentleman, short and skinny. Most of his hair was gone except for a few stubborn gray hairs around the sides. He wore a black pinstriped suit with brown cap toes. He carried a small black bag, the kind of thing doctors carried around in case of emergency.

The healer.

They brushed past me like I wasn't even there. The healer pushed Carlo's shirt up to reveal the wound. Carlo moaned as the rest of us looked on. Wasting no time, the healer opened his bag and pulled out *leaves*. Green leaves, big and healthy, from trees I was sure I'd never seen this side of Rodeo Drive. Definitely not the sort of doctor I was expecting.

He pressed the leaves onto Carlo's wound. The injured man shot up immediately with a scream. The healer pushed him back down, and Peter rushed to help restrain Carlo. He wailed so loudly I was sure the hotel staff was gonna come up and knock on the door.

"What's he doing?" I asked Malone. I didn't realize my mouth was hanging wide open.

"What's it look like?"

"I … I don't know. Healing him?"

Malone nodded an affirmation.

I squinted at the healer, like squinting would help make more sense of this.

"How?"

"Magic," Malone said, without irony or sarcasm. Genuine.

I stared a little longer. Carlo calmed down, and finally his eyes closed. Asleep, not dead.

The healer began wiping the blood from his hands. He collected the leaves together. Peter tried to help, but the healer silently pushed him away.

"Magic," I whispered to no one but myself. Magic … healing? "Can he make a limb grow back?"

"No," Malone said, after a long pause. "You need a little stronger magic to pull off that. Stuff we couldn't even dream of."

I nodded slowly. "You didn't kill Billy."

"Of course not. I liked him."

He hesitated. He started to say something, but it didn't leave his lips.

"What?" I said.

"You're right, though. Someone did kill Billy."

My apartment wasn't the sort of palatial residence I thought I'd be living in by the time I reached this age. Not that I was old, I just thought I'd get rich young. Most of the money I made from singing went to my closet. Some months I couldn't even keep up with the electricity bill.

Roger swung by at the normal time to take me to Olivia's. I could smell another woman's perfume on him again.

"I haven't seen you wear my grandma's bracelet yet," he observed.

"It's too heavy."

"It's made of *iron*. Of course it's heavy. Should've been donated during the war for scrap metal. But it should be on your wrist."

"Doesn't match a thing I have."

I didn't see the slap coming. The entire side of my face burned like I'd been stung by a thousand bees.

"I'll buy you something to match later," Roger said.

I locked eyes with him coolly. He made no indication he would attempt an apology.

I went into my bedroom and dug through a drawer. I'd tossed it there the night after he gave it to me, hoping I'd forget about it. I'd wear it now, if he'd shut up about it.

"Anything new on Billy?" I asked sullenly.

He shook his head.

"No evidence of foul play. Coroner didn't find anything new. We're just gonna call it an accidental death. Another dead Negro." He shrugged. "You're gonna sing for me tonight, right?"

The greedy smile on his face reminded me of the first time he asked, my hands still shaking from firing the gun. Trembling from killing a man. Roger didn't have to say anything else.

"Yeah," I muttered, looking at my toes. "I always do."

Roger took me to Olivia's, listening through the first set then headed off to handle his own business, whatever that was.

During the show, I spotted Malone and Kyle sitting at the same table. They didn't look like they were talking to each other, or, if they were, they didn't look happy about it. A little while later, Malone was gone and Kyle was alone.

Kyle was a healer, too, wasn't he? Whatever he did with my eye the other night, I couldn't explain it any other way.

He sat at the usual table, and most nights he was there he watched me with deep intent. Tonight, he could barely stand to look at me. Took could, though. Took watched me constantly.

After we finished our set, I went directly to his table.

"Aren't you gonna tell me how pretty I am?" I opened.

Kyle turned his attention to me, looked me up and down, then looked away.

"I would, but I simply just can't stand what you've got on tonight, dear."

I'd worn this dress before in Kyle's presence. Silvery, gray, with pearls and long white gloves to accompany it. It didn't go so well with my complexion, but it was the fairest match I could find for Roger's damn bracelet.

"You're not usually so frank."

"I apologize, little songbird. Favor for a favor?"

I smiled faintly. "Of course. What do you need?"

"Don't wear that bracelet again, and I'll tell you how pretty you are until you're old and gray." He turned his attention to Took. "I'm feeling a tad ill. Shall we retire for the evening?"

The chauffeur grunted his assent, then stood up. Kyle left without saying so much as a farewell or giving me a wink.

The backstage dressing room was the quietest place on earth after the crowd died down and the band left. I looked at myself in the mirror. I'd done an admirable job covering up Roger's latest bruise, but it was still visible if you looked hard enough.

Roger said he'd be coming to take me home, but it was way past midnight and he was a no-show. Usually meant one of two things: he was stuck late on a case, or he was with another woman.

I thought about Billy. Billy told me it didn't have to be like this. Billy said one day he'd give Roger a good talking to, show him how to treat a girl right.

The door burst open with a loud, sickening crack. I shrieked. Malone came flying through, landing on his back and rolling a couple times before coming to a stop. His suit was torn, and his face beaten and bruised. He looked up at me and pleaded, blood coming from his mouth.

"Get—" Malone struggled to say. "Get out of here."

Loud footsteps approached the door, rushing like a bull in a rage. Took stepped in, and, for the first time, I *really* saw him.

Took wasn't just big. He was enormous. He looked like he'd been carved from stone and the trunks of the thickest, oldest trees. His eyes positively glowed, and his muscles had ripped through his clothes. Brown, gray, and *green* hair covered his limbs.

What the hell was he?

He roared, and the power of his roar almost knocked me to the ground. The mirror on the vanity shattered. I forced my hands to my ears, trying to block the sound, but it came through, deafeningly painful.

Malone reached into his jacket and pulled out a gun, a snub-nosed revolver. From his prone position, he took aim and fired off two shots. Both hit Took square in the chest, but he didn't even seem to notice. Took ran forward, every step an earthquake. Malone squeezed another shot off, but it went wide. Suddenly, Took was on top of him. In one hand, he grabbed Malone's face and picked him up. He threw Malone through the air like a ragdoll, into the opposite wall. Malone slammed against the wall so hard, pieces of it flew off.

The gun fell to my feet.

I didn't even think about it. I picked it up, aimed, one eye closed, and focused. Took began walking toward Malone's limp body, his back to me.

I fired.

I wasn't a good shot. Not really. This was the third bullet I'd ever fired in my entire life. But I hit Took in the back of the head. I could tell by the way he suddenly jerked and roared. He turned around. The bullet didn't kill him. It just made him more upset.

Took turned to me, charging in my direction like a ram. I squeezed the trigger a few more times. I don't know if they hit or missed. All I heard was the telltale *click* of an empty gun. I threw the empty piece at Took's face. He swatted it out of the air like it was made of paper.

Next thing I knew, Took's hand was around my throat. He squeezed and squeezed. I couldn't breathe. I tried kicking him with my heels, but my shoes fell off after the third or fourth try. He squeezed harder.

My eyes were going to pop out of their sockets. My lungs burned with every breath I couldn't take. I tried kicking some more, but it only made me tired.

Shadows. I could see the silhouette of Took's enormous shape beside someone else, someone small. Kyle. I saw hunger. I saw … children. Babies. Infants. Newborns. I saw Took *feasting*. Everything spun around in wisps of black smoke and tendrils. I couldn't see the gore, but I could hear the sickening crunch of Took chewing on young flesh. If I wasn't being strangled to death, I would've puked.

I grabbed his huge muscular arm with my tiny hands, trying to force him off me, trying to free myself. It didn't work. I swatted at him with my arms, but I couldn't even reach his face.

Took shrieked and suddenly let go.

I plopped onto the ground, grabbing my own throat as air suddenly rushed back into me. I gasped for a few moments, my heart pounding.

What the hell made him drop me?

I smelled something burning. I looked at Took clutching his arm near the shoulder, black smoke emerging from underneath his fingers. He was holding a spot at the edge of where I could reach while he was strangling me.

The bracelet.

Roger's damn bracelet.

I took it off and clutched it. Before Took fully recovered, I lunged at him, the bracelet squared in the palm of my hand. I grabbed around his shoulders and wrapped my legs around his enormous chest, latching on as I slammed the bracelet into his face.

Took roared and I wondered if I was going to go deaf from being this close. He thrashed to one side, then to the other, trying to shake me off. His huge arms tried to force me aside, but, with every passing second, he was getting weaker.

He fell to the ground with a loud thud, me still riding him. The impact of the ground almost knocked me off, but I held the bracelet firm. Strange black and gray smoke erupted from his face, like it was burning off. Took roared louder, thrashed harder and harder.

And then he stopped.

I held the bracelet in place a little longer. I wasn't going to get suckered into thinking he was dead when he really wasn't. I wanted to make sure.

When I finally stepped off him, Took's face was hardly recognizable anymore, half of it charred, black from whatever wound I'd inflicted with the bracelet. An eye was gone, and the bone underneath the flesh was exposed.

In death as in life, I couldn't look at Took for too long.

I rushed over to Malone's side. He looked like he'd seen better days. I was surprised he was still alive. He was lying on his chest, unable to lift himself up. I didn't know if he *wanted* to stand up to begin with.

"Two things," he said quietly, when he noticed I was beside him.

"Are you okay?"

"One: Billy knew Kyle. Better than you think he did. Kyle isn't his real name. You can't pronounce it."

"Don't try to talk—"

"Two: Call my damn healer."

"Okay. Just … just don't move."

"Three."

"You said two things."

"Three. I want Kyle dead before he gets me dead."

It was late.

Everything hurt. I looked at myself in the cracked mirror of the vanity and I couldn't recognize myself.

I called Malone's healer, then Thomas. I didn't need Roger to see me like this.

Thomas swung by a few minutes later to pick me up from the club.

"What the hell happened?" he asked the second he saw me.

"I need you to drive."

Thomas blinked. "Uh. Sure. Where to?"

"Kyle's."

Thomas didn't even need to ask *which* of Kyle's houses to drive to, or where it was. It was the biggest damn place in the Hills.

Kyle's house could make even the richest people seem small and unimportant. There were three levels to it, designed to look something like a cross between a French chateau and a sultan's palace. The lights inside were still on, even at this hour. Kyle was expecting company.

Thomas killed the engine. "Really, Margaret. What's going on?"

I shook my head. I could tell him that Billy was dead because of some strange magic. Part of me thought he'd just think I was crazy. The other part of me thought Thomas was already crazy enough to believe it.

Instead, I said, "Just wait for me here."

I stepped out of the car before he could say anything else. My dress was torn and had blood all over it. My blood, or Malone's, or Took's. I didn't quite know. My feet ached in the heels I'd put back on, the swelling making me force them through the straps. All I wanted to do was go home and sleep. But I had to know *why* Billy was dead.

I didn't have any illusions that Billy was my last and only ticket out of this kind of life. I knew he was poor, that maybe if he'd been born years earlier he could've been as big as Duke and had a band to call his own. I didn't even pay attention to him until after I started seeing Roger. But Billy was sensitive.

He knew the right things to say, the right places to touch, and when I needed space. I *had* to know. How did he get tangled in all this? Why did this happen to him?

I knocked on the door. Or tried to knock on the door. It swung open as my hand came up.

No one was on the other side.

I looked into a wide room, greeted by a majestic staircase leading up to a balcony overlooking the entrance. Beautiful paintings of people I didn't know decorated the entrance.

I stepped inside.

"In here, Miss Reese."

Kyle's voice. It came from the main floor, toward the back of the mansion. The words floated on the air like lilting butterflies, and I could *see* where they were coming from.

I followed the source. I came into a round room, curved into an oval shape that overlooked an enormous pool the size of the Silver Lake reservoir. Kyle stood with his back to me, looking out the windows.

"How'd you know—" I started.

"Please," Kyle cut me off. "I know when another blessed with magic is present. Also, I saw you pull up in Thomas's car."

So. Magic it was.

"You killed Billy," I blurted.

Kyle didn't shift. "Yes. How did you know?"

"Women's intuition."

He turned his head to face me. I had his attention.

The shadows of Kyle's memory played around the room. I saw things more vividly here than I had anytime else, though things were still in silhouette and shadow. I saw Kyle, with Billy. I watched as Billy appeared at Kyle's door, outside the very mansion where we stood. I watched as Kyle took Billy in and hugged him like a father would hug a son.

Kyle's eyes went where mine did. He was watching the same scene.

"You restored his hand," I said.

He smiled and nodded.

"But you always want favors for favors."

"Go on, little songbird."

"Malone's in your pocket, isn't he? It's how you make your money. You put Billy in with Malone's boys."

"Malone's performance has been rather lacking as of late. I was hoping Billy would be a boon to business. I was correct, for a little while. But with Billy gone now, Malone's back to disappointing me. It's time to clean house." Kyle shrugged nonchalantly. "If only it were possible I could just create money from thin air, but alas. I'll make do with what I have."

"How come he's back to missing a hand now that he's dead?"

Kyle chortled. "I blame myself for my own hubris. As I restored his hand before, I took it away when I was done with him. I figured it would baffle the police and the reporters for a while—what fun headlines those would be. I didn't think it would lead you to me."

Billy's death didn't get much news traction. Dead Negroes were dead Negroes. LA didn't care unless you were rich, pretty, and white.

"How'd Billy come to know you?"

"The girl he saved in Belgium," Kyle said. "She's my daughter."

"Then why kill him?"

"I was grateful for what he did, but one does not defy a faerie prince and simply walk away."

The room grew colder at the sentence.

"Who are you?"

"You wouldn't be able to pronounce my name properly, and I'd rather not bear the insult of listening to you try."

The shadows around me shifted. I saw Billy in his room, hours before Thomas came home, but it was the same scene. He wasn't the only one there. Kyle stood nearby, watching as

Billy played the trumpet. I could see all the movement of a
trumpeter in heat, every note ringing crystalline. Billy played
on and on, and the more he played, the more he struggled to
just *breathe*. Then, he finally collapsed.

"I gave him clothes, a home, and I put him in contact with
the right people. He had enough chances to return my favors.
I enjoyed his music well enough, but times are changing
and Olivia's is failing. The other clubs on Central Avenue are
going to overtake it within a year or so. Billy could've been
spectacular, if he played the way I wanted him to play."

"But Billy hated bop."

"So he did. And I asked him for a different favor instead. You
see, Took does not eat often, but ogres can be funny like that.
When they get an appetite, they have a very specific taste."

I remembered the vision I had of Took while he was
strangling me. My neck still hurt from it.

"You wanted Billy to abduct a child for Took's dinner."

"Took was hungry, but he was patient. It wasn't just any child
he wanted."

Kyle raised an eyebrow at me.

I gripped the bracelet at my wrist. Kyle saw the movement.

"Obviously, it won't come to pass," he said, still eyeing me
cautiously. "You've seen to that yourself. And he wouldn't go
through with it anyway."

"Why me? I'm not even pregnant."

"Oh, but one day, perhaps. Took especially liked the taste of
children of a magical bloodline."

I almost retched. "Why are you telling me this?"

"Because you asked. A faerie cannot tell a lie. I also know
you're not going to do a blessed thing about this."

"What do you mean?"

"You could go to your man Roger and tell him what a
naughty boy I've been, but Roger would just beat you again.
Or you could try to harm me with your bracelet, but I'd just

kill you the same way I killed Billy."

"I don't play the trumpet."

"No, little songbird, but you sing, and I do so love your voice."

I eased my grip on the bracelet. I exhaled deeply, then I slipped it back onto my wrist. Kyle watched me with a slight grin on his face.

He left the view of the windows and walked to a side table, an open bottle of wine and an empty glass. He poured.

"You know you have a gift, yes? You see the shadows of the past, the things that people cannot help but remember, even when they don't want to."

"I figured."

"It's quite a powerful tool, Margaret. One you should learn to control."

"Are you asking me for a favor?"

Kyle smiled widely. He took the other glass of wine in his hand, then turned his gaze to me.

"Favor for a favor, little songbird. Keep my little transgression to yourself, and I'll see to it that you learn to develop your wonderful gift."

He held the glass up, presenting it to me. His eyes sparkled, and I felt a strange, intoxicating warmth pulse through my body.

There are two things I take from men.

Jewelry.

And fine wine.

Hearts at Rest

by Michael Willett

bang. bang. bang.

Three shots ring out, conjured thunder for the rainy night.
She drops the smoking revolver, the weapon skidding on the
wet pavement to rest against the foot of the man she shot. His
features are frozen in shock, his body seeming to refuse the
knowledge he has been killed. Drops of blood fall to the cement,
followed by his knees, and then the satisfactory thud as his face
plants fully upon the ground. Gathering her wits about her, she
runs towards the wounded cop behind the corpse, her shoes lost
to the night and her feet slapping the wet stone beneath her.
Sliding to rest at his side, she tears her skirts in an effort to catch
him as he slides to the ground, his head falling to rest in her lap.
She mumbles at him for a moment, as if searching for the right
words to say.

"CUT!"

A klaxon sounded, and lights came up on the sound stage.
The woman smiled weakly, embarrassed for forgetting her
lines. The two men in the scene stood up, crew moving to
clean them up and preparing to re-shoot the sequence.

Frankie smirked, pushing his hands deeper into his trench
coat as he strode through the building. *I guess my hat and*
jacket are going to be another cliché, thanks to movies like this.
Pushing the door open leading to the storage areas, he left
the fantasy behind and stepped firmly into the reality he had

come for.

Two officers looked up as he entered, nodding a curt greeting before they returned their gaze to the crime scene. He acknowledged them, but moved past, towards the detective and the desiccated body in the security uniform on the floor. Sliding his hand out of his jacket pocket, he flashed his own silver shield before speaking. "So, what do we have?"

"Janitor came in to clean the room and found him this morning. At first he thought it was a prop, but then he recognized the uniform." He eyed Frankie with suspicion. "I am surprised you got here so quickly after my call, Schwegler."

"I was in the area. Consulted on a triple a few blocks from here."

"Oh? Anything interesting?"

"Wasn't my department." He kneeled next to the body and, removing a pen from the inside of his jacket, used it to probe at the neck of the victim. No lacerations or punctures. Doesn't look like a Red List attack. "Any profile on the stiff?"

"Security. The I.D. tag says 'Johnson.' Waiting on the employment records for a first name. Body looks to have been here for a few weeks, but janitor remembers him reporting to work yesterday. No obvious wounds; not a stabbing or shooting. Poison? Broken neck?"

Frankie shook his head as he stood. "Nope. Bones and skin are intact, no signs of bruising or discoloring on the face or neck." He looked at his pen a moment, then motioned one of the uniformed officers over. "Get on the radio and ring up the downtown precinct. Ask for Donovan; tell him this is a List killing, and to send up a couple of our guys." He handed the officer his pen with a thin smile. "Put that in something and tag it for evidence." He watched as the officer scurried from the room.

The responding detective sighed audibly, closing his notebook and pocketing it in his suit pocket. "Well, that's a relief. I was hoping I could push this one off on someone else. Studio killings are a nightmare to handle with all the publicity. I officially release the crime scene to your department, Schwegler."

So formal. "Frankie."

The suited man paused a moment. "Excuse me?"

"I prefer people call me Frankie. It puts them at ease." He leveled a blank gaze at the other man, clearly disinterested in speaking with him further. "I take custody of the crime scene and all responsibility for the contents. You can take your officers and go."

The detective gave a short nod, taking the hint to get out of the building. He tapped his remaining uniformed officer on the shoulder, motioning for him to follow. Once Frankie was alone, he turned his eyes to the room, seeking answers to the questions dead Mr. Johnson posed. The storeroom was a repository for various movie props, set sections, and the occasional costume. It was filled with items from a horror movie, which probably lent to the idea the body was a property and not flesh. He stepped between shelves laden with arms and heads of various beasts, fake weapons, and foliage of mythic plants; within moments, he stood at the back of the room facing the biggest victim of the break-in.

A cabinet's doors had been melted off, but there was no evidence of a fire or heat on the items in the room. The doors themselves lay upon the floor, twisted metal pools solid and cool to the touch. The items in the cabinet were likewise untouched by harm, film canisters whose contents would burn if exposed to the slightest heat. At least eight canisters missing if this cabinet was full. Most of the canisters were labeled as monster movies made in the decade prior to the war, low-budget films never important or successful enough to warrant storing in the studio vaults. No Orange Lister did this; anyone strong enough to melt these doors would have torched this half of the room.

"FRANKIE! Oh, shit. Dead guy. Frankie, there's a dead guy here!"

Sounds like my backup is here. "Yeah, Molina. I saw. Which diviner you got with you?"

"Cooper. Hendricks was uptown trying to read some mystic graffiti."

"Send her back here. I need her to recreate a scene for me. You do your thing with the stiff."

The sound of footsteps echoed in the room for a moment, but soon a shorter woman in a LAPD uniform stepped to his side, her eyes hidden from his view. Her hands were gloved, a scarf covering the lower half of her face; she was as hidden from prying eyes and casual touch as she could be. Her voice was soft, almost a whisper. "Good morning, Detective Schwegler."

"Morning, Sarah. What do you make of this?"

"I shall endeavor to perceive it, with your permission. Would you like to see as well?"

No, I hate this part. Is there a stronger word than hate? "Sure, give me a moment." He spread his legs and steadied himself; Sarah removed her gloves, hat, and scarf, placing them on a shelf nearby. Frankie was used to the eerie glow of the diviners' eyes as their power spun up, but the icy chill of her touch on his hand and sudden flashes of memory behind his closed eyes were enough to knock him off his feet. He began to perceive what she was seeing in her mind: the near past, what had occurred in the room.

The room was dark, so dark, it was hard to see where they were; the sudden hush that fell over his ears was unsettling. They stood in the storage room, outlined in the faintest glow that illuminated nothing of their surroundings. After a few moments, a small pair of reddish-orange lights appeared at the far side of the room; as the orbs came closer to where Sarah and Frankie stood, it was obvious these were eyes moving unerringly through the darkness to the cabinet. Without sound, it was hard to know what was happening as the eyes paused for a few moments. Then, faint lines began to appear on the cabinet doors with a golden glow, forming into a series of pictographs or runes. The steel began to slide off the frame, the doors pooling upon the ground like luminescent gray water, before solidifying to the state Frankie found them. The thief moved, and Frankie lost him in the dark, assuming he was pilfering the canisters. A movement from the storeroom entrance caught Frankie's eye; the door opened and light reflected off the guard's badge as he entered, his flashlight sweeping the room. He paused as it illuminated the back of the creature's head and shoulders. Frankie was surprised as Sarah squeezed his hand. Tendrils of shadows curled to mask the perpetrator as it hissed or reeled from the light. Knowing they were viewing events that already passed, he tried to call out a warning voicelessly to the guard; helpless to change the events, they watched the criminal step into the shadows outside the flashlight's illuminated cone and reappear behind the guard. With a touch on the man's head, the killer smiled to reveal jagged, silvered teeth. Fear crossed Johnson's face as the creature seemed to inhale deeply. Dropping his torch, Johnson twitched but a moment, and then fell to the ground already dead and shriveled. Obstacle removed, the burning eyes strode slowly back towards the cabinet, kicking the torch under a shelf as it moved. Frankie lost sight of it as darkness fell over the room once more.

Sarah broke the connection, rubbing her temples and looking around, blinking. She stepped over to the cabinet and touched where some of the canisters had been. "I did not see the man in question, but he does appear to be a Lister, as you surmised, with powers that transcend the List system. I do not understand how this could be."

Frankie leaned against the wall, trying with all his might not to fall over; he hated piggy-backing a diviner as they worked. "Did you see anything that might help us track him down?"

Sarah nodded. "The canisters were all tagged with director and two or three actors' names. In this case, each one had a particular actress' name: Leah Morgan."

"I recognize the name, but that's about it. Still, a lead is a lead. Let's see what Molina has for us." He pushed himself off the wall and walked back towards where the body lay.

Crouched over the corpse was a slender man with an immaculate uniform, but the face that looked up at Frankie was nothing more than bones. The skeletal face moved, and sound came out of the gaping maw that once was a face. "Nothing to get from this guy; no one home to answer the door." Standing up from the side of the body, he tugged his face back on over his skull, fussing at it a bit to put it back into place.

"What does that even mean?"

"No soul, *jefe*. Not here, not up, not down. Just… gone." Molina scratched the fake beard on his false face as if deep in thought. "No *criatura* or Lister I know can do this kind of voodoo. You got me on what did this."

"All right; someone from the studio offices should be bringing a staff list, so don't leave without it. I'll radio for a meat wagon, so stick with the body until they get here, and follow it back to the shop. I want to talk to Leah Morgan and see what she might know." With a nod that conveyed his thanks for their assistance, Frankie left the same way he arrived, headed towards the parking lot and his rusty '38 Packard Coupe.

After a short radio discourse with dispatch to obtain the address of the actress' agent, and another argument with his car whether it would start without hammering the engine,

Frankie was underway. It was a short drive up to the hills between Hollywood and Studio City, and traffic was light at this time of morning. He didn't have a lot of time with his thoughts before he found himself at his destination. Frankie took little notice of the opulence of his surroundings, sliding out of his car and walking purposefully towards the front doors. Not even bothering with the bell, he raised his hand and pounded on the doors. After a couple minutes, a rather dour old man answered, opening the door with the intention of admonishing the man he saw. Pushing his badge into the butler's face, Frankie moved through the portal and into the foyer.

"Detective Shwegler, right?" The voice sounded East Coast, either Jersey or New York. What Frankie saw, however, was a rotund man who barely came up to his chest, dressed in a loose suit jacket covering a garishly flowered shirt. "What is that, German?"

"Swiss, actually; call me Frankie. Is Ms. Morgan here?" He looked in the direction from which the man arrived, but the greasy little agent pointed him in the opposite direction and began walking. Frankie followed, pausing a moment as he did to remove his hat.

"Name's Carl. Carl Wallace. Wallace Talent Agency. Best talents in the biz." Carl puffed himself up as he spouted his sales rhetoric. "Frankie, eh? Is that for Francis or Frank or something?" Well, if I ever need an agent, I know who to avoid.

"No. Nickname someone gave me during the war when they heard I spent some time studying near Frankfurt; Darmstadt, actually." That is bound to pique his interest. The questions that followed were not new, and never ceased to be annoying.

"Figured you were a Kraut. Probably the only job you could get when the war ended, goose-stepping around and intimidating people. My brother killed a ton of Krauts; maybe you were related to some. How did you end up state-side?"

"My parents immigrated in '29; I served with US Allied forces in the war." He placed a hand on the man's shoulder and was satisfied when the agent went rigid at the touch. "I am not going to ask again. Where is Ms. Morgan?"

"In here, Detective. " The voice was such a contrast to Carl's, it made Frankie pause; silken and soothing where the agent's was abrasive and nasal. The woman stood near the window in what Frankie assumed was an office, watching a pair of dogs play in the yard and sipping something from a glass. She did not turn to face them as she continued to speak. "I was surprised to find out Los Angeles' police were looking for me. Have I done something wrong?"

"Ma'am, someone broke into a studio storeroom last night and stole a number of your films. Usually this would only warrant a phone call and some paperwork, but in the commission of the crime there was a murder."

She paused, the glass brushing against her lips as she considered what he said. Then, she turned to face him, leaning against the sill. "That is unfortunate. Those storerooms held all the props and master recordings for my horror films. Why anyone would steal them is beyond me." Her eyes fell to the floor for a moment, but Frankie was unsure whether her concern was for the corpse or the reels.

"I am more concerned with the dead body." Frankie pulled out a notebook and pencil to record her answers. "Do you have any enemies who want to ruin or discredit you? Anyone who you feel capable of killing someone just to get at you?" He watched her reaction, but she only closed her eyes and drank deeply from the glass.

Carl broke the silence, and she released a slight sigh of relief. "Leah has not been in a film in over fifteen years, and everyone loves her. Never a bad impression in the city, this one. In fact, we were trying to orchestrate a comeback for her.

Monster movies are out, but these gangster and crime movies could be her ticket back to the spotlight. Picture it: Mob wife, mother to the lead, lonely and vulnerable older burlesque dancer or club singer…" *How is any of this relevant? Quit speaking, you fat little rat.*

"What about fans? Any letters that stood out, public events where someone got rowdy, anything?" As soon as he asked, agent and actress looked at each other momentarily. Ah, there we go. There is something they're worried about. Or someone.

It was Leah who spoke first. "There was a letter… six months ago? It was noteworthy because I hadn't received anything from a fan in some time. This one, however, mentioned 'taking me back to where I belonged' and 'I could not deny my destiny.' Carl said it was someone eager to see me acting again and dismissed it."

"She's had her share of eager fans, sure. Figured this was just another horror nut being overdramatic. We see it all the time." Carl paced a bit, before moving to his desk and opening a drawer. He pulled out a stack of envelopes and folded papers, banded together with twine. "There's everything she's gotten in the last decade, if you think it'll help."

"It can't hurt. Do you have anyone you can stay with, just in case?"

"She'll stay here." The fact he answered for her was not as surprising as her nodding in agreement. She helped herself to another drink from the bar, and Carl handed the letters to Frankie.

"I'll have a black and white park outside and watch the house." He fished a crumpled card out of his jacket pocket and gave it to Carl, pointing at it in the man's hands. "If you remember anything else, or something happens, call my precinct." Instead of the local boys, he neglected to add. With that, he put on his hat, tipped it to Leah, and walked out of the house; he paused as he opened the front door to sneer at the butler, who was rushing to take the door from his hand.

Frankie decided it might be a good idea to check in at headquarters, catch the lieutenant up on the case and see if anything new had come in from open investigations. All List-related cases were pushed to Headquarters downtown, so Frankie's department was getting swamped. Seems like there are more Listers every year. He pulled into the parking garage and found an empty spot, killing the engine and getting out of the car.

Upstairs in the bullpen, he sat at his desk and rifled through his papers; images, reports, witness accounts. Colored folders representing verified or suspected List involvements in the crimes. Reaching into a drawer, he paused and considered what color to use for this case, his hand hovering over the stack. Black; whatever was used in other aspects of the crime, there's some sort of necromancy afoot. He pulled out the folder and a few forms, starting the paperwork.

"Hey boss." Molina came over, sitting on the corner of his desk. He tossed a folder down in front of Frankie, open to show a number of photographs and two reports. "Doc found squat on the body to verify our findings. Cooper said this *criatura* had glowing eyes? *Potentcias fuego*? Very rare to have two List entries, and this might have more. Scary thoughts, *amigo*."

"Agreed." Frankie leaned back in his chair, the wooden frame creaking beneath his bulk. At least this one lasted longer than the last two. "Any List history in the guard or his family?"

"Nada, *jefe*. He was as mundane as they come. Employee of the studio long enough to retire, but kept working to support an ailing wife. Wrong place, wrong time I guess."

"So, no doubt at this point he wasn't the target. Which just creates more questions; why steal master reels of some old monochromatic movies starring some aged show-off? Why kill the old man? Why not just burn him the same way the cabinet was melted? Something like that would have destroyed all evidence of the murder."

"You're the detective, *amigo*. You figure it out." Molina tapped the desktop and stood, brushing down his uniform and winking one of the dead eyes in his mask.

Frankie flipped him off as he walked away, then returned to drafting his own notes and reports to add to the ones completed by his assisting officers. He had just wrapped up when the lieutenant sat down in the chair next to his desk, announcing himself with a low cough and an angry scowl.

"I don't have to tell you I'm getting heat from the studio suits, do I?" Frankie shook his head, but that didn't stop the admonishing. "Nor do I need to tell you I've been on the horn with both the FBI and the HHS regarding this case?" Makes sense; the Department of Human Health and Services handles the requirements and registration for the Lists. "Seems a lot of folks are interested in your investigation, Frankie. A lot of very anxious people who would like very much to get this solved. You on the stick, Detective?"

"I got it, I got it. Get the guy, and quickly. Working on it as we speak, LT." *Some backup wouldn't hurt, either.*

"See that you do." His lieutenant tapped the desk three times and stood, before moving on to yell at another detective. Frankie shrugged, and pulled the parcel of letters out of his jacket pocket. He untied them and began reading, hoping to find a clue.

About an hour into the pile, Frankie noticed the squad room getting louder. He lifted his head and looked around, noting the arrival of a handful of uniforms and two men in handcuffs. They were forcibly seated into chairs; one seemed resolved to his fate, while the other looked around wildly. An officer sat down with each to start the questioning, while the rest of the officers moved to the locker room or chalkboards to update the roster. Wild Eyes became more agitated, tugging

at his cuffs enough to cause his wrists to bleed. Frankie
scooted his chair back away from his desk slowly. This isn't
going to end well.

As if on cue, Wild Eyes howled and stood, growing larger.
His clothes started to tear, and even the handcuffs failed to
hinder him as the short chain shattered and fell to the floor.
Great, a Brown, and my revolver is in my locker. The werewolf
clawed at the officer assigned to him, rending flesh from
his face and chest. As other uniforms scrambled for their
revolvers, Wild Eyes turned towards Frankie's side of the
room and bolted towards the windows. *Idiot! We are seven
floors up!* Frankie stood quickly, closing the distance with
the creature. He leaped at the wolf, grappling it about the
midsection and knocking it to the floor. Arching his back
against the clawing at his clothing, he pressed his forearm into
the throat of the beast to keep it from biting him long enough
to get assistance. He punched the werewolf twice as it tore at
his back, the second strike dazing Wild Eyes.

"Get the beast shackles, you fools!" He pressed his weight
against the werewolf as someone grabbed a pair of silver
bracers off the wall, linked by a golden chain and etched with
glowing runes. Two uniforms pulled Wild Eyes' arms together
over his head, as a third clamped the binders in place.
Immediately the werewolf reverted, as the power imbued into
the shackles went to work.

Frankie stood, kicking the man once more for good measure,
before turning to the group of uniforms trying desperately
to keep the wounded officer alive. He thought about yelling
at them for their oversight, but figured the dead comrade
would be lesson enough. He shrugged, stretched his shoulders
and felt the cloth tear over his skin, and decided a change
of clothes was in order. Gathering up the file and evidence,
he tossed it all in an old leather briefcase and headed for the
squad locker room.

***

Freshly clothed, revolver in his shoulder rig, and evidence in the seat next to him, Frankie drove to the best place he knew to focus: the Mocambo Nightclub on the Sunset Strip. Most of the officers avoided clubs frequented by the Hollywood elite, but he found the noise and crowds more comforting than a quiet room. As he pulled up in front, he could see it was another busy night, lines already long despite the early evening. Sliding out of his car, he tossed his keys to the valet and walked through the zebra-striped doors with his briefcase.

Once inside, he dropped a coin into the phone, letting the Sergeant's desk know where he was in case something came in and he needed to be alerted. He had just hung up the receiver when a familiar voice spoke behind him. "Cigarettes? Try the new Winston brand? Cheaper than Pall Malls, sir!"

"Sure, a pack of regulars." He turned and smiled at her, reaching for a couple coins in his pocket. "How are you this evening, Lili?" He tossed the coins into her tray.

"Gig's all right, Frankie. Hip place like this, get to see all the show-offs." She handed him the pack of cigarettes before adjusting the bodice on her bunny-themed outfit. "I think your table's ready, Daddy-O." With a short curtsey, she wandered into the crowd to peddle her wares.

Frankie pocketed the pack and picked up his briefcase, moving to his usual spot. He waved off the waitress with a hand, not interested in drinking. Unbuckling his satchel, he dumped the contents upon the tabletop and began reviewing what he had so far. An hour stretched into two as he finished going through the fan letters, noting the ones mentioned in his meeting with Leah earlier in the day. He looked at the pictures, the reports, but he was no closer to finding out what it was he saw in the divination. As he thought about the vision Sarah shared with him, he began drawing the runes used on the cabinet on a spare sheet of paper. He fished another cigarette out of the half-empty pack, lighting it with his idle hand.

"Frankie… how do you know how to do that?" Lili dropped her tray onto the table, leaning over to look at the paper in front of him.

"Something I saw. You know what this is?" He turned to look at her with a more discerning eye than he had in the past. Her features were soft, but she suddenly looked older than he remembered, despite the heavy makeup. Her outfit did not seem to fit as well as it appeared earlier in the night, and the ears and tail seemed almost… real. "Lili, are you registered?"

"Registered? *Nil, mo mhúirnín bán.*" Gone was the East Coast accent and the modern vernacular; Frankie was surprised to hear the thick brogue from someone he had known for years. "My kind has no need of your little Lists. Forgive the cliché, but we were ancient before the dawn of humans." She sat down in the chair next to him with a smile, placing her small hands upon his. He wasn't sure why, but the difference in their size suddenly bothered him.

"What do you mean, your kind?" Frankie looked around to make sure no one was listening to them, but, between the music and the din of people talking, they seemed safe enough.

"There are humans, aye? No-powers. Then you have your magi, casters. These are the ones you write down in your Lists. Then you have the naturals; the ones born with powers. Shifters. Reapers and Diviners like you use in your department." She gently stroked his hand, and he was confident he saw one of her rabbit ears twitch. "But before that, there were those who were born from magic, of magic. The Sidhe. Fae, some call them. We are they who are in legends and myth, who live not in the world but outside it."

"Faeries? With wings and dust and Tinkerbell?"

Lili rolled her eyes and snorted, her ears lowering to echo

her frustration. *Okay, those things are attached.* "A year that movie has been out, and already everyone forgets the stories about us. I can't wait until he finishes that monstrosity of lies in Orange County." She sighed and looked at the photographs. "I know what did this. Tell me you aren't going after it, love; you cannot go after this." Her ears rose once more, and her eyes turned to lock with his, pleading.

"I swore an oath, girl; uphold the law, bring them to justice. If you have information on this, I need to know." He leaned back in his chair, sliding his hands out from underneath hers. She glared at him for more than a moment.

"Sluagh; they are what we call Underfae. They are dark hunters summoned to gather items, kill things, and, on occasion, gather or kill people. The Sluagh are capable of manifesting a number of powers native to the Unseelie, if empowered to do so to accomplish their tasks." She paused, and wrapped her arms around herself. "They kill by taking the soul of a thing, consuming it. When this happens to a mortal… you can see the result."

"Summoned? So someone is controlling them. Probably one of these crazy fans." Frankie passed his hand over the pile of letters. "Any suggestions for dealing with one of these?"

"Don't? But you won't listen, so here you go." She picked up the half-pack of cigarettes and kissed it, leaving a perfect reproduction of her red lips upon the wrapper; it almost seemed to glow in the nightclub lights. She tucked the pack into his jacket breast pocket, and placed her hand over it. "*Mo sheacht mbeannacht ort, mo mhíle stór.*" Her words echoed in his ears, causing him to feel sad and comforted at the same time.

"What does that mean?"

"It is an old Seelie blessing." She smiled, blushing slightly. Her ears rose up a bit, and took on the color of her cheeks.

"Lili, are you a Sluagh?"

Her sudden laughter was loud enough to cause a few people to look their way, but no one seemed interested in the conversation between the heat and a costumed cigarette girl. "No, no, no. I am a Pookah, love. Hence the ears and tail; no matter what form I take, I just can't shake them. Looks good in this place, though, right? Fit right in. No one pays attention, and I can pay my rent. Just the other night, some big shot from Chicago said he would fill a club full of girls dressed like me." She stood, gathering her tray up once more, then touched his face momentarily. "There are good and bad Fae, Frankie. I promise I'm one of the good ones." Her nails dragged along his jaw line as she turned to walk away.

Frankie sat there a moment, torn between arresting her and grilling her for more information on the Fae. His eyes returned to the pile of letters, pulling a couple of the creepier ones out to view again. It has to be one of these, but which? His thoughts were interrupted by a hand on his shoulder. He looked up to see the club manager.

"Detective? There is a call for you in the lobby."

Frankie motioned to the other responding officers to surround the house, as he and Molina moved towards it. The call to dispatch had described someone lurking around the outside; when they arrived the doors had been bashed in and no light illuminated the residence. Molina moved to the threshold of the entrance, revolver at the ready. Frankie drew his own revolver and checked the cylinder before entering the agent's home.

The foyer was quiet, so Frankie gave Molina the signal to enter and watch his back as he moved to the office hallway. *My guess is whatever we will find, it won't be anywhere else.* Sure enough, he almost tripped on the body of the butler, dried and twisted like the first corpse. He must have been surprised by the door bashing in and came to see what the ruckus was. Frankie stepped over the body, pointing it out to Molina before moving further down the hallway. He was just about to go to the office when he paused, hearing something rustling inside the room.

Moving through the doorway, he saw four figures in the room; Carl and Leah he could see easily enough in the moonlight filtering into the room, the woman slumped over the desk. Despite the light, the two Sluagh were harder to perceive as more than glowing eyes and hissing. One of the Underfae grabbed an unconscious Leah around the waist, hefting her up onto its shoulder; the other touched Carl's face and grinned, sharpened teeth suddenly visible. It began to inhale deeply, and Frankie was reminded of what he saw in the divination. He raised his firearm, pulling the trigger three times: two bullets sliced through the air, passing through the Sluagh attacking Carl; the third passed through the forehead of the one holding Leah. Neither seemed affected or even concerned at being shot.

"Guns don't work!" Frankie leaped over the chaise, flipping his revolver in his hand and swinging it at the head of the nearest creature as he yelled. "Drop them, fiends!" Carl's body hit the floor, and the butt of the revolver passed right through the Fae, rewarded by a hiss. The shadowy thing turned and looked up at Frankie, reaching for him with clawed hands, but something repelled it; something burned it. It shrank back, its teeth bared at him, holding the smoking stump of its wrist.

"The *criatura* can't hurt you?" Molina stared at him in disbelief, his weapon holstered and a curved blade now in his hands. He swung it at the retreating Sluagh, but it passed right through like the bullets and the revolver. "What are these things, *jefe*?"

"You wouldn't believe me." Frankie moved forward to grapple the Fae, but the two shadowy forms leapt through the large windows with Leah, moving swiftly across the backyard.

He followed them to the fence, watching them vault over it as if it was no obstacle to them. Frankie attempted to follow, but had to dive for cover as a series of shots peppered the brick and wood; a semi-automatic handgun by the sound of it.

A voice called out as the shots faded. "She belongs to me, now! You cannot get in the way of destiny!" Another couple shots hit the fence, and Frankie returned two in kind. Then silence. He stood up and looked around, but whoever it was had left with the Sluagh. He swore, quietly at first, but then loudly.

Molina caught up, sheathing his knife and breathing heavily from the exertion. "I could feel them take the soul from the fat one. I felt it. These are terrors. Horrible things. Now what do we do?"

"Get the uniforms on the bodies and call the coroner." Frankie turned to face his friend. "I'm going to knock down some doors and hope for the best."

It was near dawn before Frankie arrived at the warehouse. It had taken all night to find a magi capable of scrying and willing to work for LAPD, but he was able to discern the location the eerily-familiar letter had originated from. *I hope I can expense out the cash for that asshole; there went two month's salary.* He emptied the five spent shells from his revolver, replacing them and locking the cylinder in place. *Maybe bullets will work on whoever is controlling the Fae.* Frankie took a deep breath and entered the building.

The building was obviously rented out by a studio, as there were all kinds of sets on the main floor. The majority of the warehouse was dark, but it appeared the office was illuminated, the light steady on one half of the room and flashing on the other. Within moments, he was close enough to hear soft music, and voices.

"Remember how wonderful it was on set? You were ideal to

direct, not that you needed it. The camera loved you, the cast loved you. I loved you, from the moment I saw you." A male voice.

"Robert, you have to let me go. What you are doing is wrong. You could go to jail." Leah Morgan.

"Leah, you don't really mean that. Admit it; you want to act again, and I can make that happen. I can make your dreams come true. You belong with me. It's your destiny." Robert was starting to sound more frantic. "Have some wine and relax, my dear." The sound of something pouring, and then a glass shattering upon the floor, followed by the sound of flesh slapping flesh. Leah cried out from the pain from being struck.

Frankie entered the room, revolver leveled at the man in the center. The room was crawling with Sluagh, hissing and moving just outside the circle of light created by the desk lamp. Robert stood behind the aged piece of furniture, next to Leah; a small line of blood drew a crimson path from the corner of her lip to her chin, her face starting to swell from the slap. A film was playing upon the wall, with musical accompaniment. Frankie locked eyes with Leah for a moment, hoping to comfort her with his presence as he spoke. "Are you alright, Leah?"

She nodded. "I'll heal." She glared at Robert's back, and then back to Frankie. "Be careful, Detective. He's insane."

Frankie turned his focus towards the other man. "Don't move, Robert. You are under arrest."

Robert just smiled, and spread his arms. "I think you are out of your element. My Sluagh will kill you where you stand, and that large firearm you hold can do nothing about it." He began to step around the desk, moving towards Frankie.

"You're right, bullets don't affect your minions. Do they work on you?" He sidestepped towards the desk, keeping his distance from Robert and moving closer to where Leah was sitting. He could now see she was held with iron shackles, probably from one of the sets in the warehouse. The Sluagh shrank away from him, going so far as to move to the other side of the room from him.

This angered Robert immediately. "Stop! Not another step near her. Why do my pets avoid you, Detective? What is it about you… are you Sidhe?"

"No, nothing special about me. Tell your fiends to stand down, then you kneel down, and put your hands over your head." Frankie moved closer to Leah, reaching out to her.

"Well then." Robert paused a moment, reaching behind him and drawing a wide, silvered blade with runes similar to those the Sluagh used to melt the film cabinet. His face spread into a disturbed smile, and he began to close the distance between them. Frankie fired his revolver, emptying it at Robert. As the bullets approached him, they suddenly veered off-target, some invisible force pushing them away from their goal. Robert laughed, running forward and plunging the knife deeply into Frankie's chest. Frankie stumbled back from the force of the attack, falling over a chair onto his back and sending his revolver sliding across the floor. The Sluagh all seemed to make a collective cry of favor as his vision started to blur, and his limbs weakened. Robert kneeled next to him, still smiling that sadistic smile. "That blade is coated with a Fae poison, Detective. It will kill any living person it pierces, within moments. You were foolish to pursue me, and it has cost you your life." As if to punctuate his statement, he wiggled the blade in Frankie's chest, shooting pain through his chest.

"Oh Robert, what have you done?" Leah stood, bound wrists at her waist, moving away from him towards the door. Sluagh moved to block her path.

Robert stood, moving towards her. "No one will come between us, beloved. Not the studio, not your agent, and certainly not some giant brute with a badge."

Leah looked over to where Frankie lay on the ground, and smirked. "Your story, about your name… I knew it was fake when you told it to Carl. I could sense it as soon as I looked at you. I wonder why you don't tell people the truth, Frankie."

Robert paused, turning to look at the body on the floor. "He's dead, Leah. Forget him." Still, he moved towards Frankie to confirm, kicking at him to make sure he was dead. "See? Dead." He returned his attention to Leah, drawing his handgun. "Now, sit back dow-"

Frankie grabbed Robert's ankle and twisted, feeling the satisfying crunch of bones beneath his grip. He pulled the man off balance, his other hand pulling the blade out of his chest. Robert cried out in pain, and the Sluagh echoed him; they moved as it to help him, but whatever kept them away from Frankie also kept them away from their master. Frankie rolled onto his hands and knees, crawling over towards Robert, who tried helplessly to get away from him. "They call me Frankie, Leah, because I'm on the organ donor list."

"Not with holes in them!" Robert emptied his firearm into Frankie, eleven shots passing through his torso and arms. *I always forget how much getting shot fucking hurts.* Frankie pulled Robert to him, lifting him up by the collar and punching him in the face as hard as possible. Twice. Three times. "How… in the… hell…"

"Im on that list as a recipient, asshole!" He continued bashing Robert's face in until all that was left was a bloody mess on the floor, and bony knuckles stripped of skin on his hand. He stood, the toxin from the stab wound still making him dizzy; he braced himself on the desk, eyeing Leah. "How did you know? Only department Reapers can tell I'm not living."

"I could smell the glamour of life upon you. Fake. An illusion." She offered up her bound wrists, and Frankie pulled the bindings apart. As the iron shackles fell to the ground, she seemed to change; her hair went wild, her eyes started to glow, and she rose up off of the floor as if suspended. Eldritch lightning arched from her hands, and she pointed towards the Sluagh gathering near Robert's corpse. "*Go hifreann leat, slògh sìdhe*; the Mórrígan commands you!"

With a unified howling screech, the Underfae sank into the floor and disappeared. The room seemed to get brighter, but that might have been the poison's effects wearing off; Frankie wasn't sure which to believe. He was about to ask a question of Leah, but she stopped him.

"He was the director on a number of my movies; had a great love for the monster genre, that one. He was attentive, and we went out a few times, and I let it slip once that I was Fae. After that, he was very interested in all things Sidhe, so I lent him some books of stories and lore." She sat against the desk next to Frankie, and looked at Robert's body. "The war came, and I went back to Ireland for a time. I guess in the years after we stopped making movies, interest became obsession; not just with the Fae, but with me as well."

"How did you banish the Sluagh?"

"I am the Mórrígan, Queen of the Fae. He must have figured that out before he sent them after me. I could have dismissed them at any time, but they knocked me out at the house and then he kept me in iron shackles to cut me off from my powers. But then, I am not the only one protected from the Sluagh tonight." She turned towards him and smiled, patting his jacket. "It looks like you carry the blessings of the Fair Folk as well, granted by someone who cares a great deal for you, or the integrity of your soul, Frankenstein." She laughed, melodically.

"Frankie, please." He grumbled at her as he steadied himself upon his feet. "Frankenstein was my creator's name, and Schwegler is just a fancy way of saying 'Smith.'" Frankie considered her words as he walked over to pick up his revolver. Lili, you sly little girl. *I will have to thank you properly when I see you next.* "So, what happens now?"

There was no answer. Frankie spun around to find her gone, along with her films. *Great. How in the hell am I going to put all of this in the report?*

-Fin-

Mr. Mean

by David Perlmutter

1.

The Cat took off his straw boater, flipped it in the air, put it back on his head, thumbed the armbands of his purple vest,and cursed his bad luck.

"They're *late*," he thought. "Every goddamn *one* of 'em! This is *all* I need! Now, my *old* mob would have gotten here without a problem. But *this* bunch of tools- geez! I can't believe we were *created* by the same guys!"

It was the summer of 1972, and the Cat, along with some of his colleagues at Hannigan-Barbarossa Studios, in whose comfortable and spaciously-appointed board room he now stood, was preparing for a heist in order to replenish their increasingly depleted collective funds. However, nothing would work out exactly as they planned it.

2.

The Cat and his associates had been created at various times and under different circumstances by the animation production team of Bill Hannigan and Joe Barbarossa. Each of them had, at one point, been the star of his own nationally broadcast television series, chiefly in the 1950s and 1960s, and all of these series had brought in a considerable amount of money - for Hannigan and Barbarossa. This is not to say that these beings of ink, paint and celluloid were not well compensated for their efforts, for they were. But they compromised themselves through constant gambling, alcohol abuse, drug abuse, partner abuse and a variety of other issues, some punishable by law. The once exorbitant sums of money they had earned dwindled down to a pittance, and now they required money to pay their debts. The sooner the better, as far as they- and their debtors- were concerned.

For cartoon characters had no legal "rights" in this "real" world. If they were caught by the police, they were typically beaten severely before being released and, if they were brought to trial, they inevitably ended up imprisoned for indefinite lengths of time, usually lengthy. While arrests were commonplace, trials were not, since the studios were quite effective at making sure charges and arrests were properly "hushed up" and addressed in ways that could be more easily dealt with in terms of advancing local causes and charities (i.e. bribes).

Of course, the 'toons were not always passive victims of human misdeeds and prejudices. As they were physically strong, able to manipulate their bodies fluidly, and virtually indestructible to any of the works or diseases of man (with the notable and costly exception of fire, which burned down the nitrate film interiors of their bodies easily), they could survive and take punishment no mere human could survive. But, in trying to live life successfully *off* camera, they were discovering this was both a blessing and a curse.

The planned heist - and meetings accompanying it- was designed to correct the misconceived assumptions about cartoon characters dealt with on a regular basis- as well as take down one man they assumed to be responsible for many of them.

3.

Eventually, they came, one by one, in their cars, under

cover of recording the new series that they had, in fact, been brought out of retirement specifically to do. The group consisted of The Dog, blue furred and red bow tied; The Bear, wearing a green pork pie hat on top of his brown pelt and starched white collar; The Horse, white-maned and wearing a red cowboy hat, holstering a pearl handled six shooter on his hip as he entered the studio; Mr. Stone, driving a foot-pedaled canopied steam roller device; and Mr. Space, who piloted his anti-gravity spaceship. All either gave the lot guard "the finger" or mouthed a series of words to him that resembled the phrase "same to you, fella!" but was, in reality, something more profane in nature. The Cat was bemused, if only temporarily, since he had done exactly that upon entering the studio earlier that day, although he had done so on foot and had added a kick in the guard's groin to boot. Still, he was displeased at their tardiness, and, scratching his yellow pelt to relieve an imaginary itch on his butt, he planned to cuss them out over it as soon as chance provided.

The Cat coughed loudly into his paw, signaling that the meeting was to commence. Then he began speaking, in his nasal but very commanding Bronx accent.

"Well, gentlemen," he said, putting his "thumbs" in the armpits of his vest, "and understand that that term is used *loosely* for most of you, I believe it is fairly obvious what we've gathered here to do. Isn't it?" Some of the group tried to speak at that moment, but he silenced them. "No, don't answer that! That was a *rhetorical* question, meaning it was *not* to be answered! I say this in acknowledgement of the fact that most of you are incompetent pea brains…."

"Hey!" Mr. Space said. "I *resent* that!"

The Cat walked over to where Mr. Space was sitting and flicked him right on his needle nose, making it bounce up and down several times.

"I resent you *back*!" he said, returning to the center of the room and resuming his customary position at the head of the table. "Any *other* questions?"

A general chorus of "no" was uttered, with the exception of the Dog, who raised his hand rather gingerly to ask the Cat a question.

"What?" the Cat demanded petulantly.

"Ah just wants to be sure," said the Dog in his deceptively mild Southern accent, "that this here deal will work for us well and good, on account of we's having to pony up the plane fare for Washington and all...."

"Would you *relax*?" the Cat said. "I told all of you before that the offices are bound to be loaded with enough money to keep us on easy street for the rest of our lives. Plus, there's our fee. So what the hell are you complaining about?"

"Well, uh, I don't mean to do no complainin', 'cause I ain't the complainin' type," added the Bear in his singsong voice, "but I am desperately in need of a significant amount of money or else I will have my pelt mounted on some gangland leader's wall! And I am not particular as to the means by which this is achieved- heyeyeyeyeyEY!"

"Ain't none of you got to worry with *me* 'round!" said the Horse in his dumb goofy voice. "I'll be *protectin'* all of you *good* with my old *sick* shooter!" He demonstrated his "skill" by firing one of the bullets in his gun, which bounced off the reinforced rosewood of the walls and hit the Horse square in the shin, causing him to yelp in pain and mutter softly, "That smarts!"

"What the *hell*, man?" uttered Mr. Space, displaying a profane version of the fatherly outrage he once displayed on television, face turning as red as his hair. "You could've *killed* us with that goddamn *trick shot* of yours!"

"That," the Horse cut in angrily, "was *no* trick shot, *sor*! In the days of the Old West..."

"You're not *in* the Old West!" Mr. Space countered. "You

no more *lived* in the Old West than *I lived* in the future TEN YEARS AGO - or Stoney here actually *lived* in the Stone Age!"

"That's right, pal," Mr. Stone said as he took a long drag out of a hip flask removed from a concealed pocket in his red leopard skin suit. "Of course, ever since I got cancelled, I've been living in the *Stoned* Age! And, I tell you, it's no fun! NO GODDAMNED FUN AT ALL!" He dropped his now empty flask on the ground and went off into a corner to cry out his drunken sorrows.

"If the *amateur theatricals* are now *concluded*," said the Cat, more than a hint of annoyance in his voice, "I would *appreciate* receiving your *undivided attention* again, if you consider it *fit* to *give* it to me!"

"What the hell *for*?" Mr. Space scowled at him. "What gives *you* the right to lead..."

"Because *I* have been more successful running con games and hair brained schemes than *any* of the whole goddamned *lot* of you!" said the Cat. "And, if you know what's *best* for you, you'll *keep* it that way!"

"Why, you," said Mr. Space. He lunged at the Cat, but the Cat caught him with a punch to the face that knocked him to the ground.

"*Don't* piss me off *again*!" the Cat said, directly to Mr. Space and indirectly as a warning to the others. "I wrecked *all* of my boys soundly when they pissed me off like that, and *damned* if I'll let any of *you* pull that crap on me, either! So *shut the hell up* and let me explain the way things are going to go so you won't screw up this up the way you did your *lives*!"

"And *you* did *yours*!" Mr. Space said from the floor.

"You keep what I did *out of this*!" the Cat said, kicking Mr. Space in the ribs. He then signaled to Mr. Stone to return to their conference, or, more specifically, to "drag [his] drunken old fat ass back" there. It was only then that he revealed the heist he had carefully planned in his own mind- and which he expected the others to follow to the letter, with no exceptions or screw ups, something he had warned them about so many times before.

He pulled down a map of the complex to burglarize, which he had the studio staff install the previous evening.

"This, gentlemen," he said, "is the Watergate complex, consisting of a hotel, two office buildings, and three apartment cooperatives." He pointed to each with a large branch that served as his "pointer." "Our target is this office building which, I know for a fact through my informants, contains the headquarters of a certain political party - which shall remain nameless - that all of us supported in our younger and more successful days. My informants have also noted that a certain group of men, affiliated with our nemesis, code name "Mr. Mean," are planning to knock over the building in an attempt to prevent their opponents from succeeding in their political goals. Fortunately for us, they are utterly unaware of our presence in the equation.

"Now comes the *remunerative* aspect of this whole torturous ordeal. A member of the opposing political faction, who is as anxious as we are to see Mr. Mean removed from his current position of office, forthwith- that means 'soon,' in case, unlike me, you did *not* receive the benefits of a P.S. 32 education - has offered each of us the cool and complete sum of $1 million to perform the ridiculously easy task of halting our opponents in their tracks. This will provide all of us with substantial money to settle our various debts - plus a few extra bucks!

"Now, today is June 13th, meaning that we have exactly three days to get to Washington before the deal goes down at the Watergate. We'll stay at a Howard Johnson's across the street, posing as a family of brothers whose mother went to the well too many times too often, so to speak. I have made all the arrangements and reservations in advance, so there's no need for you fellas to further deplete your funds. We go there, we do it, we get out. Simple as that. Then we have something for our the declining years that this blasted *immortal* condition has granted us. Be at LAX first thing in the morning. Any questions?"

All of the others raised their hands immediately. But the Cat knew they were all asking the same question, his firm answer prepared: "NO! We do *not* get paid in *advance!*"

4.

On the evening of June 16, 1972, police surrounded the Watergate complex after reports of an attempted burglary. At the same time, *another* group of police surrounded the Howard Johnson's hotel on the other side of the street, after the manager reported an altercation between a group of masked beings and some of his guests. The masked beings were our friends from Hannigan-Barbarossa who had indeed, as the Cat had feared, "screwed up" the seemingly simple task they had been given.

The members of the team disembarked from their flight at Dulles Airport, after which they proceeded to a nearby men's clothing store and bought six identical black sweaters and toques. This was followed by a trip to a nearby Walgreen's, where they individually purchased six cans of black shoe polish as a form of disguise. However, the Cat was the only one who used the polish as it was intended. He decorated the pouches under his eyes, in the manner of a football player. The others had the wrong idea entirely. The Dog used his as a powder puff, the Bear ate his, the Horse shot a dime sized hole through his can, and Mr. Stone and Mr. Space decorated their entire faces and upper hands with it, looking like an old-fashioned blackface minstrel show comedy team. They managed to do a dialogue routine in this fashion, before the Cat slapped them harshly on the face and told them to "stop fooling around".

Having donned their newly acquired disguises, the sextet headed towards the Howard Johnson's adjacent to the Watergate complex. The original plan was to take five separate rooms, and then to coordinate their movements. However, they learned that several mysterious men, claiming to be engaged in work for the federal government, had already commandeered several of the rooms, and had paid the hotel manager handsomely for allowing them to use the facilities. No amount of pleading, cajoling or threatening could allow the 'toons access to more than two rooms, another severe crimp in the Cat's plans.

Finally, after some intense negotiation, he agreed to a somewhat more truncated version of the planned assault. This proved to be the group's undoing.

Later that night, disturbed by what he figured to be an intentional disruption of his peace by the people in the next room, who had the television on far too loud, the Cat directed his hastily-assembled colleagues to invade said room. Hastily donning their disguises, the group barged in to demand a halt to the noise.

One person in the room was watching television, but many more encircled a brace of closed circuit television monitors, observing what appeared to be a burglary in progress across the street.

The man at the television set turned it off and demanded to know what the group wanted. The Cat and the others responded as planned, not with words but with actions.

Conflict and profane words resulted from their confrontation, but it was buried by the growing confusion and conflict on the other side of the street. Consequently, little notice was taken of this more minor shibboleth until the victimized men finally escaped from the room into the embrace of the police across the street, who were somewhat confused by the whole thing.

In any event, the heist conspirators and the 'toons were soon discovered in the room, each somewhat but only superficially injured, and were carted away to the now surprisingly crowded Washington, D.C. jail.

5.

Joe Barbarossa, five thousand miles and three hours away in Hollywood, was awakened abruptly by the telephone after falling asleep over a bottle of his favorite Chianti. He quickly stumbled to the phone and picked up the receiver.

"Hello?" he said.

"Do I have the pleasure of speaking with Mr. Joe Barbarossa?" a gravelly voice asked.

"Yes," Joe answered. "What the…"

"Joe, you may not know me, but my name is Dick, and I'm calling from Washington…."

"'Course I *know* you!" Joe said blearily. "Who doesn't? But why are you calling *me*, and why *now*?"

"Well, Joe, as my esteemed predecessor in this position used to say, your boys just shat on my flag. By that, I mean that they were caught trying to interfere with some government business I was conducting this evening at the Howard Johnson's across the street from the Watergate building…."

"WHAT?" Joe said, suddenly sober. "You mean some of my *employees*?"

""Employees' is too elastic a term for them, Joe. I think the more accurate term is your 'stars.'"

Barbarossa soon realized what this caller meant. He had only a few major stars in his stable of animated characters and, if their careers fell, his company would collapse. And those stars had all taken the weekend off from filming their new series to go on vacation to Washington.

Washington! Now he remembered. There had been reports

of a burglary earlier that night in Washington - at the
Watergate complex. He'd seen it on the news. And didn't they
say something to him about being able to be reached at the
Howard Johnson's ?

"You don't mean to say that they were involved in that
burglary at the Watergate tonight?" Joe said.

"Not with the burglary itself," said "Dick," "but they *were*
taken downtown, along with the rest of the people involved.
The police knew they had to be with your company because
they didn't look like my…any of the other people who were
picked up that night."

"Well," Joe concluded, "I suppose you'll want me to say
something to them. Probably make some sort of 'campaign
contribution' to your coffers. That what you want?"

"Look, Joe," Dick responded, "you're in the media, and I
depend on the media to keep my good name in the headlines.
We both know that bad publicity never improved anyone's
career. So I'm not gonna press charges against your boys- I got
enough trouble with my own right now! Just make sure you
keep 'em in line next time, okay?"

Barbarossa breathed a sigh of relief. "Can do," he said.

6.

Once they had been expedited back to Los Angeles, the
would-be heisters were summoned to a meeting with
their employers. Hannigan, white haired and stocky faced,
remained in the background, allowing Barbarossa, deceptively
youthful looking in his appearance despite the fact that he
and Hannigan were the same age, to conduct the business
with their performers. Normally, due to Hannigan and
Barbarossa's kindness, wit and gregariousness, these meetings
were entertaining and mess free. However, due to Barbarossa's
earlier encounter with "Dick," his good nature was at low ebb
as he addressed the wayward performers.

"I can't *believe* you guys!" Barbarossa said angrily, adding a couple of curses in Sicilian. "Here we give you enough cash to live out your lives and settle your debts like gents, and you go ahead and squander your good names by getting involved in CRIMINAL ACTIVITIES!"

"Boss, you got it all wrong," the Cat said. "We…"

"SHUT UP! Didn't I tell you guys all the time *not* to besmirch our good names by doing stuff like that? What you got between your ears, anyway? Paper?"

"Come on, Joe!" Mr. Space said. "They were offering us each $1 million to do the job! That's more than you ever paid *any* of us! Why *wouldn't* we jump at the chance?"

"Because," Barbarossa said, gripping Mr. Space's shirt collar, "you are *all* our *employees*! And anything you do or say reflects as badly on Bill and me as it does on any of you! Do you think we want to get our firm mixed up with the biggest political scandal of the *century*? Well? DO YOU?"

"Damn it, Joe!" Mr. Stone said as he got to his feet. "Do you even *know* how long it's been between gigs? We can't pay off our bills and stuff if you keep us on this cheap pay, non-negotiable contract indefinitely! Maybe if you laid off this third degree stuff and let us explain our situations…"

Barbarossa laughed with none of the warmth he saved for the sponsors, the human staff and his wife.

"What the hell have YOU got to explain?" he snapped. "You got the idea that you were big-time crime fighters and stuff, 'stead of the clods you really all are! You forget one thing, boys- Bill and I *own* your asses, and that's how it'll always be. You entered this business with us, and you *stay* with us! No outside work, no deals behind our backs, and especially no more of this 'hit the government when it's not looking' crap you seem to like pulling now!"

Angrily, the 'toons tried advancing on Barbarossa, but he pulled out his cigarette lighter and stuck it out like a sword towards them.

"None of that!" he ordered. "Now, here's how it's gonna be. We'll just *forget* about this whole damn thing! You were NEVER anywhere NEAR Watergate if anyone asks! And, if *somehow* you manage to slip up that task, like you did *this* travesty, I'll throw *all* of your goddamned films into a bonfire and you'll *all* die in agonizing pain from the burning- LIKE YOU SHOULD HAVE DONE TEN YEARS AGO!"

He stalked out of the boardroom, cursing in Sicilian and Italian loudly under his breath, leaving his partner, who had lurked in the shadows all this time, to take over the task of addressing the stars.

"Well, boys," Hannigan said in his understated fashion, "looks like you screwed up in D.C. Let's just hope you don't screw up your lines on the set today!" He laughed at his bad joke more than he should have.

"You're not *mad* at us, Bill?" the Cat asked. "I mean, Joe was all…."

"That's just the way he is- you know that. I'm different, as you also know. I've already gotten over it, just like he'll have to eventually. You actually didn't do too bad compared to what those fellows did at the Watergate that night, did you? And I figure that it's going to be *them* that end up taking the heat for what happened that night, not *us*."

He was absolutely correct.

Tainted Hooch

by Michell Plested

The rain beat down on the Buick like a hammer as I arrived at the crime scene. Barricades had already been setup around the brownstone and the bulls on the scene were hunched down in their overcoats trying to stay dry. The gas lamps along the street only highlighted that this was a night not fit for man nor beast.

I parked under one of the street lights and readied myself for the onslaught. I wasn't worried about the rain. I was no witch who would melt under its power. No, I was more concerned about what I would find in the building.

I flipped up my collar, adjusted my fedora, then stepped out into the night.

Within moments, the pounding rain had me wishing I hadn't bothered getting out of my nice warm bed.

"Detective?" One of the bulls dragged himself reluctantly from the relative shelter of the building's porch. That he actually sounded glad to see me only proved how miserable the night's weather truly was.

"Whadaya got for me, Sergeant?" I asked.

"Another stiff, just like the last two. This one's a Jane."

Just like the last two. I shook my head. One was just another crime. Two dead could be coincidence. But three? Three was a pattern.

And not a pattern I particularly liked.

"You sure? Just like the last two?"

"Course I'm sure!" The sergeant, an unimaginative bull of a man, sounded offended. That was fine by me. Offended meant he might pay closer attention to try and trip me up. Catch something I might miss. Keep me sharp and on my toes.

"You better get in there. The lieutenant's waiting and ready to start chewing on the upholstery."

"The lieutenant! Swell. Things are looking up already." I brushed past the sergeant and made my way up the stairs. I ignored the two bulls huddled in the doorway and stepped into the building.

It was like every other brownstone I'd been in. A long corridor stretched away from the entrance, doors set on either side of the hall. A wooden staircase climbed up to a the second and third floors.

I heard voices from above, so I played a hunch and took the stairs. They creaked under my weight as I slowly made my way to the upper floor.

I reached the landing and saw the source of the voices halfway down the hall. The two bulls were making no effort to be quiet. This time of night, that wouldn't make us too popular with the neighbors.

A few heads poked out from the doors along the way, prairie dogging, trying to catch a glimpse of the goings-on.

"You boys want to keep it down to a dull roar? Maybe so the folks across town don't know what's happening here?"

The two men, cast from the same mould as the beefy sergeant I'd left in the rain, turned their dull eyes, sneering as they recognized me.

"Detective, come to test out your hay fever?" The one in the doorway asked, trying to be funny.

"Nah, McGready. That isn't hay fever. I'm just allergic to the cheap cologne you wear. Maybe if you washed up once in a while, you wouldn't have to bathe yourself in it."

"Why you, dirty...."

"Kincaid!" The lieutenant called from inside the room. "Stop teasing the animals and get yer butt in here!"

I stepped into the room just as a flashbulb went off. The photographer gingerly unscrewed the hot bulb out of the camera, giving me an apologetic look.

"Nice of you to drop by, Kincaid. I trust we didn't pull you away from something important?" I knew how much the lieutenant hated leaving his cozy little family. Something about this death had to be big. I took a deep breath, trying to detect the signs of magic.

Nothing. If magic was involved, it was subtle.

"The boys downstairs say this one looks just like the last two," I said.

"Did they now? Well, I guess we didn't need you after all, did we, Kincaid?"

I walked right into that one. Nothing quite like giving the lieutenant an opening to rip off my head. "You tell me, Lieutenant. I don't get called into these things unless somebody thinks magic was involved." As I spoke, I did a quick surveillance of the room. Small, with a woman's touch. Photographs were on every surface showing a choice piece of calico mugging for the camera.

"Maybe there was and maybe there wasn't. That's why you're here. To tell me the difference," the lieutenant all but spat at me.

I didn't know what had the lieutenant all in a lather and I wasn't about to ask. I focused on the job at hand. "Where's the victim?"

"Back in the kitchen," he answered, a shake of his head to show me the way.

I went around him and into the kitchen. Whoever the victim was, someone had thoughtfully laid a sheet over her. I bent down and peeled back the cloth to take a look at her face.

I was expecting to see the girl from the pictures, but I was in for a shock. Picture girl looked to be in her twenties. This creature could have passed for a hundred. Emaciated would have been a kind way to describe her face.

Just like the other two.

I stood up. "Who is she?"

The lieutenant shrugged. "As far as we can tell, she was a young actress by the name of Sissy Deville."

"Young?" I scoffed. "This dame looks like she hasn't been young in decades."

"Don't you think I know that, Kincaid? You gotta do a lot better than that or I'm gonna starting wondering what I pay you for."

I'd heard that threat before. The lieutenant didn't much like me. The feeling was certainly mutual.

I considered the scene for several moments. The two earlier deaths had happened in alleyways, one not far from Temple Street and the other near Fifth and Main. Just like this one, the bodies appeared to be extremely old citizens. There were no evident causes of death; the boys down at the morgue were still working on it. It could have been totally natural for all we knew.

This was different. The victim looked old, but, by the lieutenant's own words, she was young. How could that have happened? "You talked to the neighbors, Lieutenant? Maybe she looked after her old granny?"

"Give me some credit for having brains, Kincaid! I've already been up and down the corridor talking to anyone who'll answer. The girl lived alone. If you check some of the pictures you can see the same jewelry as the corpse."

I grabbed one of the pictures and compared it to the body. The lieutenant was right. I held the picture next to the dead woman's face. If I turned my head just so and squinted a little, I could just make out some similarities.

"Okay, Lieutenant. I can see you've been busy and I can also see some resemblance to the picture. I ain't sniffed a trace of magic in the room though. What makes you think…"

"Kincaid," the lieutenant interrupted, "how else do you suppose a young skirt like this Sissy Deville would suddenly turn old, huh?"

He had me there. I certainly didn't know of anything but magic that could change a person so drastically. Once again, I was struck by the oddity that the lieutenant was involved.

"You got me. I still haven't sniffed out anything. Has anything been taken from the room?"

"No, nothing."

I nodded. "Okay. I need a bit of privacy so I can go over everything. Your aftershave is throwing me off."

He gave me a dirty look, but cleared out of the room with the photographer, closing the door behind him. He may not like me, but he knows I do my job. I'm the only one in the department who CAN do what I do, which is detect traces of magic.

One of the questionable results of my mixed parentage. Not every guy had a succubus for a mother and a priest for a father.

Not that I advertise.

I pulled off my dripping coat and hat, hanging them on the stand by the door. Sniffing around for magic, literally for me, was not something I enjoyed. When I did it, it was out of necessity. And when I found anything magical…well, let's just say I needed a good supply of clean mops.

I slowly wandered the room. Nothing but a bit of dust tickled my sensitive nostrils.

I ended up at the body. I knelt down beside her and breathed deeply. Other than the faint odor of decay, I got nothing. I glimpsed a whiskey bottle laying near the body and picked it up, taking a careful sniff.

I almost dropped the bottle as a fit of sneezing struck me.

The lieutenant, burst into the room. He must have had his ear glued to the door. "What did you find, Kincaid?"

I held up the bottle. "The alcohol stinks of magic."

"That has to go to the Feds," he said stiffly. "Contraband is their jurisdiction."

"Lieutenant, if we turn this over now, I won't be able to find out what's happened. This is our third death and only our first piece of evidence."

"We've got to turn it over. There is no room for discussion."

I thrust the bottle at the man. "Fine! Turn it over. And while you're at it, I would like to formally request to be pulled off this case. The first evidence we find and you want me to get rid of it? I guess you're right. I'm not worth keeping around."

It was a calculated move. I knew the captain and Chief wouldn't let me go. I knew the lieutenant knew that too. The truth was, I was sick and tired of being treated like the department bloodhound without any support. I couldn't do anything with my hands tied, exactly what the lieutenant was trying to do.

I grabbed my hat and coat and started to walk out the door.

"Where do you think you're going?"

I looked at the man. "Like I said. I'm out." I pulled my coat on. "You'll just have to find someone else to handle the case."

"That's not your call, Kincaid," the lieutenant said. He tried his best to look imposing. "You'll work on this case until I say different."

"Not this time, Lieutenant." I flipped my badge at him. "You can keep that for a souvenir. The piece I'll keep for mine. Give my regards to the Chief."

He paled at that. The man may be miserable, but he isn't a fool. "Kincaid, I need you on this case."

"And I need that bottle or I haven't got a chance to find out what's going on!"

"And you'll take your badge back?"

"For now." I had to fight hard not to smile. I was winning this little battle and we both knew it. No point rubbing the guy's nose in it.

He didn't think about it long. "Fine! You have twenty-four hours and then you turn that back in to me. If you haven't found anything, you might as well turn that badge in again too."

Ouch. Seems like I might have won the battle on the way to losing the war. Twenty-four hours. Not a lot of time. I knew it was just enough for the lieutenant to make a case against me with the powers-that-be. That was fine. If I couldn't turn this little sample into an answer, I didn't deserve the job.

I nodded and pulled on my hat and coat. "See you in twenty-four hours."

I knew where I had to go. My boy at the King Eddie would be able to point me in the right direction. On the surface, it looked like a legit business. A piano store to the law-abiding citizens at street level, to the citizen looking for more… sophisticated entertainment, there was a whole underground side to it.

Not put too fine a point to it, the King Eddie was a speakeasy.

I drove past the place and left the Buick a couple blocks away. The rain was still sheeting, so I wasn't expecting to run into anyone I knew. Still, a fella couldn't be too careful.

I made my way down the alley to the back of the store.

Why the back of a piano store? Turns out, there were tunnels under the city. Lots of them. The back door led down into the tunnels where could be found almost any degenerate, illegal or immoral activity you might want. That included illegal hooch and the King Eddie's underground speakeasy.

I rapped my knuckles against the steel door. A small window at eye-level slid open. "Password?" a gruff voice asked.

"Glamorous life," I promptly replied. A source had provided me with the password months before. I hoped I would find my boy who worked here. Twenty-four hours wasn't a lot of time.

The eye slot clicked closed and the door opened, spilling dazzling light into the dark alley. "Come on in," the same gruff voice said.

I stepped into the light and was grabbed by a set of strong silent types. They pressed me against the wall and frisked me, pulling my .38 Special out of my shoulder holster.

"You'll get the piece back on the way out…Detective," the bimbo said with a grin. He handed me back my badge.

"What, no kiss?" I wasn't surprised at the treatment. I wasn't even bothered to have been found out. It was pretty well known that the Mayor's office ran the supply of hooch. I was just another crooked cop to these jokers.

The stairs took me down to the tunnels and I followed the crowd to the King Eddie. My boy Ralphie was at the bar where I expected him. He blanched white when I sat down in front of him.

"Whaddaya want, Kincaid? I'm busy!" Ralphie continued to pour drinks and pull beer as he spoke.

"Ralphie, boy. Is that any way to talk to an old friend?" I asked. "I just came down here to draw on your expertise."

"My…expertise?" Ralphie sounded surprised at that. "Look Kincaid. I don't know what you think my expertise is, but I'm just a bar jockey."

"That's what I need." I pulled the partial bottle out of my coat and set it on the bar. "What do you make of this?"

Ralphie finished pouring his drinks and came over to take a look. "By the bottle, I'd say it was produced by Jack Dragna's crew." He popped the cork and sniffed the contents. "Phew! This batch has something wrong with it."

It surprised me that Ralphie would notice the whiskey

wasn't quite right, but I didn't say anything. "Where can I find Dragna?"

"Oh, you don't want to find him. He's pretty hard-boiled. Going after him is a sure way to disappear for good. You might find the harps he uses to cook the giggle water though."

The kid gave me the address and I threw him a couple bills for the information. I picked my .38 up on the way out and fought the rain back to my Buick. It was late, but I didn't think a bunch of moonshiners would be keeping regular hours.

I drove to Glendale to the moonshiners' hole. It was a big factory-type building, the windows dark. I suspected they were probably painted. The palooka standing in the rain having a cig trying to look inconspicuous told me I was at the right place.

I didn't bother to be subtle. I pulled the Buick right up beside him and rolled the window down.

"Hey! You can't be here!" the palooka said. "Move yer wheels along, fella!"

When I didn't move the car, he came forward. I could see he was carrying a Thompson, but didn't seem too motivated to use it. He leaned toward the car and met my .38 Special up close and personal.

"Drop the chopper, buddy and you won't get hurt. I need to talk to the boys doing the cooking. I need information, not bodies."

The guy looked startled and set the tommy gun down on the ground like a good boy. I climbed out of the Buick, keeping the gun trained on him.

"Okay, fella, now march."

He turned to start walking and I clipped him behind the ear with my gun. He collapsed to the ground and I trussed him up like a Christmas goose. He'd wake up with one heck of a headache in the morning, but he'd live.

I grabbed the chopper and carefully went into the building.

Either this Dragna character was really confident he wouldn't get busted or he was stupid. The palooka outside was the only muscle.

I walked between the kettles of cooking whiskey to a room in the back, the only one with lights. Four guys sat around a table playing poker. I walked in on them, holding the chopper where they could see it.

"Okay, boys. I don't want no trouble. I've got some questions to ask you and I expect answers right quick."

"What the…." The men jumped up from the table, expressions of shock on their faces. One started to reach for…something, but thought better of it when he found the submachine gun pointing in his direction.

"Like I said. I just want some answers. Now, all of you sit down and put your hands on the table where I can see them. The first of you to make me nervous is going to get you all killed."

They sat down like I ordered and watched me and the tommy closely. I pulled the partial bottle out of my jacket with my right hand, keeping the gun trained on them with the left. I set it on the table. "Any of you boys recognize this?"

I saw a look pass between the boys. "Okay, fellas. Spill! You tell me what I want to know and I'll let you get back to your game. No one needs to get hurt tonight."

Nobody seemed too willing to talk, so I pulled out my .38 Special. That gave me a gun in each hand for any of you keeping score.

"What…what are you going to do with that?" the boy closest to me asked.

"I figured I'd shoot you, Smiley. Maybe in the leg, maybe in the knee, maybe between the eyes." I said this with a smile. "See, I don't have all night like you jokers. Your pal outside isn't going to come charging to your rescue either."

"Well, we ain't gonna talk," an older fella across from Smiley said.

"Really? Maybe I can change your mind." I pointed the gun at Smiley. "You got until the count of three, Smiley. And then we all see how good a shot I am."

I looked him square in the eye. Sweat was starting to bead on his forehead. I pointed the .38 at one of the glistening beads just about exactly between his eyes. "One…Two…"

I didn't quite reach three when the older fella tried to make a move. I only had to move the .38 a short distance. The sound of the shot was deafening and then there were three.

The men sat very, VERY still, making sure not to antagonize me.

"Look boys. I wanted to do this peaceful, but your buddy there wouldn't have any of it. I could just mow you down right here and call it a night. It would mean less paperwork for me and a chance at some sleep." I made a show of considering the option. "Or, you could be cooperative and tell me what I want to know."

"What DO you want to know?" Smiley asked. From the smell coming from him, I was pretty sure his trousers were due to be washed.

"Didn't I tell you? I want to know about this bottle. I know the joy-juice you're brewing is laced with magic and I want to know who's doing it and where they are. You tell me that and you can get on with your game."

Smiley looked at his buddies and then at the dead man slumped over the table.

"Don't worry about the squealer there," I said. "He won't be going back to your boss with anything. Heck, if it makes you feel better, give each other a few bruises when I'm gone and tell your boss that you put up a fight." I pointed the .38 back at him. "Or, if it makes you feel better, you can join the stiff. Your choice. And I ain't about to start counting this time either."

Smiley made his decision. "We cook the stuff and some warlock does some hocus pocus over some special bottles for some Big Cheese. That's all we know!"

"And where can I find this warlock?"

"I don't know. He comes here, grabs a case of the good stuff and does his thing. A courier comes by after and takes it away."

"So, this warlock. Does he have a name?"

"I've only ever heard Bruce over here," Smiley nodded at the dead man, "call him, Professor Mortimer."

Professor Mortimer. I could almost picture him in my mind. Tall, dark, brooding. Demons didn't have much imagination and the story the boys told me before I left them sure sounded like a demon to me.

I paid a visit to one of my more trusted informers who always seemed to have a finger on the pulse of L.A.'s bigwigs. I found him in his rooming house on Bunker Hill.

"Tommy, I need your help," I said by way of greeting. I flashed a bill at him to get his attention.

His eyes lit up. "Living or dead, Kincaid?"

"A little of both, I suppose," I said.

I noted his confusion. "The guy calls himself Professor Mortimer. Ever hear of him?"

Tommy took a moment to consider my question. "I think my memory might just be jogged a bit with a little kale in my hand," he said, rubbing his fingers together.

I handed him the bill and waited.

"Yeah, I've heard of him. Some mystic from Europe, I think. Lives up in Highland Park."

"You have the address?"

"Sure, sure," Tommy said. "But, I think my memory needs a little more jogging.

I gave the kid the money and he scribbled down the address.

I found the gated building Tommy had described. If this was the place, the money was well spent.

I rang the bell and waited, hoping the Professor was the night owl I suspected him of being.

I didn't have to wait long. A manservant came down to the gate. From his demeanor, I'm pretty sure the Professor had many late-night guests. "May I help you, sir?"

I held up my badge. "Detective Kincaid of the LAPD. I have some questions for Professor Mortimer."

"Do you have an appointment, sir?" The man's calm was almost unnatural. In hindsight, it probably was supernatural.

"No, I don't. However, if I am forced to get a warrant, the Professor will be forced to come down to my precinct instead of the two of us getting cozy over a brandy."

"Very well, sir. One moment." The manservant went still for almost a minute before he addressed me again. He unlocked and opened the cast bronze gate as he spoke. "Please follow me, sir. The master is expecting you."

Creepy. But then, I've seen a LOT of creepy things in my time.

I followed the man up the cobbled pathway and into the house. He bid me wait in the foyer.

I didn't have to wait long. The tall, shadowy, and especially sinister figure of the Professor came sweeping down the grant staircase in a display meant to impress.

"Detective Kincaid. How very nice of you to visit!" The voice of the Professor boomed and echoed through the chamber. I resisted the urge to sneeze at the special magical enhancements he was obviously making.

I stepped toward the man as he stepped off the stair. "Professor Mortimer. Thank you for seeing me." I maintained a polite guise, not sure how far I could press this creature. My .38 wouldn't be much help despite the silver bullets I'd taken the liberty of loading. Demons were tricky and my own meager abilities only extended to the detection of magic. Silver bullets would only slow him down…and make him angrier.

"Please, will you join me for a nightcap?" the Professor asked, leading me to an adjoining room.

"Thank you, no," I said. "I'm on duty." The on-duty part was true, but really had no bearing on whether I would take a drink or not. My distrust of all things demon was the clincher.

"Do you mind if I partake, Detective?"

"It's your house," I said. "I hope you don't mind answering a few questions?"

"Of course, Detective," the creature said. He poured himself a snifter of brandy and sat down in a padded armchair, gas lamp giving his features a sinister glow. "Please, have a seat. I await your questions."

The Professor was certainly confident. I had to give him that. Which meant I was probably way over my head. I was beginning to have difficulty seeing clearly. I realized that the room was saturated with magic and my allergic reaction to it was much worse than my normal sneezing fit. I was losing the ability to see and think straight.

I had to move fast.

"Professor, what can you tell me about this bottle?" I asked, pulling it out of my coat.

The Professor leaned forward to get a better look. "Ah yes. That is a bottle I magicked for a client of mine. One of several, I believe."

"And just what is the spell you put on it supposed to do?" There was no time to beat around the bush. I had to get my answers and hope I could make it out of the house alive.

The Professor steepled his fingers and looked at me in amusement. "Why, Detective. I would have thought that obvious. The spell redirects life energy."

"To where?" I asked, almost wheezing.

"Why, to my client, of course. He wishes to remain strong, young and viral. Since he is mortal, there is really only one way to achieve that, isn't there?"

"Magic," I whispered.

"Precisely."

"And, who is your client?"

"I'm afraid that is privileged information, Detective Kincaid." The Professor stood. "And now, I believe it is time for you to go."

The way he said, "Go!" told me very clearly that I wasn't going to be leaving under my own power. More like I would be carried out and laid low in some farmer's field.

I drew my gun.

Professor Mortimer laughed. "And what are you going to do with that little pea-shooter? Surely you know it can't harm me." It might have been a trick of the light, but he seemed to grow a little.

The light! "No, Professor, but I can slow you down a little, at least." I pointed the gun at the only thing I could clearly see any more. The gas lamp. I fired and the bullet flew true, shattering the lamp and creating a small burst of flame that immediately caught on the table, armchair and, best of all, the Professor.

The Professor howled as he became a torch. The human flesh burned away, revealing the creature's true supernatural form beneath. His human form had been tall and brooding. His trueform was anything but. Shriveled and scaled with tiny nubs of horns protruding from his forehead, he looked almost comical. That is, until you saw the serpentine eyes and razor sharp orange fangs that crowded a too-small mouth and split wizened lips.

I knew better than to laugh or discount the little guy. It wasn't the big ones you worried about. The small ones like the former Professor were far more dangerous.

I sprinted from the room, bouncing off walls and furniture in a desperate bid to escape the house that was becoming a blazing pyre. Somehow I managed to find my way out into the fresh, cool rain. I sat down and watched the house burn. The Professor didn't come out.

As my vision cleared, I realized I had a problem to deal with. Well, another problem besides tracking down the tainted hooch.

The partial bottle was still in the house. The lieutenant was going to have puppies when he read my report in the morning and know it was gone.

But that was a problem for another day.

STARCROSSED

"Miss Maurus, there's a wizard here demanding to see you. What do you want us to do?" The young imp standing in front of her wrung his small, green hands looking frantically between the front door and the lively room where they now stood. If he hadn't been so obvious with his hand wringing, his clipped German accent would have given away how nervous he was.

"Can they hold him at the door, Mr. Bird?"

"Not for long. I mean, they're throwing everything they have at him, but they're only minor magicians at best. They can't keep a wizard at bay too long."

Roshanara nodded, her long black hair waving in a gentle wind no one else in the room felt. She twisted her wrist, taking her hand from her side to palm-side up. In it appeared a small glass bell. Wasting no time, Roshanara climbed onto the bar, grasped the handle and rang the bell once. The sound of crystal upon crystal had the desired effect in the boisterously loud room: absence of sound.

"We have a situation, guys and dolls. There's a wizard at the door. You know the drill, right?"

A chorus of "Yes," peppered with a few growls from those so inclined, reached her. It was exactly what she wanted to hear. These were truly her people. A smile, a blink and snap of fingers later and the Djinn Joint became a tea room rather than the speakeasy it was rumored to be.

Rather than change everything, Roshanara kept the jazz combo along with the bar itself: chandeliers, bright wall paper, round tables, fortune tellers and the dance floor. The only thing changed was the drink. Instead of absinthe, vodka, and her famous bathtub gin, her clients were now sipping a selection of teas that included orange pekoe, jasmine and green. It was good that the majority of her clients were unaffected by natural alcohol and just came for the inventive flavors rather than a buzz. The wizards who worked with the Feds would be able to tell exactly who had been drinking and how much regardless.

That was the kind of attention she didn't need, and one of the reasons she kept natural humans from darkening her doors. That and she didn't trust, or care for, naturals. She preferred when they stuck to their kind so her kind, supernaturals, could live in peace.

Seconds later, the pounding piano took up the rhythm restarting the frenetic dancing, one favored by only the surest feet. Smiles pasted back on and an aura of pure joy drifting through the joint, and she deemed the house ready.

"Alright, Mr. Bird. Tell the magicians to let the wizard in."

The imp grinned mischievously as he blinked out in a flash of smoke. Roshanara knew exactly where he was heading. The speakeasy was in the back half of a beautiful Victorian along the funicular known as Angel's Flight in Bunker Hill. What once was an area filled with the idle rich was now falling downhill towards the middle class, the perfect place to hide in plain sight. Mr. Bird would head toward a platform along the Angel's Flight's path which hid the secret door to the Djinn Joint. There he would grant the wizard a one-time pass to the speakeasy, allowing him to step upon the magic carpet. The carpet would transport him inside the front door and into the ongoing party that had started January 16, 1920. Rather than wait at the door for her uninvited guest, Roshanara slipped invisibly into the shadows, utilizing one of her many gifts as a djinn.

A puff of smoke rose from the oriental rug decorating the foyer, drifting from nothing to solidity. Wisps became feet, then shins, then legs and on until, finally, moments later, a fully realized wizard was fuming in the foyer. The man standing on her carpet was not one Roshanara was familiar with, which meant he was not a regular to Bunker Hill. Not terribly tall, his muscle bound frame would still be able to squash her if they were to fight without magic. Good thing she never intended to test that theory.

It was the crumpled suit and unbrushed fedora that truly caught her attention. This was a man who knew his fashions, but didn't care enough to maintain them once owned. It was even possible that she was staring at his only suit and hat.

"Where is she?" he growled at Mr. Bird. The small imp danced around the edges of the carpet, trying to keep one step ahead of the full-sized feet that could stomp him in an instant.

"Master, I do not know who you are talking about. I told you that before."

"I. AM. NOT. YOUR. MASTER!" the wizard roared before grabbing Mr. Bird by the front of his well-pressed suit and raising him up to his face. A softer growl grew from his stomach and exited through clenched teeth. "Now, imp, you go get Janelle Fisher from whatever monster has her and tell him I am here to rescue her. You'd better not get in my way. Got it?"

"But, sir. I don't know Janelle Fisher. What is she? Nymph? Witch? Vampire? Fairy?"

The wizard looked as though he was about to explode, or at the very least destroy the speakeasy if he didn't get an answer soon. But Mr. Bird was right; he didn't have an answer to give the man. As far as he knew Janelle Fisher had never stepped foot into the speakeasy, just as Roshanara intended.

"I'll take it from here, Mr. Bird." Roshanara stepped from a small blue flame, a bit of trickery really, but theatrics helped calm the worst rules offenders.

Unfortunately, it did not work on this wizard. Instead of stepping back or dropping Mr. Bird, the wizard just turned his ire on her. She felt the heat of his anger burn the outer edges of her aura before she threw up a shield of water. That would keep any accidental spells at bay, but it would not diffuse the situation. Only words could do that. Hopefully, she had the right ones.

The wizard turned his cold, grey gaze towards her, electricity snapping from every pore as he looked her up and down. The sneer on his lips was fake, there to intimidate her. Roshanara knew without prodding his mind. It was a good thing she didn't need to, as his shields were some of the best she had ever encountered. Every tendril of power she pushed toward him reflected back. There wasn't one thing she could learn from him using her powers, something she had yet to encounter. The two of them stood in the foyer sizing each other up, neither sure how to proceed.

"I'm sorry. Where are my manners. I am Roshanara Maurus. Welcome to my establishment."

"I know who you are."

"Then you have me at a disadvantage, Mister?"

"I know better than to give a djinn my name, let alone a dame djinn." The wizard's sneer was real this time.

Roshanara felt the green fire inherited from her mother flash through her before she could suppress it. The wizard's eyes widened slightly at what he must have seen. She knew the green fire's effects and how most people quaked in fear when they saw it. Her normally blue eyes would turn green, followed by the stone at her neck changing from emerald to sapphire, trapping the controlled Marid djinn magic and releasing the wild magic of her mother's people, the Ifrits, while flames danced across her skin.

But these changes didn't affect the wizard. Most supernaturals would have fallen to their knees begging forgiveness the instant her eyes changed color, but this one leaned back before calmly reaching into his pant's pocket for a hand rolled cigarette from a slim silver case.

"Those flames light one of these? I seem to have forgotten my matches."

Infuriated, Roshanara snapped her fingers in the general direction of the wizard's face. The cigarette burst into green flames before he even put it to his lips, half of it silvery ash before his first puff.

"Neat trick. What else can you do?"

Blue and green fire warred inside Roshanara. Her eyes and necklace spiraled between the two before finally settling in to the controlled blue eyes she typically kept. She needed to be in complete control with this potentially very dangerous wizard.

"Please come with me, Mr. Wizard," Roshanara said, her voice liquid smooth tinged with ice. She turned silently and walked through the main room of the speakeasy never looking back to see if the stormy man followed her.

Roshanara glided through the bright room that now smelled like the most exotic of teashops. Her guests were enjoying themselves as if nothing had changed. Ghostly banshees dancing the Charleston with scruffy werewolves passed gnarled gnomes and stately elves dancing the Fox Trot to the lively music that seemed to come from all sides even though the combo was in one corner. At the bar, vampires drank donated blood in glasses rather than from the necks of unsuspecting victims while witches and warlocks flirted. Everything you could expect to see in a natural human speakeasy. And, best of all, smiles decorated every face, something that did not often happen in the supernatural community these days.

All noise stopped as soon as she stepped through the wide
doorway. Rashanara realized instantly that the wizard must
have followed her into the common room. Wizards were
not the most popular people in the supernatural world, self
appointed cops who felt the need to be in complete control of
all supernaturals, no matter the crime, or lack thereof. They
lived within the lines, never stepping over regardless of the
reason. This wizard seemed to be no different, except he was
in her joint and she needed him to leave. Sooner rather than
later.

"He's with me. Carry on. There's nothing wrong with a bit of
legal whoopee, even if there is a bull in the crowd."

That was enough to turn everyone back to their diversions
and make a path. While she heard a few mutters as they
passed, Roshanara's guests were mostly polite and made her
proud. The wizard on the other hand? She could feel him
bristle behind her. The best way to get him out of her hair was
to find out exactly who he was looking for and why. Maybe
she could help, maybe not. Either way, she would hear him
out. This wizard was keen for a promotion, most likely at any
cost, so this Janelle Fisher was in a great deal of trouble even if
she hadn't done anything wrong.

They wove through the joint, past the bar now exclusively
selling tea, past the combo playing as though their lives
depended on it, and finally through a curtain separating
the brightly lit speakeasy from the offices. Mr. Bird hopped
at Roshanara's feet, trying to get her attention. She could
sense that his feelings on the subject of a copper in the
establishment might not be the most prudent, but she had a
sense about the guy. No particular reason, but her feelings on
the matter were typically never wrong.

Once through the curtains, the entire space changed.
Roshanara turned back to her uninvited guest and waited for

him to get his bearings before saying anything.

"Welcome to my humble abode, Mr. — ?"

"Again with wanting my name. What if I refuse?"

"This is America. I can refuse you access to my club."

His grey eyes flashed. "That would be your biggest mistake yet."

"I'm not so sure. Want to give it a try? I can give you the bum's rush and no one would be the wiser."

The strong scent of cigarette smoke began to fill her head, causing dizziness plus a short cough.

"Nice digs you've got here. They supposed to look like they have curved walls?"

"Well, I am a djinn. Where do you think I live?"

"In a bottle, unless called. At least that's what I've been told. It's not what I've seen so far."

"And what have you seen?"

The wizard laughed, one hand in his pocket and his cigarette's long cone of ash dangling such that Roshanara wanted to walk around him with an ashtray so he did not burn the ancestral rugs that had been in her family for over one thousand years.

"You're both a Mirad and Ifrite djinn, but not a member of either clan. No one claims you, which means you're a pushover. Damaged goods. Right?"

"Not even close. But that's not why you're here."

"No. I'm looking for a doll named Janelle Fisher..."

"I got that much from your rather aggressive inquiry in the middle of my *perfectly legal* club."

He barked laughter, waving his hands in an attempt to apologize. When he finally got his breath back, he dropped onto the pillows, which lined the circumference of her office.

"You slay me! No, really, you do!" The laughter was raucous, but finally calm enough for him to talk. Rashanara wished he hadn't recovered quite so quickly. "Lady, you've got some daddy giving you sugar for this joint. That part isn't illegal. You worked as a hoofer for a while, where you must've found your dapper daddy. I'm just as sure of that as I am the drinks your tenders usually serve have very little to do with tea."

"I don't know what you're jammering on about over there, sir. Perhaps you'd like a cup of tea to calm yourself?"

The wizard laughed again, nodding his head as though he were keeping time with the musicians down below. Between the music, which Roshanara typically enjoyed, and cigarette smoke, she was in sensory overload. She knew there was a reason the djinn preferred bottles and lamps to the large mansions they could create.

The cold sapphire eyes returned. Blue fire coursed along Roshanara's skin forcing the hair on her arms and neck to stand up with static electricity. He was a wizard which meant he had at the very least a wand. They couldn't actually do magic without a prop. Only truly talented magicians, witches, and druids, those with natural magic, could cast using just a flick of their hand. Wizards had to be careful with the manner they flicked everything, always.

Rashanara, on the other hand, had enough of her own magic. Blue fire coursing through her body never meant anything good. Once blue danced through her body she had to release it somehow. This time she had just the target to use it all on.

"Why are you here?" she asked, her ice blue turned directly on him. Time he learned what a truly pissed off Marid djinn was capable of.

"I need Janelle Fisher."

"Not good enough." Lightning gathered in her arms and hands, dancing down her body from her third eye.

"Well, it'd better be, 'cause that's all I got." If he knew he was in danger, he never showed.

"Who is she?"

"Daughter of an oil man."

"Why are you looking for her?"

"Daddy thinks she was kidnapped by some rag-a-muffin were-beast named Ronin. He asked me to look into it."

Rashanara circled the room, forcing him to follow her with his eyes as a manner of captivation. The technique had quieted his rage.

"So, you're a cop who's a dick after hours?" This one was becoming more and more intriguing. All wizards reported directly to the LAPD. Each was given a badge, a gun (usually unused), a car, a place to live and a larger salary than anyone in town, except for the movie people, of course. But this one was moonlighting as a P.I.?

"I never said I was a cop."

Her blue eyes flashed green again. He really didn't understand his precarious situation if she couldn't control this half of herself.

"You really haven't said anything," she said quietly.

"I'll tell you what," he said, putting his feet up on the ottoman while he sank back into the rounded sofa. "You guess what I am, I'll tell you who I am."

Roshanara was not keen on the game, but felt trapped. At this point, she hoped he would not try to take her bottle away as police evidence. Not having a place to sleep would be horrific. "This should be interesting."

"Oh, you can't use any magic but your own to figure it out. Djinn magic is limited by distance, if I'm not mistaken."

"How many blue-green djinn do you know, Mr. Wizard?"

"Does it matter?"

Roshanara stopped. Getting information from him would require a different tactic than her normal seduction routine. Most wizards were pushovers, so excited to meet a djinn as rare as her they jumped over backwards for a look inside her private room. And an offer for a private dance? That was just amazing! This one, however, was a true killjoy.

"Fine," Roshanara said, dropping onto a cushion across the room from the Wizard. "Let's talk."

"I don't want to talk with you, djinn. Unless you know where Janelle is. Then again, there's our game." His eyes flashed quickly. If Roshanara hadn't been looking for it, she wouldn't have seen the desire. Desire for what she wasn't sure, but he wanted something more than to solve the case.

"Alright. I'll play your game. But your name isn't much of a prize. So, what else do I get if I win?"

"Depends on what you guess."

"The more I guess, the more I win?"

"Something like that."

Roshanara grinned a sharp-toothed grin. Whether she liked it or not, this was the type of game she was most suited to play. No one had ever bested her in a guessing game, which meant this wizard knew who he was dealing with or had never heard of her. Roshanara was pretty sure he knew something, though. The angry storm crackling around every inch of his aura spoke volumes. This was a man on a mission, just not the one stated.

Roshanara stood in the middle of the room and pointed towards the curved wall, releasing a small burst of blue energy. A low drum beat filtered throughout the room, starting from where she had pointed before moving lazily towards the wizard. Right after came a quiet tambourine which led to a guitar, then a subtle piano. The music was exotic, inviting her hips and ribs to move in different directions while her feet drew small circles in the rich carpet. Columns of smoke, either blue or green, drifted up from the exact point her toes touched the floor. As the columns of smoke rose towards her waist, Roshanara's hands began their work. Circling fingers and palms, each hand took the smoke in and wove intricate patterns. As each pattern completed, she released them into the room, never taking her eyes off the wizard's face.

His expression was frozen. Most men would be panting and dreamy-eyed by now. The djinn magic Roshanara carried brought a man to his most base point where he would do anything for her. This primal magic was one of the reasons men sought to harness the djinn, to use the magic for their own purposes. Wizards, however, wanted to ensure they didn't use their magic on mankind. Roshanara typically chose not to, unless her clients were threatened. Like a wizard who wouldn't share his name showing up on her doorstep.

"It won't work."

"What won't?"

"Your dance. Just in case you haven't figured that out yet, I can't be seduced."

Roshanara kept moving if only to try to distract the man sitting in front of her while she considered her next move.

"Who says I want to seduce you?"

"Isn't that what all djinn do? Wiggle your hips and lick your lips, then suddenly all naturals, and most supernaturals, fall to the ground begging you to give them favors?"

"What makes you so sure I am like others of my kind?"

"If you aren't, why are you dancing?"

He had her there. There was no reason for her to continue to dance other than to cover her thoughts. If she moved constantly, perhaps she would be able to keep her thoughts from him. But that didn't seem to be working either.

With a snap of her fingers, the room fell quiet. Another snap and drinks were brought in from the bar. A full tea service from the old world, complete with a tall pot, saucers and lumps of *qand*, rock sugar. The wizard watched quietly as Roshanara sat and poured the tea into the saucers before taking a lump from the pyramid of rock sugar and placing it in his mouth. He lifted the saucer like a pro, sipping without spilling a drop, something most Americans had difficulty with, even after several attempts. Roshanara realized why she had such little power over him, allowing herself a secret smile.

"Who was she?"

"Who was who?"

"The djinn you met before you met me."

The wizard's eyes sparked while the rest of his face remained still. "Does it matter?"

"Only from curiosity. You see, I am unique, no others like me. But you already know this."

"The seeker spell I put down showed this bar as the last place Janelle was."

"And yet she's not here."

"No."

"So how can you trust your spell?"

"It's never wrong."

A wizard with a never-wrong seeker spell could destroy everything she built here.

"Let me tell you a story."

"I don't have time for stories. I need to find this girl."

Roshanara's eyes glinted harshly in the soft light. "Humor me. Call it payback for storming into my joint and threatening my friends."

"Whatever blows your skirt."

"There was once a prince who ruled the air. He was wise, led his people with wisdom and care and did his best to ensure their safety above all else. He was called upon by many princes and kings, mostly of other peoples, to do what these rulers could not: ensure the safety of their people. Some said he was magical, but a few knew his true secret."

"This prince lived in an oasis in Persia. This oasis had several small pools, each surrounded by a grove of fig, olive, and orange trees. There were caverns situated around the water, high enough up so they did not flood but close enough that it was easy to walk out in the morning for a bath in the warm pool followed by a drink alongside the cold pool. The two pools carried water from different sources. One from the cold rivers to the west, the other from the depths of the world along pipes of warm, molten rock."

He fidgeted with his pocket watch, opening and closing the cover. "Does this fable have a point?"

"Patience. I do not tell stories just to hear my own voice."

"No, but one of your ancestors did. You are related to Scheherazade, right?"

"That woman was nothing but a Sheba who stole my family's stories to save her own skin." Roshanara spat.

Green fire crackled off her skin, prickling as it rose higher this time. The wizard cocked an eyebrow and stared at the flames.

"You going to do something about that, or do I need to?"

"I can control it, Wizard."

"Not what I've heard."

Roshanara fiddled with the triple ring on her finger, focusing on the blue stone set in the antique gold, willing the fire to soak into the stone. Slowly the stone turned green and her breath went from ragged to smooth.

"Now, wizard, you will let me finish my story or I won't work so hard to control myself."

His eyes were skeptical. Regardless, Roshanara felt a truce of sorts. At least she hoped so.

"As I was saying, this hidden oasis was a paradise to all who visited. You could only visit if you were invited, for the oasis moved every night. Only the prince knew where they would appear when they woke in the morning. Which is why, one morning, he was very shocked to see a naked woman bathing in the warm pool outside the entrance of his cavern.

"She was a beauty beyond compare. Emerald green eyes, olive skin and hair that was rich, full and as smooth as the silk of the prince's tunic, curling slightly along her face. The prince knew he was witnessing a rare sight. He dropped to his knees to watch, to thank Allah, the Prophet, and the Sun for allowing him the honor. He stayed still as the woman dipped herself under water three times. After the third time the woman looked over her shoulder catching his eye.

"'You can come out now, prince. I promise I will not harm you.' This shocked him, as he was sure he had done his best to hide himself. He stood quietly and walked towards the woman. He saw her clothing laid out a step or two from the pool, but no towel, so he offered his own which she gratefully accepted, covering herself so the Prince's eyes would not see her nakedness.

"'You know who I am, lady, but I am at a disadvantage. May I have your name?'

"'My name is reserved for my husband.'

"The prince hesitated. This statement meant that perhaps someone else knew this vision's name and he would not be allowed to know it.

"'And your husband? Is he near?'

"'That depends.'

"'On?'

"'On whether or not you are willing to go against both our castes and be the brave man I know you can be.'

"The prince's heart skipped a beat. He could hardly believe his blessings, for, in those few moments since meeting the woman, he had already fallen in love. Now that he discovered she was not married, his only wish was to take her into his arms and make her part of him. Every inch of his body, from skin to his groin, screamed to touch her.

"So this wise prince, who always thought of the good of his people before his own, did the one thing no one would ever have considered possible. He knelt before a strange woman and declared his love and intent three times before Allah, the

Prophet and the Sun. He would be her husband and she his wife. They would live together for as long as Allah thought it proper, forsaking all others for the love of one another.

"As soon as he declared his oath, the prince stood and stared into the green eyes of the woman who's name he did not know and fell into the depths of their coolness. In seconds, she was in his arms, draped as one would carry a treasure, and he carried her back into his cavern.

"The cavern was plush, richer than even the richest room in a palace, but the Prince paid no attention. He was intent on reaching the soft bed with his precious burden.

"They stepped over the threshold and the Prince leaned towards his new bride. As their lips touched, sparks flashed, striking him deep in his heart, his belly, and his straining groin.

"The woman moaned, for she too had felt the lightning that melded them together. Her whole body burned in his arms as he stumbled towards the bed. Within seconds the towel around her was unwrapped and his robe was ripped off. They stopped, staring at each other fully for the first time. Each took in the beauty of the body before the other. He breathed in as he saw her perfectly rounded breasts and flat stomach. She gasped as she took in the strength in his chest, his striking blue eyes, and the cut of his hips. They were both mesmerized.

"The prince's bride lifted her body off the mattress, kneeling on the soft down as she reached up to touch her new husband's face. With one hand, she guided his face while her other hand gently caressed him from chest to groin, forcing a groan from behind his teeth. Unable to bear it anymore, the prince grabbed his bride's back and pulled her into his chest. He bent her backwards over the bed and, with only a moment's hesitation, entered her, piercing her tightness and taking the first of two things she had been saving for him, her husband, alone.

"They rode each other throughout the morning, each bringing more pleasure to the other than ever felt before. The prince was amazed at the joy he felt with this strange magical woman he held. Wracked with pleasure, he even forgot that he still didn't know her name. All that mattered was the tightness felt as she came, squeezing his member until he could no longer hold back and was forced to release his own passion into her womb.

"When finished, they broke apart to breathe, talk, and laugh. But those pauses lasted only moments before the need in them became great again. A finger on his chest, a palm on her stomach, a brush against her breast, a lingering kiss on his lips, then their desire would intensify again, breathing ragged and passions bursting through skin, forcing them to become entwined over and over and over.

"The prince didn't notice that during this time not one of his servants entered the cavern. They didn't eat nor drink. They dined only on their desire to be a part of one another.

"'I prayed for you,' she said quietly, as she lay in his arms.

"'How so?'

"'I prayed to Allah that I would meet my husband and he brought me to you.'

"His heart swelled when he heard these words, for it meant Allah had also heard his prayers for a wife. This was not a prince who wished for a harem, yearning instead for just one woman who would stand by his side, share his bed, and love him as he loved her. It seemed he found the treasure he sought.

"They lay in bed for what seemed like hours, never realizing they had been left on their own for longer than the prince expected, even on his honeymoon. The cavern where they lay was a room worthy of a prince of the blue djinn, a room where time stood still. To the prince and his princess, time didn't matter, good in some ways but devastating in others.

"As they lay there, a loud explosion ripped stones from the ceiling of the cavern. That none struck either was a miracle. The prince was furious, his skin dancing with blue fire as his servants prostrated themselves in front of him and his new bride.

"'What was the meaning of this?' he roared, barely listening as servants who had been with him since he was a baby explained that the cavern closed itself a month before. They had been trying to rescue him, fearing he had been stolen by a rival caste to leave them in the desert for eternity. But the camp and the oasis continued to moved daily, giving them hope.

"The prince and his bride stared at the terrified servants, dumbfounded as they digested the facts. So tied up in each other, they had abandoned the fates of all those who travelled with them. The woman turned as many shades of red her pale green skin allowed. As the prince reassured his people, she quietly dressed and sank into the shadows, hoping she could blink out of the cavern before anyone noticed.

"But the prince felt her absence immediately.

"'My lady, I need you. Without you, how can I run this oasis?'

"'The way you have run it for eons before me and will for eons to come. Don't worry, love, you will see me again.' With that she blinked, vanishing from the oasis and leaving the prince stunned. She also left a red rose and two words - 'One Year.'

"Once a year, the prince was ceremoniously sealed into the cavern for a month, fully stocked with all the comforts one might need with the love of one's life - silky sheets, luxurious foods, rivers of wine, and access to the oasis pools. On the morning of the day they first met, the princess appears, stepping out of green flames and into his arms. For a month, they govern together, mostly from bed or the warm pool, but

they are together. And when they are together, the stars are
brighter in the night sky. It is as though Heaven blessed their
union and shared in their joy."

"Huh," the Wizard said, reaching for a date on the tray.

"What do you mean by that?" Roshanara's emotions ran high
when she told this story, which was why so few had heard it.

"It's swell your parents told you about their honeymoon so
dramatically. That's all."

Roshanara blushed, atypical for djinn. For them, sex was
an activity, something to do when one had an itch. But the
story was about her parents. While she walked away from the
fire they created to craft her, they were still hers. The images
filling Roshanara's mind were enough to make a flapper blush
and a swell go running from the speakeasies back to his wife.
He made her anxious, heart racing while breath came in
ragged gasps.

"I'm going to need that back, you know."

The Wizard was looking down at the cushion where they sat.
Roshanara saw their hands entwined and fingers threaded,
making it impossible to figure out who's hands were whose.
Roshanara tried to jerk back. It was unseemly for her to hold
the hand of a wizard, inexcusable one unnamed. Yet the
harder she tried to escape, the stronger the grip became.

"So, I come here following a seeker spell, and all you do is
tell me a story about your parents. How they had a love affair
most people didn't quite like, and how they chose to live apart
for most of the year. Am I with you so far?"

Roshanara nodded, trying to disentangle herself.

"This natural doll I'm tracking. The one her daddy says was
kidnapped? He has a bounty on the werewolf, too. Just like
it's a real kidnapping. But, is he telling the truth? Was she
kidnapped?"

Roshanara couldn't look into his stormy grey eyes. She knew
his electricity would never strike her. Manipulating storms

was djinn magic. But she also she knew that lying to this man would be impossible. She stayed silent, praying he would never came back to the Djinn Joint.

He studied her awhile, sly smile creeping across his face. One of the rules of the Djinn Joint was predatory magic was to be avoided - no duels, no murders, etc. But somehow, Roshanara knew, the wizard didn't care. Rules made by the Council of Castes were to be enforced, that's all. Then he just dropped her hand, placing them one on the other, holding them to the divan.

"Your parents. What really happened to them?"

"That is a story I will only tell the man who takes me on, lock, stock and barrel," Roshanara waited a beat. "To include sharing his name."

The wizard laughed. "And the natural girl? What happened to her?"

"Isn't it your job to figure that out? I've given you all the information I can, Mr. Wizard."

Roshanara pulled her hands free and stood with as much assurance as her wobbly legs would allow. She opened the door and stopped by an imp named Mara, one of the many who called the Joint home.

"Make sure he leaves."

"Can I pinch him until he does?" The imp only came to her knee, but was filled with boundless energy dedicated to teasing as many men as she possibly could.

"Whatever you feel is necessary to get him out of the Club."

"Sure thing, boss! We've got you covered," Mara smiled brightly, fire shooting from the tips of her ears in short bursts.

"I am confident you do," Roshanara smiled back before turning back to the wizard. "Until you decide, I think it would be best that you not return." She snapped her fingers and vanished, leaving a curling column of blue-green smoke in her wake.

***

April's warmth filled the Djinn Joint and Bunker Hill
with warm breezes and the scents of blooming jacarandas.
Roshanara smiled as she stepped off Angel's Flight and onto
the front walkway. The Joint had been without major incident
for almost a year, unless you counted the Wizard With
No Name. Roshanara did not. He was a blip, a night to be
forgotten.

And yet, she could not forget that night from the moment
the young werewolf and his natural love came in, desperate
for help, to the moment the wizard left the Joint. Each
moment was etched with acid into her brain. Thankfully,
she knew better than to share too much information. These
memories were the stuff of dreams. Well, at least some of
them were.

"Miss Maurus! Miss Maurus!" Mara was running down the
sidewalk, contrails floating after her.

"What is it?"

"He's back. He's back!"

Roshanara laughed at the warring emotions on Mara's
face. The poor imp couldn't tell if she should be excited or
distraught.

"Slow down. Who's back?"

"The wizard. The one from last year?"

Roshanara didn't even wait for Mara to finish speaking
before she snapped her fingers, calling a column of blue-green
smoke. As it materialized, her impatience got the better of her
and she stepped through without waiting for the column to
form fully.

She scanned the room quickly as she stepped in, glittering
green eyes landing on the back of the man she had banished
the year before. At least she wouldn't have to go looking for
him. Instead, she just walked up to the bar, trying her best to
control the anger threatening to erupt from inside. The crowd

of customers scattered, leaving her a parted Red Sea on the dance floor.

She sat on a stool next to him, taking care not to disguise her anger. A year had not changed him physically, still striking with grey eyes starting flames in her stomach that spread to every limb. But if he was here, it could not be for a good reason. He was a wizard after all.

"So, I did some digging and found out something interesting. Seems the natural and the werewolf were goofy for each other. They found a way around her body guards and the spells her father paid for to keep them apart."

Suddenly there was a crystal flute in front of her filled with a green champagne cocktail, an absinthe soaked sugar cube rather than one soaked in bitters sitting in champagne. The bartenders called it a Green Djinn.

"And your client? How did he take his daughter's elopement?"

"She's pregnant. He's getting over it. His heart isn't complete ice."

"That's nice."

"Ain't it though?"

He took his last swig from the tumbler. He stood and grabbed one of her fingers in his, squeezing gently.

"The name's Sheridan." She inhaled to protest, but he smiled. "You can call me Dan."

Roshanara smiled just as discretely. "It will be on the list."

He walked out of the Joint, not for the first time and definitely not for the last.

SEEING DEAD PEOPLE

By Adam Remington

"Wow. She's beautiful."

"She's dead, Mr. Lincoln." Detective Kelly Porter shielded her eyes from the late afternoon sun. "Perhaps we can get on with this?"

Jet Lincoln crouched beside the corpse of Mrs. Harper, carefully placing his battered old backpack on the ground. Dressed in well-worn blue jeans, an equally well-worn white t-shirt, and brown leather cowboy boots, he cast a cursory glance at the victim. Despite the fact she was dead, the body of the deceased looked remarkably healthy. Rigor had not yet set in, and some color remained in her skin. Her facial expression was relaxed, and, as she lay there in her yellow summer dress, Jet thought she looked like the embodiment of freedom.

"I doubt I'll be of much help, Detective. I mean, you know I specialize in ghosts, right?"

Detective Porter surveyed the Harpers' landscaped backyard. It was alive with activity. Forensic technicians scoured the site for physical evidence, while uniformed police officers manned the external access points to the Cleland Avenue residence. "Yes, I know. But the cause of death in this case is undetermined. I wanted to get an independent opinion before I refer the body to the coroner. Ghosts or no ghosts, your assistance has proven helpful in the past."

Jet ran a hand through his mop of greasy dark hair. He certainly appreciated the opportunity to work with the LAPD Detective Bureau, but, as Kelly stood over him, looking stunning in her sharp black suit, he was terrified of letting her down. In his area of expertise, it takes a long time to earn credibility, and he knew full well it only takes an instant to lose it. "Actually, now that I think about it," said Jet. "I haven't seen a single spirit since we crossed into Mount Washington. I mean, I see them everywhere. All the time. If there are larger forces at play here, the ghosts would be the first ones to detect it."

"Let's not get ahead of ourselves Mr. Lincoln." Kelly drew her thin auburn hair back into a pony tail. "Instead of concerning yourself with what's *not* here, try focusing on what is."

"What's this?" Jet pointed at the forehead of the deceased. Partially obscured by Mrs. Harper's fringe was a horizontal dark pink mark, an almost perfect oval. "If she died from a blow to the head, I'll be terribly disappointed."

Detective Porter crouched beside the corpse opposite Lincoln. Snapping a latex glove onto her right hand, she carefully brushed back the hair to reveal the mark more clearly.

"The medical examiner would be of more assistance here," she said. "But I can tell you it's not a lesion. It could possibly be a contusion, except there doesn't appear to be any swelling. Honestly? It looks more like a burn to me."

At the precise moment the detective finished speaking, the burn mark abruptly moved an inch sideways across the corpse's forehead. Kelly leaped to her feet with a yelp, while Jet fell backwards onto his behind.

"Did you see that? It looked at me!" Jet was astonished.

"I saw something... But I don't know what it means." Kelly fought to compose herself. "Maybe it's some sort of beetle larvae underneath the skin. Lets not jump to any hasty conclusions."

Detective Porter helped Jet to his feet, when a voice came from the side of the house.

"Everything alright out here?"

"Yes, thank you Jack." Kelly hid her embarrassment by pretending to brush lint from her suit. "Jet, you remember my partner Jack Rollins?"

"I wish I didn't," said Jet.

Jack Rollins was an imposing figure. Tall, military haircut, chiseled facial features. His broad chest and shoulders threatened to rupture the seams of his charcoal gray suit.

"Ah, the psychic detective. This is a crime scene, Lincoln, not a public relations exercise."

"I've never claimed to be a detective, Detective." Jet veiled mockery in his tone. "I'm the Hollyweird consultant. I'm only here to help. I have reason to believe there's something preternatural about this case."

"Of course you do," Detective Rollins turned his head and raised a fist to his mouth. "Charlatan!" He coughed.

Kelly opened her mouth to intervene, but was interrupted by a scream from one of the young forensic technicians. The corpse of Mrs. Harper slowly arched its back. The arms and legs remained lifeless, and flopped to accommodate the movement of the body. The head slowly rolled from side to side, and the arching of the torso became interrupted by short, violent, downward spasms. Detective Rollins braced an outstretched arm in front of his partner, suggesting that she remain still. Jet crept forward in an attempt to see if the mark on the forehead was moving again.

"Lincoln," said Detective Porter. "Stay back."

Jet turned in response to her voice. "Do you feel that? The temperature just dropped something fierce."

Kelly shook her head, though she did see the goose flesh covering Jet's arms. Rollins just stared at Lincoln blankly for a moment, then returned his bewildered gaze to the former Mrs. Harper.

With back fully arched and head now tilted back, the neck of the cadaver bulged, causing the jaw to slowly open. Jet and the detectives watched with wide eyes as something foreign emerged from the esophagus.

The head of a snake protruded from Mrs. Harper's open mouth, its tongue flicking the air as it writhed its way from within the carcass. The python had only gotten a foot of its body free when a smaller snake slipped out of the corpse's right nostril. Further activity outlined the fabric of Mrs. Harper's dress as more snakes slithered from between her legs and sought shelter amongst some nearby shrubbery. It was at this point that the young female forensic scientist fled the scene, sobbing frightfully.

"A little help!" An enterprising technician had retrieved a blue recycling bin from beside the house. "They're Burmese pythons. They aren't venomous, but be careful."

Jet, Rollins, and two of the crime scene attendants helped gather the snakes and contain them in the bin. The serpentine torrent appeared to have reached its climax, and, despite their frantic writhing, the pythons did little to resist capture. It took all four men to wrangle the initial snake, first dragging it to fully remove its length from the corpse's throat, then the full team lifting five and a half feet of undulating muscle.

"I think I know what's going on here." Jet panted slightly as he mopped his brow.

"This ought to be good." Rollins braced the lid of the makeshift serpent container.

"Kelly was right. That mark on the victim's forehead is a burn. Not externally, mind you, but underneath the skin." Detective Rollins rolled his eyes as Jet continued. "Mrs. Harper had her third eye incinerated. I can't imagine the power required to manage something like that. We're dealing with a heavyweight practitioner here. The energy that was sucked out of the air when the serpents were conjured, and that dead third eye. Man, it moved. It saw us. Whoever did this was watching us. This isn't your garden variety magick. This isn't even black magick."

"What is it?" asked Detective Porter.

Jet looked her soberly in the eyes. "It's dirty magick."

"You're not buying this, are you?" Detective Rollins almost pleaded to his partner. "For all we know, Lincoln made the snakes appear. He's probably playing us for publicity... or something. I mean, who has the most to gain here? Are we honestly ready to attribute the cause of death to magic?"

"I'm sorry, Jack," said Kelly. "I saw what I saw. It's not a lot to go on, but I think his explanation may be the only one that makes sense."

"Let me talk to the husband." Jet recovered his backpack from the ground, and carefully checked it for snakes.

Detective Porter contemplated the request before nodding her consent. "Okay, but you have got to be respectful. And *no* mention of snakes erupting from his wife's remains. Am I clear?"

Jet nodded, and the two of them entered the Harper residence. Though the exterior of the house was modern, the interior was that of a homely cottage. The kitchen had been decked out in timber. Polished birch floors accentuated the maple cabinets, which were lined with dozens and dozens of tins and jars. Colin Harper was sitting at the kitchen counter, a large slab of polished wood. In one hand he nursed a mug full of cold coffee. The other hand covered his eyes as he leaned on his elbow. Mercifully, the kitchen was far enough away from the backyard that the commotion with the serpents had gone unnoticed. Even if Mr. Harper could have heard it, he was in a state of shock. Not to mention that the police officer stationed at the doorway would have kept him confined to the kitchen. Detective Porter entered first, tenderly approaching the counter.

"Excuse me Mr. Harper? It's Detective Porter again. I have someone who would like to speak with you for a moment if that's alright?"

Jet stepped alongside Kelly, and bowed his head. "I'm sorry for your loss, sir. But your wife was a witch wasn't she?"

"Mr. Lincoln!" Kelly barked with disdain.

Harper raised his head to look at Jet. His eyes wet, bleary, and bloodshot. "That... that is correct. How did you know?"

Lincoln pointed about the kitchen. "There are more herbs and spices on those shelves than the Colonel's secret recipe." Jet shrugged at Kelly to negate her scowl. "That and all the candles, and the mortar and pestle on the bench over there. It was an educated guess." Of course, he was careful not to mention seeing the burned tissue of Emily's third eye.

"True enough, I suppose," said Harper. "It was her hobby. She would boil her concoctions, and cast her spells of luck and fortune..." His eyes began to well again. "I can't say they didn't work. We led a blessed life. Great house, great jobs. We were so happy."

"I'm so sorry, Mr. Harper," said Kelly as Colin lapsed into a burst of sobbing. "This may be hard, but I really do need to ask. Do you know anyone who would wish to do harm to your wife in her capacity as a witch?"

Colin wiped his eyes and stiffened a little as he considered the question. "No. Of course not. Who would ever want to harm my Emily? She got on famously with everybody. Are you saying she did something wrong?"

"Goodness no. She didn't do anything wrong. We just have to cover all the angles. Someone attacked her in your yard. Possibly someone she knew."

"I... I guess I understand." Harper rose from his stool and

fumbled amongst some papers at the end of the counter. He uncovered a small red pocketbook and slid it towards the detective. "Here, this may be of some help. Emily was part of a club. Call themselves Mothers of Earth. All the members dabble as witches, I think. That's her phone book. They all share spells and whatnot."

Kelly took possession of the notebook. "Thank you, Mr. Harper. I will return this soon."

He nodded and returned to his seat as Jet and Kelly took their leave.

"We'll find whoever did this," said Jet. But Harper just stared vacantly at the kitchen counter.

***

"Thank you for ditching Rollins." Jet shifted in the soft leather passenger seat of Detective Porter's unmarked cruiser.

"I didn't ditch him. I had him accompany the body in case something else extraordinary happens en route to the morgue." Kelly drove south along San Rafael Avenue. "Who are we seeing first?"

"Ah, Melanie King. Just looking through the list, there are five members of the Mothers of Earth who live here in Mount Washington. It's funny that Louise Huebner isn't listed as a member in this book."

"Who?"

"Seriously? She's the only officially recognized witch in the country. Maybe even in the world. And she lives in Mount Washington, too."

"So what kind of power do these witches have?"

"I guess it's hard to say. White witches like these are all about positivity. Their spells and practices are subtle. They give and get in return. The darker and more powerful witches are blunt. They just take. I've seen white witches write a spell on a piece of paper, and then set it to flame on a ceremonial candle to cast a spell. They boil scented oils, speak poetic incantations, and burn incense. Power like we saw tonight, that requires sacrifice. Sacrifice of the mind, soul, or body. Or worse."

"Blood." Kelly turned onto Etta Street.

Jet nodded grimly. "If Mrs. Harper's murder was part of a ritual designed to take her power, we could see a lot worse than snakes tonight. The pythons were a warning shot."

"You're not chickening out on me now, are you?" Kelly asked with a smirk.

Jet didn't reply, just smiled as they pulled up outside a two-story villa at the end of the street. As Jet exited the vehicle, he noticed graffiti on one of the four palm trees lining the opposite side of the road. "What do you make of that?"

Kelly regarded the scrawl briefly. The design was a circle with a bullet hole in its center. "That's one thing that bothers me about L.A. Gangs tagging the trees. It's bad enough what we do to each other at times, but when mother nature is defiled... it's an indictment on humanity."

"Wow," said Jet. "Yes... there's that. But that symbol to me, looks like it's meant to ward off the evil eye. There is a large Hispanic presence in these parts. This could be a sign that they've been noticing a lot of bad luck lately. A lot of them still believe in it, though not many will talk about it out of fear. I spotted at least four more of these tags on the way here."

"I guess it means we're on the right track. Come on, let's go."

Jet and Kelly ascended the concrete stairs to Ms. Melanie King's front door.

"Emily is dead? Oh my god. This can't be true." Melanie steadied herself by placing one hand on the back of her black leather sofa. Her other hand pressed to her heart. "She was the best of us. So loved."

Melanie King was a heavy set woman in her late forties with dark curly hair, a little over dressed for someone who was home by herself. She wore expensive jewelry, and proudly displayed priceless paintings and vases throughout the house.

"I'm sorry Ms. King, but we need to know if you knew anybody who could have done this."

"Oh no. Nobody I know. Surely not one of the Mothers of Earth. I mean, the only one of the Mothers to even have *words* with Emily was Hannah Britten. And she would never do such a thing."

"Have words?" asked Jet. "What kind of words?"

"Oh goodness, it was nothing really. Hannah felt a little upset when Emily rejected her submission to the collected 'Mothers: Great Book of Spells.' A storm in a teacup. Though Hannah *is* a little young and inexperienced."

Jet shot Kelly a worried look, and she saw the goose flesh raise on his arms.

"She may have flown off the handle this one time, but she's certainly not a murd..."

Melanie did not get to finish her sentence. All that she could manage were hocking noises and gurgles, appearing to choke on thin air. Her face went from pink to blue, then purple. Jet rushed to slap her on the back in an attempt to dislodge the apparent blockage.

"What's happening?" Kelly took King's left arm and tried to help keep her upright.

Before Jet could answer, Melanie arched backward, then violently bent forward with an almighty screech. The wail dispersed into burbles as a torrent of insects burst forth from her mouth. Beetles, centipedes, millipedes, crickets, all fell to the floor in waves, black shelled and glistening with bile. The room filled with the sound of exoskeletons clicking against each other as the bug avalanche crashed to the carpet, battling to disperse. Melanie's eyes watered heavily, and rolled back into her head as she fought to retain consciousness. Kelly struggled to keep Melanie from falling face first into asphyxiation, and tried equally as hard not to think about the bugs she could feel crunching under her shoes as she continually repositioned herself. Just when the two women were about to give, the insect flow came to a halt. Melanie slumped to her knees and gasped for air, stark in contrast to the proud sense of propriety she had held herself in moments prior. Around her lay a smattering of squashed insects on the expensive-looking rug. The remaining survivors scuttled away to safety, disappearing under furniture and behind curtains until they were all out of sight. Jet and Kelly helped Melanie sit on the sofa. Still breathing heavily, she began to sweat profusely.

"My god, are you okay?"

Melanie nodded and brought a hand flat to her chest. She was now able to take deep breaths through her nose, and exhale via her mouth.

"I think so." She croaked in a whisper. "Water!"

Jet absconded to the kitchen to fetch a glass of water, while Detective Porter sat next to King on the sofa to console her.

"I think we need to pay Hannah Britten a visit."

Kelly had begun to notice more circular spray tags as she drove through the streets. Though the sun had set while they were occupied with Ms. King, the graffiti glowed in the dusk. She thought it odd she hadn't noticed them before, but, now that she was alert, they appeared to pop up everywhere.

"It makes sense that the killer would be here in Mount Washington," said Jet. "Proximity plays a part in the strength of one's magick. The closer you are to the target of your spell, the more powerful the result."

"Much like a bullet."

"Yes, exactly."

Jet trailed off as Kelly slowed to take the left turn into Museum Drive. He watched as the ghost of an elderly lady

shuffled toward her mailbox at the house on the corner. She
had died in her bathrobe and slippers. The spectral woman
noticed the approaching vehicle, making eye contact with
Jet. Her eyes widened, and her face distorted as she pointed a
crooked finger at him. She hobbled in an attempt to chase the
passing car, but fell into a tumbling heap upon the road. Jet
closed his eyes and took a deep breath.

"You okay?"

"Don't tell me, I look like I've just seen a ghost." Jet gave her a
tired smile "Sunnyhill Drive is just around this corner."

They shared a moment of comfortable silence as Kelly
cruised up the steady incline of Sunnyhill Drive. That was
until Jet noticed the smoke.

"Holy sh..."

The pair stared open mouthed through the windshield as
they arrived at the Britten residence. The house was on fire.
Kelly brought the car to a halt.

The Spanish mansion belched towering flames from every
window. Overhanging trees had caught, and thick black
smoke bellowed into the sky. Flakes of paint peeled from the
rendered exterior and wafted in the slight breeze. Jet and Kelly
emerged from the car, swatting at the falling ash. There was
no doubt about it, they were too late. All they could do was
stare in silence for the next few minutes.

"Wait," said Jet. "You notice something? There's no heat in
this fire. Even from this distance we should be uncomfortably
hot right now."

Detective Porter processed the information for a moment
before nodding in agreement.

"I guess I've seen stranger things tonight. Let's go."

The two of them ran up the steps toward the front door,
stopping near the closest window. Fire roared from within
the frame, licking the eaves and blackening the wall with
soot. Gingerly, Jet reached out and tested the flames with his

fingers.

"It's just an illusion," he said. "A damn good one."

Kelly drew her firearm and approached the entrance. "You think you can kick the door open for me?"

Jet regarded the solid oak door with trepidation. "I dunno." Almost as an afterthought, he reached for the doorknob. A quarter turn brought forth a deep clunking sound from within the lock. It was open. Jet regarded the handle with surprise, then looked at Kelly for approval. Her game face at the ready, Detective Porter nodded and stormed through the front door.

"LAPD!"

The threshold was clear. All four internal doors were closed. Muffled noises of activity emanated from the door to the right, accompanied by faint moans of pain. Kelly responded swiftly. She covered the distance to the door in three strides, then paused to take a steadying breath. Unleashing her mightiest kick, the detective broke through the door to the next room. "LAPD! Nobody move." She screamed with adrenaline-laced authority. "What the hell?"

Even with all her experience, Detective Porter was ill-prepared for the scene in that room. From his safe distance behind, Jet peeked around the door, and abruptly spurted a short laugh through closed lips. The expansive sitting room was heavily populated with people. Some seated on canvas folding chairs confined to the far right corner. Some standing and manning various equipment, including lights, cameras, and boom microphones. The remaining civilians were completely naked. Closest to the detective were two men, each afflicted with what could only be described as painfully heightened states of arousal. Behind the men were another four naked women. All eyes had been on the couple fornicating upon a classy chaise lounge to the left side of the room. Evidently the moans of pain they had heard through the door had actually been those of passion. Detective Porter had burst onto the set of a porn shoot.

"Hey, point that thing some place else," said the nearest male talent, nervously eying the detective's outstretched weapon.

"I could say the same thing about you, buddy," said Jet with a school-boyish grin.

"Cut. Cut. Cut! What's going on here?" The director emerged from the congregation of folding chairs and marched up to Kelly.

"Uh, Detective Porter LAPD." The flustered detective holstered her handgun. "I think there's been some kind of mistake."

A little more at ease now, the director leaned back and regarded Kelly with an artistic eye. "Are you sure? Because what you did there, with the entrance, that was dead sexy."

"What? Sir. No! I... Can I please speak to Hannah Britten? Is she here?"

The director smiled and nodded. "Sure." Then he turned and beckoned to a petite blonde standing behind one of the cameramen.

Hannah made her way toward them, tightly adjusting the lilac silk bathrobe she had hastily thrown on. "Can I help you?"

Kelly led Hannah and Jet back into the foyer. Jet took a lingering farewell glance around the room as he departed the scene. "I'm sorry, Miss Britten, We're here to ask you a few questions about the death of Emily Harper."

"The what?" Tears instantly welled in her eyes. "No. Please, tell me it's not true. Em is like a mother to me." With that, she broke down crying.

Jet immediately came to her aid, putting his arms around her for comfort. Kelly glared at him. Jet returned the look with a wide eyed "What am I supposed to do?" look of his own.

"Listen, Hannah," said Kelly. "I'm sorry to have been the one to break the news to you, but I need to ask about an argument you had with Mrs. Harper."

Hannah snapped out of her sobbing with a look of surprise. "Argument? Me and Em? We've never had an argument. I've been her protégé going on six years now. We have the best relationship I've ever had with anyone, ever! The only person that had issues with Em was that grouchy old Melanie King bitch."

Kelly and Jet exchanged a glance.

"She was always trying to undermine Em, and, boy, did she kick up a stink when Em rejected her spells for the 'Great Book.' She's the one you want to look at for this. She's the most selfish, hard-nosed, belligerent woman I know, and the Mothers of Earth should have no place for an old cow like that."

"Thank you, Hannah," said Kelly. "I'm so sorry for your loss."

Jet and Detective Porter left Hannah weeping on the stoop.

"Well, what do you know?" Jet eyed the now-pristine exterior of the mansion. "No more fire."

Kelly frowned. "I'm beginning to dislike magick with extreme prejudice."

"I'll bet the illusion was dropped as soon as we went inside. We're being watched again."

"We've been had," said Kelly. "King led us here by our noses."

"You have to admit, conjuring up a non-fatal bug spewing spell was a nice touch." Jet approached the passenger side of the car.

Kelly paused. "Something's not right. She must have known Hannah would immediately contradict her story. Is she simple minded? Or are we being played again?"

"We're not being watched," said Jet, opening the car door. "King just needed us gone long enough to work up something nasty for our return."

"Perhaps we should be heading back so we can work up

something nasty of our own."

Jet and Kelly entered the vehicle.

"Things could have been worse," said Jet, looking back up the stairs to see Hannah retreat inside. "King could have been the one shooting porn when we arrived at her place." He laughed heartily to himself. "I love L.A."

The pair fastened their seat belts. Jet continued to chuckle as the car accelerated back down Sunnyhill Drive.

Detective Porter leaned beside the front door of Melanie King's house, gun raised and braced with her free hand. Taking a last glance into the Los Angeles night sky, she took a deep breath and nodded to Jet. At the signal, Jet booted the door open with a satisfying crack. Kelly darted inside, moving with precision and scanning the room with her weapon. Jet took his backpack upon his shoulder, and cautiously followed her lead. All the lights inside the house were off, not a sound to be heard. Kelly skipped stealthily from room to room, her footsteps fast and delicate and her resolve sure and steady.

With the ground level clear, Jet followed Kelly as she ascended the carpeted staircase in the vestibule. Jet took pause to look over his shoulder every few feet. Each of the first three doors they encountered upstairs were closed. The fourth lay wide open, and candlelight from within cast a faint glow upon the hall carpet. As they crept closer, whispering became audible. Though the words were unclear, the sentences were punctuated with spite. Even as the speaker's breath exhausted, the words continued unbroken with the intake of air. Kelly paused at the door. She turned to regard Jet, her eyes studying his to ensure he was ready. Jet returned a single nod and followed as she spun into the room.

Melanie King sat cross-legged within a red pentacle painted on the hardwood floor. At the five points where the pentagram touched the outer circle were five thick, red candles. Laid neatly on the floor in front of her were her witches' tools. Her athame — an iron dagger with runes carved into the black handle. A pewter chalice which could have contained either red wine or blood, impossible to discern in the low light, and a black thurible which burned fragrant oil acting as a cauldron. So entranced was Melanie as she whispered, her eyes remained closed as the intruders approached.

"LAPD." Detective Porter spoke slowly, her weapon aimed squarely at King's third eye. "Lie face down on the floor, and keep your hands where I can see them."

Melanie, still reciting incantation, opened her eyes and stared at Kelly with indignation.

"I repeat. Lie face down on the floor and keep your hands where I can see them, or I will shoot."

Though her whispering had grown in volume, Melanie remained unmoved.

"This is your *last* warning. Kiss the fucking floor right now, or I'll blow your goddamned head off."

Jet looked at Kelly with astonishment, yet Melanie did not move an inch. The only evidence she had acknowledged the detective's demands was that she began chanting at a yell.

"I have an idea," said Jet. "Whatever she's working, it requires all her concentration. In fact, if she does break the ritual, whatever she has planned for us will probably turn on her."

King shifted her glance nervously to Jet.

"If you shoot her, and she survives, she's still going to be able to use her dirty magick."

Her voice wavering, Melanie's face grew red as a bead of sweat rolled by her right eye.

"And if you execute her, well that just looks bad for you." Jet looked Melanie up and down, before returning his attention to Kelly. "If I told you I could finish this without laying a hand on her, would you let me?"

Kelly considered her options thoughtfully. Her firearm remained trained at Melanie's head. She bit her lower lip, then turned her face to Jet. With a serious brow, she looked him squarely in the eye. "Do it."

Jet rubbed his chin. Retrieving a pen and notepad from his pack, he wrote two words, then tore the page from the pad. Melanie's efforts were beginning to come to fruition. The ghostly form of a daemon appeared, rising through the floorboards behind her. It twitched in torment, unimpressed that it had been summoned. Its eyes flashed yellow, and, realizing it was imprisoned within the pentacle, bore its fangs at the summoner. Sensing the vile rage from the apparition, Melanie delivered her incantation with a more authoritative tone. Speaking plainly now, she issued her commands to the daemon.

"Daemon Samael. I evoke thee. Cast the mortals known as Jet Lincoln and Detective Porter from this Earth."

The daemon gnashed its jaws and snarled. It flinched as though lashed by an unseen bullwhip. Jet stepped towards the pentacle and produced the notebook page, displaying it so that Melanie could read the words. Her eyes widened. She shook her head in fear and repeated her command.

"Daemon Samael! I evoke thee. Cast the mortals known as Jet Lincoln and Detective Porter from this Earth!"

Jet crouched at the edge of the pentacle. He raised the paper to the closest candle flame. The paper ignited, burning fast as if laced with sulfur. The resultant smoke drifted within the pentacle. The daemon lifted its nose to the air, sniffing the new scent and flashing its eyes in excitement. Tears welled in Melanie's eyes as she chanted her command for the third and binding time.

"Daemon Samael. I evoke thee. Cast the mortals known as..."

Her voice transitioned into a blood curdling shriek. Under its new orders, the daemon Samael gripped Melanie by the throat, and sank its fangs into the crown of her head. Much as she throttled, Melanie was held fast. Even in its ghostly form, the daemon's grip was vice-like. With one last guttural scream, Melanie's whole body clenched. She then fell completely limp as her eyes rolled back in her head. Tears streamed down her cheeks as her bowels evacuated. She would use magick for harm no more.

The daemon released its grip on the husk of Melanie's body and withdrew its long, snaky tongue. Glancing menacingly at the onlookers, the daemon spoke. "I know your names now."

With a final flash of yellow eyes, Samael dissolved into thin air.

"What the hell happened?" Detective Porter holstered her weapon.

"Oh yeah, I forgot. You couldn't see it, could you?"

"See what?"

"She summoned a daemon. Right there. I had it eat her brain."

"You what? It killed her? What the fuck did you write on that paper?"

"She's not dead. At least not biologically. I wrote two words. 'Lobotomize me.'"

"Holy shit," said Kelly, feeling Melanie's carotid artery for a pulse. "That was the first thing you thought to do? Jesus Christ."

"Under the circumstances, I figured the only way we could stop her was with her own weapon of choice."

Kelly looked up at Jet. "Dirty magick." She had mixed feelings about the outcome. The detective side of her knew that what Jet did wasn't kosher. But, as she observed King in her vegetative state, Kelly Porter could accept that the punishment was just. Maybe not for Colin Harper or Hannah Britten, but Melanie King had gotten no less than what she deserved.

"Are you okay?" Jet asked, almost apologetically.

"Yes, I'm fine. It's just..." Kelly stood up and wiped strands of hair from her face. "I don't get it."

"You don't get what? The magick?"

"No I get the magick, I just don't get why she did what she did? Why she felt she had to kill Emily Harper? Why she wasn't content with the abilities she had as a witch? Why she couldn't just move on with her life?"

"I think the answer you're looking for is more." Jet scratched the back of his head and gestured toward the window. "This is Los Angeles, honey. What does anyone here want? More. More power, more respect, more money, more attention, more friends on Facebook, more cheese on their freaking pizza. Hannah said it earlier. Melanie was the most selfish person she had met. I mean, take a look around. Everywhere, every day, all you see is unadulterated, insatiable lust for more. Some people are willing to sell their integrity or their dignity for it. Some sell their bodies for it Other people... people like Melanie, they'll even sell their soul."

"Perhaps, but you and I aren't like that. I'm not prepared to give up on an entire city just because of the selfish people in it."

"I guess if we knew what made people do stupid things, you'd be out of a job."

Kelly looked out the window at the lights of the L.A. skyline. She felt herself sigh. "At least we can agree on that."

THE WINDS

By Paul K. Ellis

There was a rainbow in the gutter. The colors shimmied and swayed, sparkling in the early morning. It was a trick of the light, those vibrant hues, but pretty nonetheless. Of course, if the oil hadn't been there, it would have been just plain old dirty water running down the street from an open hydrant. Truth be told, I would have preferred that. I hate oily water. But that was L.A. for you, looking pretty on the surface.

I could hear the shrieks of kids playing in the spray. It sounded odd given the circumstances. I stepped over the curb and onto lifeless grass. It was hot out. Hot and dry. The type of weather that brought out the worst in folk.

It certainly brought out the worst for my old pal Bobby Tremain, what with him being a bloody mess dead on the yard and all.

"Jackie," Patrick O'Connell called from the doorway of the prefab rancher, one of dozens exactly like it in the neighborhood, a product of the post-war housing boom.

I hate being called Jackie.

He waved me closer.

I stepped around what was left of Bobby and up to the stoop. "Lieutenant," I nodded.

He mopped the back of his neck with his handkerchief. "What do you make of this?" He motioned to the yard with his free hand.

The front window had been blown out and scattered across the ground, Bobby smack dab in the middle of the wreckage.

"Looks like he was shot out of a cannon," I said.

"Yeah," O'Connell said, then went into the house. "You should see it from here." His voice wavered on the heat.

I hesitated. I really didn't want to follow him, but I held my breath and stepped inside.

It was hotter and nastier. Wood paneling splintered, chairs broken, and a desk upended in the middle of the room. There was a radio smashed on the floor, its insides, like Bobby's, strewn about in an arc. It smelled of copper in the close heat of the darkened interior, blood everywhere.

The destruction fanned away from a central point in front of what had been a cheap pine bookcase. The blackened wood frame was in a direct line with the front window. The lieutenant stood beside the wreckage fanning himself with his hat. I put my hands in my pockets and strode over to him.

"What was your old buddy into, Dupre?" he said, softly.

I shrugged. "Haven't seen him in a couple of years. You?"

"Not since he left Kathleen," he said, an edge in his voice cutting into the conversation. He glanced at me and softened. "Look, I know it's been hard on you since the new ADA's decision came down, and I know you're having trouble making ends meet, so you're taking some 'odd' cases, but this," he trailed off, waving his hat about, taking in the whole room. "Jesus, this ain't none of your swamp voodoo, is it?"

"Cajun," I said, shaking my head. "It's hot enough for it, though."

"God!" he nodded, mopping his head again. "Santa Anas. They slice through you like shark's teeth and suck the life out." He cocked his head to one side, listening. "You like that guy?"

"Lieutenant?" I asked. I think the heat was getting to him. Or it might have been his son-in-law eviscerated on the lawn. I know that was getting to me.

"That Shark Guy." He saw my frown. "Oh the shark, yeah, has such teeth, yeah," he sang. Tried to anyway.

"Bobby Darin?" I asked.

He snapped his fingers. "That's the guy! Do you like him?"

"Nah," I said, tapping out a cigarette. "I prefer Sinatra."

"Me too," he said. "The wife wants to go see Shark Guy in Vegas. Wants to take Kathleen."

I lit my cigarette. Kathleen. The daughter. The one married to my buddy I hadn't seen in two years or more. I stared at the floor. I really wanted to leave, but I didn't want to see Bobby sprawled on the lawn again. So I stayed in the living room with a guy I couldn't stand, smelling stale smoke and charred wood.

My gaze flickered across the debris and caught on a flash of light. I squatted and plucked a piece of partially burned paper from the ashes. It felt like stationary, expensive stationary. The letterhead was swanky, embossed with stylized antlers. It read "The Hunt Kennels, Matilda Night proprietor. Exotic Breeds Our Specialty." It listed an address out in Topanga Canyon.

"Whatcha got, Jackie?" O'Connell asked, holding out his hand.

I suppressed a wince and passed him the remnant. "Looks like some sort of letter, Lou," I offered.

He took it and read it, then frowned. "What was that boy into? He ain't got no dog." He crumpled the paper into his fist.

"Could've been a case," I offered.

"Could've been his mistress," he barked. The outburst seemed to take all the life out of him. He sighed, mopping his eyes with his handkerchief. "It don't make no sense. Gotta be the Santa Anas."

I patted him awkwardly on the shoulder, not knowing what else to do. He was right about one thing though - the Santa Anas had something to do with this, sucking all the life out of everything.

***

North Rampart boasted a lot of new construction: warehouses, offices, and the like. My tired old building wasn't one of them. To get to my office, you went up a creaky flight of steps and down a dingy, dusty hallway. The classiest thing about it was the frosted glass on the door. One of my clients is a painter, the sign his payment. "Jack Dupre, Investigations," in bold, black lettering with a gilded drop shadow centered on the glass. Snazzy. The doorknob rocked and the door rattled in the frame, but that glass looked good.

It's Los Angeles. If the pretty looks pretty enough, maybe you won't see the decay.

My one concession to getting canned by the LAPD had been the purchase of a brand new black-on-chrome 1959 Dodge Coronet. I got it from the same guy who sold them to the department. Even had him set it up as a police special. I did spring for the dual carbs package, though.

My department rep told me that purchase convinced the shoo-flies I was on the take. I told him they had measured me for a frame well before I bought it. He disagreed. We didn't get along. Still, when I parked that car in front of my building, all the neighborhood punks faded into the shadows. Eventually they'd twig to the fact I wasn't on the job anymore. Until then, they'd keep their distance rather than risk a ride up to Hollywood Hills.

I parked my car in front the building and walked up a flight. She waited for me under a bare light bulb in the hall and she looked as faded as the linoleum. I smelled orchids.

I hate orchids.

"Kathleen," I nodded.

"Jacques," she said in a trembling, breathy voice. She liked to use my given name. It gave me the willies.

I unlocked the door and ushered her in. I didn't have an anteroom. I counted myself lucky to have an office. The last skip trace I had run for the landlord only covered me until the end of next month.

She rubbed up against me as she entered and sat slowly in the hard wooden chair opposite my desk. Despite that brief contact, she never let anyone get too close. What Bobby had seen in her beat me. He helped her out of a jam once and she never left. From where I stood, she was a clingy bag full of crazy.

"Jacques," she said after I sat down in my cracked, leather chair. Her voice wasn't unpleasant, but grated all the same. "Jacques, I need your help. Someone is following me!"

"Oh, for the love of Mike, Kathleen, it's Jack! Call me Jack! And no, I'm not going to help you!"

"But, why?" She wailed, dabbing her eyes with a hastily produced handkerchief. "He was your friend!"

"You drove a wedge between us, didn't you?" I replied, leaning back in my chair. The tired springs groaned.

"I never meant to!"

"You pulled a gun on me! And your father got me fired," I said. Suddenly it hit me and I snapped the chair upright with a bang. "Now, why do I think you had something to do with that?"

She looked horrified and hid behind her handkerchief. "I don't know what you mean!"

I stood up. "I mean, I haven't spoken to your father in over six months and I haven't heard from you in well over two years. Suddenly, both of you want to talk to me? Today?" I rounded the desk and snatched her out of her chair. The floral stench of orchids was overpowering. "What gives, Kathleen? What are you two setting me up for now?"

"Jacques ... Jack!" She gulped, nervously playing with the silver chain of her necklace. "Please!"

"Great act," I sneered. "Now, hit the road!"

I tried to shove her out of the office. I wasn't particularly gentle. She clung to my arm like a tick, shattering a couple of her lacquered nails in the process. Did wonders for my arm too. The sudden pain cleared the fog of rage. Her eyes were wide with fear, but it wasn't fear of me.

"I know why you were fired," she said, clinging to me, her eyes wide. Her hold burned like fire. I sat her down in the chair - hard - then pried myself free of her grip. I had a feeling I was going to regret this.

"I'm listening," I said, reseating myself behind the desk. I needed the barrier. The crazy broad had drawn blood.

She pulled the handkerchief gag again, dabbing her eyes and hyperventilating behind the cloth. Finally, she calmed down.

"Bobby never made it through the academy," she began.

"Yeah, I know," I said with as little feeling as I could. "I was there, remember? He was a gumshoe. Let's move this along before I miss lunch."

He washed out because of her constant harping. He wound up working as a peeper for gossip rags and divorce lawyers. So, pretty much my present existence.

She looked like she wanted to protest, but thought better of it, and composed herself in a way that reminded me of how she used to look right before she lied. I was good; I didn't roll my eyes.

"Sister, let's cut to what you know about my being fired," I said. "Word was Bobby moved out of your house and into that dump about six weeks ago. He was supposedly done with you. But he'd said that before, then gone running back. I haven't seen or spoken to him since you pulled that .38 on me and threw me out of his house."

She colored slightly at this, but said nothing.

"Last chance," I said.

"Bobby was cheating on me," she blurted. "He would go on and on about this case and how he needed your help, but he was spending all his time with *her*."

Ring-a-ding-ding! "Her? Who her?" I found this hard to believe. Bobby had walked through fire for Kathleen. He'd certainly cut me loose fast enough.

"Maddie something," she said.

"Matilda Night?" I ventured.

She got red in the face, her mouth twisting into a sneer. "I knew it! I knew you were helping him cover it up! You told him to move out and shack up with that whore!" She leaned across the desk to slap me. I blocked her swing and shoved her back into her chair hard enough it tipped back on two legs. I pulled my .45 out of its drawer and placed it on the desktop. She settled down immediately, her eyes huge.

"Enough, Kathleen!" I said. "I think I've got it figured. Your constant paranoia finally drove Bobby out. You needed someone to blame, so you chose me. You ran to Daddy and worked on him until he fired me. All so you could avoid looking in the mirror and seeing the real cause. You need to leave, now!" I placed my hand on the weapon. The cold steel shocked me. I was unsure why I had drawn it.

"Jack, please, they will get me!"

"Let 'em," I said without heat. I didn't really want to pick the gun up, but something told me to keep my hand right where it was.

"Jack," she begged. "I didn't go to my father. I came to you. He can't help me, because he'll give me over to them! Please Jack! Please! I have proof he falsified evidence against you in the corruption case. Please don't let him take me to them!"

She was on her knees, crying. Pathetic! Still, a chance to clear my name? It was almost too good to be true. Almost.

I knew I was going to regret this.

"Who's after you, Kathleen?" I asked.

"I don't know," she sobbed. "But, I see them every time I look away. I can feel their unclean gaze on me!"

Swell. Had she become a hop head? Her dress was short

sleeved and I couldn't see any track marks, but arms weren't the only place for a needle.

"Have you got anyone you can stay with?"

"No," she said between hiccups. "Bobby was my whole world!"

This time I did roll my eyes. Of course she had no other friends. Then again, neither did I anymore.

"Fine, you'll stay at my place. I'll stay here. I'll take care of your problem and you'll give me the evidence on your father. How does that sound to you?"

It sounded horrible to me. That harpy in my apartment was almost more than I could bear. It did fill me with an odd joy because my mattress was second hand.

She twisted her face into another horrible visage and tried to hug me. I realized that grimace was her smile.

"Let's keep this professional," I said. "I'll take you there and you're not to leave or call anyone, otherwise the deal is off. Oh, and I'll need a retainer."

Her faced relaxed into cold lines. "How much?"

"Just information. Who'd your old man climb into bed with in order to set the frame on me?"

"Hardwick," she said. "Judge Hardwick."

Swell. Just swell. L.A.'s hanging judge. A hot wind sliced through the opened window, stirring up dust.

I like driving my car. I like the idea that I can get away. The throaty roar of 345 horses was soothing and gave me enough speed to cool the hot air rushing in my windows. I had a troll on my doorstep and a dead buddy on my conscience. I needed some soothing.

The drive out Topanga Canyon to The Hunt Kennels was long enough for me to unwind a bit and short enough to enjoy without my legs cramping up. The business and the proprietor had come up too often to be coincidence.

I pulled into the crushed gravel drive and got an immediate sense of money. Everything was green and landscaped. I could smell the cash.

When I pulled up to the office, my suspicions were confirmed. Sitting out front was a dark maroon 1939 Bugatti 57C Cabriolet. I parked well away from it. It hurt just to look at it, and I didn't want my aching eyes to scratch the finish.

I opened the office door and walked into the blessed relief of air conditioning. What a racket! Babysitting rich people's mutts! There was no bell on the door, but that didn't stop a leggy brunette from eyeing me up and down. She must have liked what she saw because she smiled and walked right up to me.

"Matilda Night," she said extending her hand. "Owner and operator. Everybody calls me Maddie." She smelled faintly of *galant de nuit*, the night blooming jasmine of the bayou.

"Jack Dupre," I replied and reached out to shake her hand.

When our fingers met, I got an old feeling; a feeling from home when my GrandMama was "conjuring." Nearest thing I can liken it to is that sense you get when the short hairs on the back of your neck stand up, you get goose bumps, and you stick a fork in a 120 volt outlet all at once. I tried to not jerk my hand away. She was dangerous; warm and inviting, but dangerous.

"Interesting," she said, her smile growing wider and her eyes darker. She lingered over the contact before sliding her hand free. "Jack, you don't strike me as a dog person."

"I had a beagle once. Best hunting dog in Bayou Pierre," I said, trying my crooked smile charm.

"What happened?"

"I outlived him."

"More's the pity," she replied, her dark eyes twinkling with laughter. "I like hunting. What can I do for you, Jack?"

There was no way Bobby was sleeping with her. She was as

much out of his league as the Bugatti was out of mine.

"Well ma'am, I would appreciate it if you could tell me what your relationship was with Bobby Tremain."

Her smile slipped. "Was?" she asked. I nodded. She sat on a desktop and took a breath. The laughter left her face. "I asked Mr. Tremain to recover a family heirloom. He had contacted me last week and left a message that he found the item. However, I have not been able to reach him. What happened?"

"The police are still investigating, ma'am," I replied.

"Maddie," she said, a small smile hinting at the corners of her mouth. "I let you get away with ma'am last time due to the news." She looked thoughtful. "Bayou Pierre, Dupre." She ticked off on her fingers. "Jacques Dupre? Mister Tremain said he would be contacting you. He said you would have invaluable insight into the recovery." She rubbed her hand and looked up at me under long lashes. "I'd say he was right," she said in a low voice. "You are a hunter."

Man alive! That woman was anything but helpless. "That being the case, what can you tell me?"

I got that feeling again, only this time it wasn't warm and inviting. This danger was furtive and nasty, seeming to skitter just outside the edge of my vision. Maddie sensed it too. She glared about the office until the feeling subsided. It left as abruptly as it came.

"I'm sorry," she said, with a shrug and a look that said "Don't ask." "There is very little I can tell you; it's not my heirloom. Until I contact the principal and get his permission, I am afraid you'll have to make do with what you have."

I handed her my card. "Well, if you can't tell me what's going on, can I at least use your phone?"

Her laughter wrapped me in that warm and inviting type of dangerous again. "Please, please do Jacques!" When she used my Christian name, I wanted to dare the danger. "I'll call you when I can." She hopped off the desk and pointed to the handset. "Let yourself out. I have to exercise my charges."

I watched her walk out of the office. She knew I was watching. I shook my head. She was trouble, but it was trouble I wouldn't mind. Right now, though, I had the other sort to check up on. I reached for the phone and dialed my number.

I pulled up in front of my apartment, but the boys in blue had beaten me there. The place was crawling with my old pals. I saw O'Connell through the windshield. He was holding his sobbing daughter and glaring at me. I could kiss the promise of any evidence from Kathleen goodbye.

This was not what I expected when I called to check on her. She answered in a panic. Someone was trying to break in. I told her to call her father and sit tight; help would be there in minutes. I didn't like doing that, but the LAPD was closer than me at that moment.

I got out of my car and walked over to O'Connell.

"Lou," I said with a nod. Kathleen's head snapped my direction. Her mascara had run. Unattractive didn't begin to cover it.

"Damn your eyes, Dupre," O'Connell spat. "First you ruin my daughter's happiness, then you try to shack up with her? Next chance I get, I'm running your sorry ass in on a morals charge!"

"Daddy!" Kathleen exclaimed, working her silver necklace in a fidget. "Please! I told you I was being followed! Jack thought this would be the last place anyone would look for me."

"Fat lotta good that did!" he roared. "And where were you, Dupre?"

"Working a case," I said. "But Lou, how did they know she was here? They had to have been following her. The question is how long?"

O'Connell's beet-red complexion paled. He looked at his

daughter. "Do you remember seeing anyone following you lately?"

"N-no," she said.

"How about when you went over to Bobby's?" I asked. "See anything suspicious?"

"In that neighborhood," she spat. "It was all suspicious! Him living in that ratty old house with nothing of value to take from it! Please! Every time I had to go and wring my money out of him I was suspicious - of him cheating on me!"

"That's enough, Kathleen," O'Connell interrupted. He grabbed her by the arm. She clung to my jacket.

"Daddy, I only feel safe here," she protested.

He grabbed her wrist and jerked her hand free. Her bracelet snapped, spilling charms onto the pavement.

"I'm taking you home under some real protection." He glared at me again. "Stay out of this Dupre or you'll be sorry!"

"I'm already sorry," I sighed, while he unceremoniously drug her back to his cruiser. My cop shop buddies had left. Seemed no one wanted to witness how far I had fallen.

My apartment was wrecked. O'Connell must have asked them to be extra destructive clearing the rooms. I sighed again and sat on my mostly clean laundry that had found its way to my sofa. Which was funny, since it started out in my closet. It would take most of the night to clean up this mess, but at least I would be able to sleep in my own bed. Alone. After I found the mattress. And the box springs. Shouldn't take long, as it was only a three room apartment.

I got that electric, itchy feeling again. It rushed up on me like a stalking Santa Ana. Someone was in my apartment! Trouble was, I couldn't quite see them. I'd look, but they wouldn't be there. I caught movement out of the corner of my eye, though. I placed myself in front of my open door and let my eyes drift, focusing on nothing. Something rushed past me on the left. I immediately backhanded on my right and connected with something. I know because I heard it crash into my reading corner, the darkest one, since my lamp had recently been broken.

"All right," I said walking towards it. "Time to drag this discussion into the light."

I felt a stinging sensation on my back. My "feeling" exploded like a rash. It was tingling and itching so hard I couldn't stand it. I spun around and saw a blurry nothing.

I let my eyes unfocus again and when the thing moved I punched it in the "head" so hard it slid behind my kitchen bar. I got stung again four or five times in rapid succession, each sting ratcheting my "feeling" up until I couldn't move.

I fell to the floor, a numbness rushing over me. My last fleeting thoughts before darkness overtook me were: I needed to close the door so the evening winds wouldn't make me miserable; and the punks doing this were short. Solid, but short. They had silver hair and wore red hats. Red Peter Pan style hats.

I remember nights on the bayou. The hot, heavy air barely stirred, but, when it did, it kissed the senses with a breath of jasmine. I could almost smell it. In fact, I could smell it delicately lingering on the warm and inviting evening air. I pried an eye open and saw Maddie's lovely face. I could really get lost in those dark eyes.

"Up and at 'em, sport," she said, smiling wickedly. My head was in her lap; her lap was on my laundry.

I sat up with a groan, and rubbed the back of my head.

"Long day?" she asked, amusement evident. When I didn't immediately answer, she caught my chin in her hand and looked me in the eyes, concerned. "Tell me."

"You wouldn't believe it," I said. "I don't believe it."

She let go of my chin. "Try me."

So, I told her, leaving out my "feeling." And the fact I couldn't really see the guys. You know, the crazy stuff.

"Odd," she said.

"Odd?" I said. "Let me tell you about odd. Odd is waking up in your lap." She frowned. "Nice, but odd." Sheesh, how does that shoe leather taste, Dupre? "How did you find out where I live?"

"Your business card. My principal, Mister Green, has agreed to speak with you. When I couldn't reach you on the phone, I came here. I found the door open and you on the floor. I put you on the sofa and sat with you until you woke up."

Well now, my *office* address is on the card. "You lifted me and put me on the sofa?" I asked.

She smiled again. "I'm stronger than I look!"

Clever too. I stood, and the room stayed steady. I took this as a good sign. "What does your boss want with me?"

"Dinner," she said. "This evening at the Brown Derby. You'll need to change in a hurry in order to make the reservation."

I whistled. "The Derby, huh? I'm impressed."

"He's a generous man."

"Well, I won't keep him waiting then," I said and picked my way to the bedroom. Maddie stayed on the sofa.

"Maid's day off?" She asked.

I found my monkey suit under the bed frame. "Yeah, I tend to let the place go so she feels needed."

Her laughter floated down the hall. Seemed to brighten the place up. I rescued the slightly worn tux. It would have to do. I started to change.

"So, when you found me unconscious, how come you didn't call the cops?"

"Bobby made us aware of your circumstances. He vouched for your innocence. I believed him. And, maid or not, this place has been tossed. I think you've had enough police attention for one day."

I could hear her smiling. I found my tux shirt and started to take off the one I was wearing. Something was caught in the cuff. "How long have you been here?"

"About an hour, or so," she said.

I untangled the cuff and a small, silver dart fell out onto the floor. Jeez, one of Kathleen's charms! That was all I needed. "That long? And you didn't call an ambulance?" I reached for the charm.

"No need," she said. "I've seen this sort of thing before, so I knew you'd come around."

I touched the charm just as she finished. My fingers went numb. The sort of numb that stings. I dropped the charm and the stinging stopped.

"Are you all right?" she asked. The scent of jasmine was so strong, I looked to see if she had come into the room. No such luck.

"I'm fine," I said grabbing a handkerchief, picking up the dart, and dropping it into an ash tray. "I had a little trouble with my cuff links. I worked it out."

"Good," she said. "You need to hurry. Our car will be here in a few minutes ."

I got dressed quickly, even doing the bow tie. I scooped up the handkerchief and carefully folded it around the charm, then stuffed the works into my jacket's front breast pocket. Stylish, that's me.

Maddie met me at the door.

"The car's here," she said, fussing with the tie.

We stepped out and I locked the door. The mess would have to wait. The hot winds swept the parking lot. It was shaping up to be an interesting evening.

Despite the tux, I didn't belong there. The Derby is out of my class. It's not out of Maddie's, though. I wanted to think I had a shot with her, but the reality was I knew better.

She walked in and introduced me to the maître' d. She

explained this was a private meeting and she had other affairs to oversee.

The head waiter, some pretentious snot whose name I immediately forgot, didn't care for me either. By the look on his face, the tux didn't fool him. He was sure I didn't belong. Regardless, he escorted me to a private room. He knocked on the door, opened it, and introduced me. He sniffed at me when I entered. He did close the door when he left, though. Nice guy.

Mister Green was a powerful man. I don't mean big; he was athletic, but of average size. He radiated power - power that had very little to do with politics, or money, or influence. It was raw, personal presence.

His silk tux put mine to shame and he sported a nice size emerald on the third finger of his left hand. His right hand was gloved. I was a little surprised when he reached out to shake my hand.

"Hunter Green. Bobby had only nice things to say about you."

I tried not to stare at the glove. It was gray leather, so light it looked silver. Tooled on the back of the hand was the same stylized crest of antlers I'd seen on the stationary. I knew guys who lost limbs or worse during the war. Too many of them. I knew better than to gawk. I shook his hand. It had all the life of a stick.

"Jack Dupre. Glad to finally meet you, Mister Green," I said, meeting his dark eyes.

"Hunter, please," he said. "I've taken the liberty of ordering us appetizers. I understand you have some questions."

"I have a few," I said. "And I'll apologize now for going over some of the same stuff I'm sure Bobby did." He motioned for me to sit, so I sat. "I didn't know the Derby had private rooms."

"They are good enough to provide this one for me," he said.

"My family holdings are extensive. In addition to owning a share of the Derby, we have a stake in most of the supplying vendors."

His accent was hard to place, but it seemed to have some Irish brogue buried in it, like Bobby had.

"Silent partner in Maddie's kennel?"

He smiled and rubbed the back of his gloved hand. "Very good, Jack. You don't mind if I call you Jack?" I shook my head. "I am the head of an international concern, that is true."

"And what was Bobby's role in this 'concern'?" I asked.

"Bobby was engaged in a private matter," he replied and leaned forward. "I asked Maddie to find someone to look into recovering family heirlooms stolen by the Nazis. She contracted Bobby. Bobby reported he located one of the missing items here in Los Angeles. He also believed you could help find the others. You two have history?"

I smiled tightly. "When we met, I was on fire." Green arched an eyebrow. "Long story. I was blown off the docks and into the water when the Japs attacked Pearl. I surfaced covered in flaming oil. Bobby pulled me out of the harbor and put me out with his bare hands so fast both of us only had second degree burns. Others had worse." I couldn't help it. I looked at his gloved hand.

He followed my eyes. "I believe I understand," he said.

Time to change the conversation. "How valuable is the heirloom Bobby said he had found?"

"It's priceless," Hunter said, spreading his hands.

Ring-a-ding-ding; priceless! I might not know what it looked like, but I knew who had it. "And how will I know it when I find it?"

"I take it this means you will take up Bobby's charge?"

"Yeah, I'll find the item. What am I looking for?" I asked. His response was as strange as everything else on this caper.

"This heirloom is likely a small silver charm fashioned into a stylized spear," he said.

I was good. I didn't pat my handkerchief pocket. Not once.

I had the prime rib. Green, excuse me, "Hunter" and I exchanged pleasantries, pretending to be social equals. That was nice. After dinner, Green had another commitment. He apologized, but he needed his car. I took a cab back to my apartment. The evening was hot, and the winds brought no relief. I thought about hopping in the Dodge, heading back to my office, and pulling the cot out of storage. At least I wouldn't wake up to the mess in the apartment.

Despite the domestic situation, I was feeling pretty good. I didn't realize it at the time, but my "feeling" had grown to numbing proportions over dinner with Green. I had become so accustomed to it, I didn't notice it until it was absent.

"All very strange, Green and Company with their fancy cars and antlers," I muttered under my breath, walking up to my door. The cause of my yakking could have been the long day I'd had, or the realization about who killed Bobby. Likely it was the 25-year-old single malt I'd had with dinner, though. And after. Yeah, it was probably the scotch. It fuddled my ears too, because I didn't hear the jamokes who came up from behind and sapped me. They hauled me into the alley like they were taking out the trash and dumped me on the ground, right into a puddle of dumpster juice. That cleared my head enough to really enjoy the beating they gave me. It was very professional. Blackjacks and boot heels in the gut, kidneys, and liver. Not a mark on my face and not a bone broken, but they got their point across. I'd stepped on someone's toes.

One fellow, the tall one giving the orders, had a voice like broken gravel. "Gumshoe," he said, kneeling down and slapping me on the cheek. "You still with us?"

I nodded, more to make him stop than in any agreement with him. I cracked open an eyelid. Gravel Voice was in silhouette, but I could see his silver-haired buddies in their red hats. My "dangerous-in-a-bad-way" feeling was cranking out enough voltage to set me shaking.

"Okay, peeper, here's the skinny; you need to back off. You hear me? Back off. There ain't nothing worth finding that's worth dying for, you understand?" I nodded. That seemed to satisfy him. "Good. I don't want to come back. You're in over your head, little fish. Swim away."

A couple of kicks underscored their point and they left. Eventually, I hauled myself upright and staggered to my apartment. The second hand tux was ruined. That smell would likely never come out. I tossed it on the floor. I showered, wincing as the spray hit bruises and tender areas. When the water ran cold, I got out and toweled off.

The nice glow from the single malt was gone. I shuffled into the kitchen and poured three fingers of the bourbon I kept stashed under the sink. I sipped and thought. I moved to the sofa, piled the clothes onto the floor, and sat. I finished the bourbon and placed the shot glass on the arm. I thought about it until the sun came up, adding its heat to ever-present wind.

I didn't understand the players. I needed some wisdom.

I picked up the phone. "Yeah, operator, I need to place a call to Bayou Pierre, Louisiana. No, I'll pay. I need to reach Ray's This 'N That." Ray's was a grocery on the tip of the bayou and the nearest place to my GrandMama's that had a phone. Given the time difference, Ray's should be open, unless he was fishing. Maybe Ray could find someone to track her down. The line clicked open.

"Boy, you get back behind dat counter. I done tole you dis call is fo' me." Her voice was muddled. It got clear in a hurry. "Whooo-wheeee, dat boy got a mad on, cher!" she crowed. "So Jacques, you tell your Bonne-Maman what your trouble is, yah?"

Oh yeah, she did that a lot. "GrandMama," I said, trilling the 'R'. "What are you doing at Ray's?"

"Your friend Bobby, he tole me you'd be a-calling," she said.

"Bobby's dead, GrandMama," I replied.

"I am what I am, cher. He tole me all da same. It's in your blood, child. It's da responsibility of da family," she chastised. "So, wat your problem is?"

I told her. Crazy wives, dark-eyed vixens, eccentric millionaires, guys in funny hats, and all.

"Take a care, cher," she said. "Dem Lords and Ladies. The Lutin. Dem Fae."

Clearly, she had been at the still.

"I has not been at da 'shine, boy!" her voice rang over the wire. "Dem real, real as da bruises on ya."

"Who said I was bruised?" I asked. It hit me as soon as the words left my mouth.

"Bobby," we both said in unison. I could hear her smiling.

"He a good boy, cher. Just ain't got no sense about women folk. Dats why y'all get along. You same!" she chuckled, then became serious. "You watch for da Nain Rouge, yah? And da one-eye. Dey bad gris-gris. You bind yo'self in a salt circle. And you come visit your poor ole Nannan soon, ya cher? I's got to go now, bye-bye." And, she hung up. Wouldn't do to call back. She would have just left in her pirogue.

Nain Rouge. Red Cap.

I had been played. I hate that feeling.

Time to get all parties on board. It was about six in the morning. I called O'Connell, then Maddie. O'Connell was suspicious and Maddie dubious, but they both agreed to meet me at Bobby's at eight in the evening. I had to hustle. I had errands to run: a bag of salt, aspirin, and bed.

The alarm woke me at six. I had fallen asleep in my bathrobe on the sofa. I awoke to the smell of my tux on the hot evening air. I had been marinating in the odor all day. I carefully removed the charm from the jacket pocket and dropped it into an ashtray. The handkerchief was ruined, so I stuffed it back into the pocket. I threw dignity and the tux to the winds and I took the smelly thing to the dumpster. I avoided the puddles this time. I turned the fans in the apartment on high and opened all the windows. If nothing else, I'd circulate the evening heat and blow the stink out.

Another shower and change of clothes later, I felt decidedly less smelly. Either that, or my nose had gone numb. I wrapped the charm in a fresh handkerchief, climbed into the Dodge, and headed over to Bobby's.

The blasted-out window was boarded up, but the front door had been left unlocked. I let myself in and waited for my guests to show.

O'Connell arrived first, about half an hour early. He didn't bring any backup with him. I was afraid of that. That's why I'd tucked my old .45 in my waistband. I shook out a cigarette and lit it, waiting for him to finish casing the street. He came through the door and wasted no time on pretense. He pointed his gun right at my head.

"Where's the evidence, you punk?" he snarled, walking into the front room.

"Calm down, Lou," I said. "I've got someone else coming and this case too complicated to go through twice."

"You invited someone else?" he screamed. "Who, you rat bastard? Are you trying to fit me for a frame? Fat chance! I'm bulletproof in this town!"

"Daddy!" Kathleen cried from the doorway. I was actually glad to see her. For a moment, I was afraid that he'd left her at home.

"Get back in the car, Kathleen," he barked.

"Daddy, please. I'm sure Jacques can be reasonable," she said, strolling over to him and pushing his gun arm down. "Put that away. You can always use it later." She started playing with her necklace again. On an eighteen-year-old, it was coy and cute; on a thirty-five year old, it was just sad.

I sighed. "It's just Jack, Kathleen." She simpered. I fought down a retch. Then, I felt a wave of warm and inviting danger. I smelled jasmine. Maddie appeared at the door, looking confused.

"Jack," she began.

Kathleen laid eyes on her and let out a banshee wail. She charged Maddie, fingers crooked into claws. Maddie waited until Kathleen was almost upon her and quickly stepped aside. Kathleen bounced off the door frame and hit the floor, out cold. A red welt appeared on her forehead. I was stunned. Hearing a slide cocked brought me out of my reverie.

"Put the gun down, Patty. That's a good boyo," Maddie said. "Kathleen is right-as-rain, just entranced. Why did you let her dalliance with that mortal continue? Your overindulgence unhinged her mind."

She was holding my Colt in her gloved hands and bracing O'Connell who was very carefully placing his .38 on the floor. How did she get my gun?

"I got friends," O'Connell said. "You won't get away with this."

"Maddie," I said. "Do you know who he is?"

She spared me a quick, cold glance. "Yes, he's a Fomorian."

"No, he's a police lieutenant," I said.

"It's a family rivalry," she replied, her eyes never leaving O'Connell. "Kick it over and lie face down on the floor," she said to him. He complied. "If you move, I will shoot you."

She turned the gun on me. "Now, you."

I put my hands up. "Whoa, sugar! I'm not the bad guy here."

"You invite me to an ambush and then tell me you aren't the bad guy?" She wasn't smiling. "I had such high hopes."

"Who's dallying now?" O'Connell taunted, raising his head

from the floor.

She shot him in the face.

I dropped to the floor, and covered my head.

"Oh Jack," Maddie sighed, walking over near me. "I truly wished it hadn't come to this. I warned him, but changlings are notoriously slow to listen. Now, will you please get the heirloom?"

I sat up, carefully. "I'm going to stand, reach into my right coat pocket, and pull out a handkerchief. In the handkerchief is the item. Can I do that now?"

She nodded.

I got to my knees. "Funny thing, Bobby found your heirloom. Kathleen killed him for it." I stood. "She lost it last night when her bracelet broke and it tangled in my coat sleeve." Maddie frowned and my "feeling," already cool, became decidedly less warm and inviting. "Long story. The point is I found it. Now, there are two things I can't figure. One: why didn't she pawn the thing, it being priceless and all." I got the handkerchief out and began unfolding it.

"And two?" Maddie asked.

I paused unwrapping the item and waved my free hand about. "What caused all this destruction?"

I finished unfolding the cloth. I could feel the tingling voltage of the charm beginning to numb my hand. Maddie leaned over and let out an indelicate, unladylike swear.

"That's elfshot!" She said, her face turning red.

"So, not your heirloom?" I asked.

She just glared at me.

"She didn't pawn it because it is worthless?" I asked.

"She didn't pawn it because her father didn't allow it. His master would have killed them!"

"Excellent," a voice rumbled from the door. "So, the Spear is still in play." Oh good, Gravel Voice had returned!

"Balor!" Maddie said, raising my weapon at the intruder.

Handsome man, haughty and vain. He had brought company.

"Who are the thugs in the red hats?" I asked.

Maddie gave me a sharp look. "You can see them?"

"Well, yeah," I said. "Why shouldn't I?"

Her eyes flickered to my hand. "The elfshot must be theirs."

"So," I said, gesturing to the door. "Lutin?"

She ignored me.

"Matilda, put that away. It throws lead, not cold iron," Balor said. Maddie wilted. He looked at me. "Yes, little fish, we are Lutin. The 'item', as you call it, is the Spear of Lugh. It caused this destruction. You mortals pride yourself on splitting the atom. The Spear's tip boils with that power. As I told you last night, you are in the wrong pond."

"Wouldn't be the first time," I said and grabbed my gun from Maddie's hand, shoving her to the floor. I dropped the charm down the barrel and sighted on a bemused Balor.

"Really, little fish. The beating I gave you last night will not compare ..."

I shot him in the eye. He screamed and fell. His red hats scattered. Maddie looked up at me, bewildered. I offered her my hand.

"Hey, I figured elfshot might work," I said, tucking the .45 back into my waistband.

"It won't hold him for long," she said taking my hand and scrambling to her feet. "We need to find the Spear and leave before his troops arrive."

Troops? Maybe she hit her head. "You were talking about O'Connell's master," I said. I hooked a thumb at Balor's crumpled form. "That guy?"

She nodded.

I glanced over at Kathleen. Even unconscious, she held on to the necklace. Uh huh. "Did you drive?" I asked.

Maddie shook her head and blushed. "Hunter dropped me off. I was kinda hoping ..." she began.

"Hold on to that hope, doll," I said, grabbing her hand. We quick stepped to Kathleen. I knelt down and worked the clasp on the necklace. It slid from around her neck, a silver stylized spear hanging from one end. I could feel its power already. I didn't take any chances and dropped it into my pocket. If it operated like old one eye claimed, touching it might knock me out. The Santa Ana's hot breath swept through the open door, causing Balor to stir.

"Time to go," I said and we raced to the car.

We were free of pursuit until we hit Seaside Freeway. I could see headlights weaving in the traffic behind us. And something else. I floored the Coronet, the roar of its engine overcoming the blaring horns of the passed drivers.

Maddie grabbed my hand. "Where are we going?"

"Terminal Island, baby," I said. "I saw what the power of the atom did in Japan. No way I'm letting that loose in my town!"

"Jack, we can control it," she said.

I pulled into the docks and slid to a stop. "No one can control that." I jumped out of the car and raced to the end of the pier. I could hear thumping behind me. I reached into my pocket and grabbed for the chain. My fingers closed on the spear instead. The charm grew into a full-sized weapon, ripping its way free of my coat. Holding the spear, I felt its full power thrumming through me. Everything was preternaturally clear. The spear's tip glowed, casting a wide circle of light about me. I reached back to heave the spear into the Pacific. I bet I could've hit my old rack at Pearl from here.

"Jack," Maddie said carefully. "Consider what you are doing."

I heard a growl behind me. I turned and saw Maddie holding back a dog the size of a small pony. It looked like an albino Rottweiler with red ears. Its eyes were as dark as Maddie's. Or Green's. This dog was the leader. The rest of the identical pack fanned out behind him, blocking off the pier. I took the salt out of my other pocket and poured it in a circle around me.

The dogs didn't like that.

"Jack." Green appeared, moving towards me. The white dogs parted for their master and closed behind him again. He was wearing a sleeveless tunic. I could see the stylized antler on the back of his hand. The "glove" reached up past his elbow. "The Spear is mine. Please return it."

"No!" I slammed the butt on the pier. A shaft of fire burst from the tip creating a fireball over thirty feet high. "It's too dangerous."

"It's a danger I am used to living with, Jack. It's my family's responsibility," Green said.

His words echoed my GrandMama's. The Spear's power numbed me. I staggered and brushed out part of the circle with my foot. I felt a sharp pain on my chin. My head bounced off the pier. I looked up into Maddie's dark eyes.

"You hit me!"

"I'm so sorry, love," she said, her brogue thick. Her lips brushed mine. "So, sorry." She picked up the spear from where I had dropped it and left, the dogs following her.

I could hear sirens in the distance. The wild chase probably got their attention. Either that or the fireball.

"Jack, boyo," Green said, his eyes glowing in the darkness. "Come under the hill. There is a lot we can teach each other."

"Somehow, I doubt that," I winced.

"You're not Fair Folk, or Changling," he said. "I'm not sure what you are, but you have power. And you are interesting."

"There is that, I suppose."

"Well, come or stay. It's up to you. You know where we are." He turned to leave. "You're a fine hunter, Jacques Dupre. Your GrandMama would be proud." He climbed into the passenger seat of the Bugatti. Maddie was driving and sporting a new necklace. I guess the dogs had run off.

They left me on the pier, sirens closing in. At that moment, returning to the swamp seemed warm and inviting. I lay back, watched the stars disappear in waves of red and blue, and felt the wind drive her jasmine scent from me.

The hot, soul-sucking wind.

292   DIRTY MAGICK: LOS ANGELES

Contributors

Charlie Brown is a writer and filmmaker from New Orleans. He currently lives in Los Angeles, where he will soon receive his Masters in Professional Writing from the University of Southern California and also runs Lucky Mojo Press and Mojotooth Productions. He has made two feature films: "Angels Die Slowly" and "Never A Dull Moment: 20 Years of the Rebirth Brass Band." His fiction has appeared in The Menacing Hedge, Aethlon, and what?? Magazine.

Paul K. Ellis believes having been a lifeguard, convenience store clerk, bookseller, construction worker, broadcaster, web developer, network engineer, and having worked in the foodservice industry uniquely qualifies him as a professional dilettante. He has been spinning yarns since he could talk and considers himself a storyteller of some modest achievement. He considers it modest due *to Dirty Magick: Los Aangeles* being his first publication; otherwise he wouldn't stop talking about it. Paul lives in the City of the Monuments with his wife and three girls, and can be found at his website (paulkellis.com).

Michael Ashleigh Finn is a thematic consultant on Dynamite Entertainment's Hugo-nominated *The Dresden Files*, and creative consultant on the *Mana Punk* RPG from Hot Goblin Press. His short fiction has been published alongside the likes of Fred Saberhagen, Harlan Ellison, and Stephen King; he's working on the jump from short stories to novels, one of which features the narrator of his tale in this anthology.

Jeff Leyco does more things than he knows how to keep track of. When he's not writing stories, he's swinging out to Count Basie. When he's not dancing, he's making maps and geeking out. Jeff currently lives in New York with all the Chinese food he can handle.

Justin Macumber is the author of two novels – *Haywire* (Gryphonwood Press) and *A Minor Magic* (Crescent Moon Press). He is also an award winning short story writer, with his work appearing in various anthologies. The slide into middle age hasn't been easy for him, but his wife and houseful of pets have made it less painful than it otherwise might have been. He is presently located in North Texas, but once fame and fortune arrives at his door the family will fly off to somewhere much cooler and greener.

Terry Mixon, co-host of the three time Parsec Award finalist writing podcast *The Dead Robots' Society*, is the author of the upcoming military science fiction series *Empire of Bones* (book one of the same name coming in January 2014). A former soldier with the 101st Airborne Division, he now works providing direct computer support to the flight controllers in the Mission Control Center at the NASA Johnson Space Center supporting the International Space Station and other spaceflight projects. Both those careers provide plenty of fodder for his imagination.

Brent Nichols is a Canadian writer of fantasy and science fiction. His work appears in the anthologies *Blood and Water* (Bundoran Press) and *Shanghai Steam* (Edge Publishing), and in anthologies from Cruentus Libri and Hazardous Press. His novel *Lord of Fire* will be released by Double Dragon Publishing in 2014.

David Perlmutter is a freelance writer based in Winnipeg, Manitoba, Canada. The holder of an MA degree from the Universities of Manitoba and Winnipeg, and a lifelong animation fan, he has published short fiction in a variety of genres for various magazines and anthologies, as well as essays on his favorite topics for similar publishers. He is the author of the upcoming books *America Toons In: A History of Television Animation* (McFarland and Co.) and *The Singular Adventures Of Jefferson Ball* (Chupa Cabra Press).

Michell (Mike) Plested is an author, editor, blogger and podcaster living in Calgary, Alberta, Canada. He is the host of several podcasts including *Get Published*, (2009, 2011 and 2013 Parsec Finalist), the SciFi/Comedy *GalaxyBillies* (Hitchiker's Guide to the Galaxy meets Beverley Hillbillies) and *Boyscouts of the Apocalypse* (Zombie horror meets boyscouts), a part of the Action Pack Podcast. His debut novel, *Mik Murdoch, Boy Superhero* was published August 1, 2012 and was shortlisted for the Prix Aurora Award for Best YA Novel. His anthology, *A Method to the Madness: A Guide to the Super Evil* was released April, 2013.

Neal Pollack is the author of eight bestselling books of fiction and nonfiction, including most recently the Matt Bolster yoga mysteries *Downward-Facing Death* and *Open Your Heart* and the historical noir novel *Jewball*. He's also the men's yoga blogger for Yoga Journal magazine, and a certified yoga instructor in the Ashtanga vinyasa tradition. A contributor to many magazines and websites, including The New York Times, Slate, Vanity Fair, and the automotive and travel sections of Yahoo!, Pollack lives in Austin, Texas, with his wife and son.

Richard Rayner is the author of many short stories and nine books including *Los Angeles Without a Map*, *The Blue Suit*, and *A Bright and Guilty Place*. He has written for The New Yorker, The New York Times, The Los Angeles Times, the Los Angeles Review of Books and numerous other publications. He teaches at the University of Southern California.

Adam Remington is a stay-at-home father of two in Tasmania, Australia. This is his first published work.

Lisa-Anne Samuels is a wanderer at heart. Born in Idar-Oberstein, Germany, Lisa-Anne is proud to be the daughter of a family of "Wandering Jews." Growing up in a military family and moving every few years made it difficult to keep friends once the boxes were packed, so books and stories took that role until the Samuels family settled down. Well, at least her parents did – Lisa-Anne kept moving. As of now she has lived in 17 different cities, at least five of those more than once. Lisa-Anne currently lives in Virginia with her son and husband while attempting to avoid the vigorous tail wagging of the family dog, Macon.

Patrick Scaffido writes and performs The Horde, a musical and spoken word podcast novel available at www.thehordewilleat.us. He is currently coordinating the literary and new media programs for Balticon and editing The Horde for print publication. He majored in historical uses of semiotics and media and has taught both English and History to the uncaring masses. Find more about his songs, stories, poems, and machinations at www.thousandheads.com.

Michael Willett has a background in traditional publishing and web-comics. At a young age, he enlisted in the Marines and followed that with law enforcement service; he has owned his own businesses and worked a myriad of different jobs. Everything he has done gives him more experience to pour into his writing. Now, he has settled into the corporate world and finds himself with lots of time to fill with storytelling and reality-building, when he isn't spending time with his family and pets.

7938842R00174

Made in the USA
San Bernardino, CA
22 January 2014